Left by Light
C. K. Hart

Hart Cover Books LLC

Copyright © [2024] by [C.K. Hart]

All rights reserved.

No portion of this book may be reproduced in any form without written permission from the publisher or author, except as permitted by U.S. copyright law.

TABLE OF CONTENTS

Dedication		1
1.	Prologue	2
2.	Chapter 1	4
3.	Chapter 2	13
4.	Chapter 3	22
5.	Chapter 4	33
6.	Chapter 5	38
7.	Chapter 6	44
8.	Chapter 7	57
9.	Chapter 8	65
10.	Chapter 9	73
11.	Chapter 10	83
12.	Chapter 11	95
13.	Chapter 12	106
14.	Chapter 13	116
15.	Chapter 14	125
16.	Chapter 15	142

17.	Chapter 16	154
18.	Chapter 17	157
19.	Chapter 18	171
20.	Chapter 19	177
21.	Chapter 20	187
22.	Chapter 21	194
23.	Chapter 22	205
24.	Chapter 23	214
25.	Chapter 24	221
26.	Chapter 25	234
27.	Chapter 26	240
28.	Chapter 27	251
29.	Chapter 28	255
30.	Chapter 29	260
31.	Epilogue	263
Chapter		264
Chapter		265
Found in Flames- Teaser		266

When I need to be reminded of what unconditional means, I call my sister. Who, thankfully, is nothing like the sisters in this book.

This one is for you.

Prologue

"In the realm of light, a flower bloom,
    A bearer of fate shall loom.
Born of Stone's bounties, fair and sweet,
Her journey through shadows, she shall complete.
Across the realms, her steps shall tread,
Seeking the entrance, where darkness spreads.
Her heart shall embrace the spirits' cries,
Uniting the realms, where darkness lies."

They've always been vague. Deciphering it will take time. Patience. I suppose I do have an eternity.

I click my tongue in thought. "What of her Mother?" I ask Mantis, the one without eyes. He often gives more information than the others. It's still in riddles, but information all the same.

"Both mortal and Divine?" Mantis answers my question with another.

He grins as my brows push together in confusion. Could the girl have a Mother that is both God and mortal? It would not be the first time a God lay with the lesser.

Or perhaps the Goddess of the harvest has played another one of her tricks. For she is not a mortal, and her daughter is fated to be powerful, that much I know. A mere mortal or even half could never amount to such.

I will play a trick as well. For if she truly is in the mortal realm, if my visions of her destruction are correct, then it's only a matter of time before the two halves of power meet.

A naive, malleable Goddess in need of guidance. I turn from the seers, done with their services. Their whispers follow me to the door.

Hades thought he could keep me from getting my revenge. How wrong he was.

For you cannot escape your fate.

Chapter 1

Cedric is the first to go. I can see him throw his bags into the back of one of the Father's carriages. A dark-haired coachman is at the reins as my sisters say their goodbyes. Adriel pulls out her handkerchief to wipe away tears that are too far away for me to see. I don't need to. After all, it's not a rare sight. Her unending tears are as much a part of her appearance as her button nose.

Medla stands with her arms crossed. I can almost feel the anger from here. It drips off of her and onto those around her. That's why I am far away, hiding behind the tall grass that has turned brown from the summer drought. Her signature scowl is meant to let Cedric know the hate that she feels for his decision. It's not all that different from how her face normally looks. If anyone knows what hatred from Medla looks like, it's me.

Cedric takes a step back and looks up at our once-grand castle.

Overgrown weeds now invade the garden, entangling the once pristine pathway leading to the door, which has long ceased to welcome guests. He places his hands on his hips, searching the windows. For me, I realize. Why, I do not know. He has never had a kind word to share with me, or anyone for that matter.

Maybe he wants one more jab, one more shove that throws me into the mud, reminding me that I do not belong.

I am not close enough to discern the words spoken between my brother and sisters. Adriel embraces our brother, and Medla stomps her way up the stairs without so much as a turn of her head. When both my sisters are inside, and the dark-haired man at the front of the carriage lets out a whistle demanding the oxen to pull, I sink down into the tall grass before rolling on my back to look up at the cloudless blue sky. Hoofed feet pass by. The knocking of wooden wheels against rock makes my heart race. When it fades away, I remain under the hot sun until my nose burns, and there is an ache behind my eyes.

One less person in this castle makes no difference. We lost our servants and maids long ago. The once tidy home now has a thin layer of dust covering all the furniture, tables, and grand paintings. White sheets cover fine pieces of art made of marble and porcelain. Father's collection, gifted from noble men and women for his work in architecture. I close the front door, which I have not entered in so long that I had forgotten the disarray that lies within.

Scanning from left to right as I take it in, emptiness, quiet, calm. The small library past the foyer has books thrown on the floor and shoved into cushions of dirty couches. The table is full of old teacups and crumbs from when my sisters were happy and ignorant. Sunlight from the large window illuminates the intricate designs on the floor where my sisters used to host boring parties and gatherings for the other well-to-do people of Thorn Row. It's so dark in the places that the sun doesn't reach. I don't dare stare too long. The Shadows have eyes and teeth, and sometimes, they whisper their complaints to me.

Rounding the corner, I head for the servants' stairs. These, too, need dusting. I run my finger along the wooden railing, it comes away with a perfect black circle of debris. The farther down I go, the colder it gets. The bottom floor holds no heat. Father does not care for the warmth of his servants. I swipe at my arms to get rid of the tiny bumps that have gathered there from the cold. Again, the darkness shifts and whispers to me as I take the final steps that I've memorized without having to look or think.

Lupita only stayed this long because she is the furthest away from Father, in her kitchen, the corner of the house that cannot be reached easily by the people who occupy the spaces above. I often find myself here, learning how to make bread and preserves. I do not enter. The whispers coming from within are not of the Shadows this time.

Medla talks quietly to Lupita, and without needing to listen to the entirety of the conversation, I know that Lupita will not be around much longer. This is of no surprise to me. When Medla says her final goodbyes, I take a step back into a dark corner, with the brooms and various cleaning supplies blending into the unwelcoming black.

A chill runs down my spine as my imagination gets the better of me. *A trick of the mind*, I say to myself as the darkness embraces me, almost making it impossible to part from. *They are not real*. Medla passes me and heads for the same stairwell. I trail her with my eyes for a moment as she goes, irritation on her red face and determination in her steps. I know who she truly seeks, I hope she never finds me. I've always been good at making myself invisible, or maybe Medla has always been good at ignoring me. *Are you a boy or a girl today?* Her voice pops into my head from a memory I wish to forget.

Lupita cut my hair short when she could no longer brush through it. Although it has grown well past my waist since then. I prefer trousers over dresses even now, my body not rounded yet as hers and Adriel's, giving me a boyish figure. Now, my hips are wide, and although I haven't grown much in my chest, I am unmistakably a woman. "Come on out girl" Lupita calls from the kitchen. I step through the door frame, feeling the heat from the oven and the smell of yeast and sugar from the bread. "Your steps are light as a feather, but you smell like a horse." She keeps her head down as she speaks, occupied by the carrots she peels.

"You're leaving, yeah?" I say quietly as I make my way towards the oven, standing in front of it to warm my bones as I listen to the small hiss of fire. Lupita nods her head slowly but still does not look up at me. "I told your sister where to find everything. The preserves will last you a long while, and you know how to tend the garden." She finally lifts her head slightly and looks at me from the side. A strand of white hair falls from the fabric that holds her curls back. Her skin is so white I wonder if she's ever seen the sun. Her left ear is missing a bit of flesh, a notch at the top, a perfectly round hole. I can see straight through it. It shows her status, low, a mark the same as every servant that has ever worked in Thorn Row.

She puts the knife down and finds a pot large enough for the stew she is concocting—the last meal that I will taste of hers, I guess. As it clangs against the counter, she continues to fill the pot with various vegetables as she instructs me on the how-tos of the kitchen and what to look for in the garden. I already know all of what she tells me. Still, I let her fill the silence as we spend our last moments together.

Her rambling comes to an end, or maybe I just stopped paying attention. "Take this," I say as I pull the cuff from my arm. It's made of copper with a small yellow jewel on top. I've seen her eye it a time or two.

I never cared if servants stole my things. I didn't have much to give but the amount of jewelry Adriel would gift me after she was done with it, I would purposely leave out and unattended. They were always missing the day before a maid would quit or the same night that servants were fired by Medla. They probably deserved such a raise after putting up with her.

Sweet Lupita would not steal. She is too good, that's why I present her with this parting gift. "It will get you four gold at the markets, at least." I make a guess. Her hands do not move from the chore at hand, ignoring me. When I reach for her arm, she does not stop me. I watch a tear fall from her cheek. With my other hand, I open hers and place the cuff inside. She does not say thank you, but she holds my hand along with the cuff for a moment longer. I am unsure of the touch, fighting the urge to pull away from it.

When she finally clasps her hand around the jewelry and shoves it into her apron as if I might change my mind, I leave. Making sure she does not see the redness of my nose and the swell of tears in my eyes. Only when I pass the servants' quarters, empty as I walk to the back door which leads to the garden, do I let a tear drop to my boot.

That is the last time I saw her, and even though my own brother left only moments ago, this is much more devastating.

There is a knock at my door early in the morning, I know who it is before opening it. The overwhelming scent of lavender hits my nose before I can even reach for the brass knob. Medla stands there, a smile on her face, which is troubling. She only smiles when she wants something, and she never needs anything from me.

There are no harsh words about my long hair, which is unruly and hardly ever brushed, unlike hers. Surprisingly, she does not comment on how unkempt my room has become as she walks right in. She even steps right over my dirtied clothes, goes to my closet, grabs undergarments, and pushes them into my arms. With no explanation, she leaves the room.

Confused but assuming she will return, I strip off my own clothes and slip into the bright white petticoat and step into the stockings that I could have sworn I threw away. *These will dirty quickly,* I think to myself. *I was planning on fishing on the far side of the lake today.*

Medla returns with a long red dress and a leather corset hanging over her arms. I never met my Mother, but I do believe that these pieces belonged to her.

Medla then takes to dressing me, I could have done it myself, but one does not argue with Medla, so I hold my tongue as she pulls the fabric over my head. I haven't worn a proper dress in a very long time, for church when I was young but soon my family attended without me. I stop myself from letting the memory creep to the front of my mind.

Medla goes on and on about the intricacies of ladyhood, how to dress and eat and sit and blah blah blah. These things do not pertain to me.

I remember all the times I was ushered out of the ballroom or told to wait in my room while my sisters took their etiquette classes. Has she forgotten? As Medla wraps the corset around my waist, I see the shape of me in the glass of the window. I look away quickly. I don't recognize that body. It does not look the way it should. In my usual attire of trousers and long-sleeved white shirts that I snuck from Cedric's closet from when he was a boy. Paired with black suspenders that Lupita brought me when the trousers that also belonged to my brother kept falling from my waist.

Medla then shows me a trick of tightening the corset myself. She pulls the string around the bedpost and tells me to hold the leather strip tight in my hand, then, "lean forward." she instructs. The air in my lungs is no longer there, and I cannot breathe it back in due to the pressure the corset puts on my chest.

I remember dresses alone being painfully uncomfortable. Now, with the addition of a corset, I see why Medla always has a pinched look on her face.

I don't dare say anything as she looks me up and down, proud of her work. *Something feels wrong*, I think to myself, and it's not the dress. I take a good look at my oldest sister as she fidgets with a tie on my left sleeve. We could not be more opposite.

Her long light-brown hair is always up in pins, and her dresses fit her curves perfectly. Her skin is fair, and freckles line her nose and cheeks, making her unique and sought-after. She always knows what to do and say in the presence of others, all while maintaining a cool exterior. Which must be hard because I have seen the orange molten anger of her insides. I used to wish I was more like her, but it's all a façade, just as this is.

Her silver eyes catch my black ones, another opposite of ours. She takes a step back to look at me fully, and I look down at myself as well, mostly to avoid her gaze. "You're no longer a girl, Katsia." A fake smile contorts her features. Her fingers lightly pinch my cheeks. I often saw Adriel and Medla do this to their own faces to add a bit of pink to their appearances, but I never noticed the difference.

"Or a boy," I add, hoping to get under her icy layer. It remains unbroken, but she lets a breath go that I didn't realize she had been holding. She reaches into her own hair and takes out two brass pins. Somehow, even with the loose pieces draping over her ears, making her not-so-perfect as usual, she is still beyond beautiful. And she knows it. *Aphrodite must have played a part in her creation.*

Medla reaches up and secures them on each side of my head, pulling the tangled strands of black out of my face. When she turns to the door in a wordless command to follow, I do.

My dress drags on the ground slightly as I descend the stairs. Adriel stares up at me as I follow behind my oldest sister. Adriel's head tilts slightly to the left as I come closer. *She is hiding something.* The last step groans as I land on it, as it always has.

Medla turns as if she wants to say something, but I push past her and gently grab Adriel by the chin, pulling her closer.

I inspect what I now see is a swollen eye. I run my fingers over her cheek and down to her shoulder, where her long blonde hair sticks to a scrap of fabric that drowns in blood. Her brow has a bead of sweat, and her once milky skin now has a greenish hue to it. My eyes fall further, down to her abdomen. There, just above her hips is another noticeable lump under her otherwise perfect dress. Another scrap of fabric, I assume, most likely tied around her slim waist and concealing another bloody gash.

Her blue eyes, ocean eyes, I had heard them called once. Eyes that once sparkled, are now dull and bloodshot. "You need a doctor," I tell her, as if she doesn't already know. I look to Medla. "She needs a doctor," I repeat to my other sister. She nods her head in agreement.

Medla plays with a string attached to a bag at her feet before a man enters the front door. He begins to gather the luggage. "Two stops to make. We best hurry." His smile disappears when he sees the anger that heats my face.

"You're leaving," I say it as a statement and not a question. I already know the answer. My eyes are still on the man, frozen as he waits for an answer. The man holds up a pathetically small bag. Those are *my* things I realize.

"No, Katsia, *we* are leaving." Adriel takes a step in my direction. I take a step back accordingly. She tries again, and I move away from my sister once more. *I should have known, the dress, the talk, the fake smiles.*

"Medla and I will go to Fredricks." Adriel blubbers. "He has offered to take us in," she says as tears fill her eyes. Fredrick, one of Medla's many men that she has wrapped around her finger. One who would die for her, but she would hardly flinch if asked to do the same.

"And you will go to the nunnery, get a proper education" Medla cuts in. She cannot hide how pleased she is, happy that I will finally be far away, out of her hair. No doubt that part was her idea.

"Put those things down!" I shout at the man. "Don't touch my things, I'm not going with them." I turn my attention to Medla. The bag hits the ground as the man stands tall, awaiting Medla's orders.

"Father is soon to die. He isn't well," She rambles off. I laugh, a crazy laugh that comes from deep in my stomach to express my disbelief that they were just going to leave him here, alone, to die.

"Go!" I Take one more look at Adriel, sweet sister. Her small acts of kindness were wasted on me. My eyes shift to Medla once more. She shrugs, as if it doesn't matter if I stay or go, as long as *she* gets out of here. I laugh once more at the absurdity of it all. Then, I run.

Through the kitchen, past door after door of the once busy servant quarters. Into the garden, where the Shadows that live within the brick and mortar of House Luz cannot reach me. I don't stop there, I make my way down a long row of trees, counting them as I pass. *Twenty-one, Twenty-two.* Peeling away the many layers of this damned dress as I go. The corset crashes to the ground, my ribs sing with relief once freed. But even though I'm no longer caged by that contraption, I still can't breathe.

Chapter 2

The sun has fallen over the trees by the time I make my way back inside. It's quiet, not unusual, and easier now that I don't have to take alternate routes to avoid my sisters. Medla and Adriel were always together, and they followed the same routine every day. It was easy to memorize. Cedric was hardly ever home, as he spent most of his nights amongst the ladies employed at the town brothel. His absence does not bother me.

Of course, Father is in his wing of the castle, where only my sisters frequented, I was not to go near there. So, I kept to the servants' quarters or outside and only ended the days in my own room, which I sometimes think was out of the way on purpose. All the way on the east side, where no guest would need to pass by on their way to the library or picture gallery, and another way to ensure I was not seen by Father, ever.

Making my way down the long hallway, I pause as I hear footsteps above that could belong to no other than my Father now that we are the only two left. I become as still as a deer that hears a twig snap under a hunter's foot. The air feels thin, like I can't get enough into my lungs. The marks on Adriel come to mind. *Has he really become so taken by this sickness?* The footsteps are further from me. I knew he was losing his mind, but those cuts could have caused more damage or even cost her life.

When I reach my room, it's with near silence. I open the door slowly and meticulously, a practice I've perfected over the years. I take all the right steps into my bedroom so the floor does not squeak under my weight. Then, as I have always done, I light all eight candles, placing them strategically around the room so there are not too many dark spaces. Another measure I take to go unnoticed, this time it's not my sisters or Father or Cedric and his friends I hide from. Instead, it's the void, the darkness, the boogie man, the thing that makes my imagination bleed into reality. The Shadows have become more demanding as of late. Always teasing me with whispers that I cannot make sense of.

Not even Lupita knows what ails me. She has told me stories of what happens to those who suffer from insanity. Condemned as a witch or locked into asylums. So, I keep my secret, taking these extra measures to ensure they don't drive me entirely into a madness I cannot escape. I prepare myself for a cold night, curl into a ball covered in all the blankets I can find, and close my eyes, praying to the Gods for sleep to come quickly before my candles burn out.

My sleep lasts only a few hours. I'm awoken by an almost melodic sound, one I've never heard before. As if the sound senses my consciousness, it stops. Only one candle near the window remains lit. *The smaller I am, the better*, I tell myself, pulling my knees into my body. The whispers make their way to my bed. I hold as still as possible, not affording them the attention they seek.

Fear takes over, I feel myself start to sweat, which makes the cold of the night unbearable, sending shivers down my spine. *Just close your eyes*. I try to coax myself back to sleep, but the whispers are in my ear now. They surround me. It's not just dark, it's empty, there is nothing. The small blurs of light you can normally see from behind your eyelids are nonexistent.

Then, as if I'm underwater, weightlessness.

There is no more bedroom or worn candles, there are no sounds or coldness, and even the feeling of my heart slamming into my ribs has stopped. It's just black. *Perhaps I have fallen asleep once more.*

When the world recreates itself around me, when my feet bear the weight of my body, and a cool breeze blows at the hem of my sleeping garments, I open my eyes reluctantly. There is a door in front of me, elaborately carved designs, faces with eyes that do not move from me, Father's door.

I would rather have stayed in that abyss forever, warm and weightless, I would rather be anywhere but here. *Run.* To the left of me is a giant porcelain statue of a warrior. *Run.* To the right, a seemingly endless hallway. *Run.* But my legs do not move.

A pool of black spills from Fathers' room, through the cracks and into the hallway. *This can't be real. It's a dream,* I try and fail to convince myself. The darkness slithers through the keyhole before wrapping around my hand and guiding me to the handle. It seems I cannot move, cannot stop it from twisting my wrist until I'm looking into Fathers' room, my hand still glued to the knob.

The bed is disheveled, as if he were just here, and the window is cracked slightly, pulling in a breeze. Quickly I shuffle to the other side of the room to close the window. No wonder it's so cold in here. I look down at my bare feet and then around the room, illuminated by the night sky that spills from the window. "Just one more day," a voice says from far off with excitement, like Adriel used to sound when dressing for a party. It does not belong to anyone I know, certainly not Father. The Shadows have never been more than whispers and commands but short, undesired words. But these words are fully formed, nothing like what I have heard the darkness say before.

Frantically, I search for who the voice belongs to. Movement near the unlit fireplace catches in the corner of my eye, but when I try to trace the object, I see nothing. *Brush, thump, brush, thump.* Footsteps from the hallway, they make their way closer to the door. I'm not sure who I'm more afraid of in this moment, an intruder or my own Father. Silently, I wait for someone to enter the room. I begin to make up things that I know can't be true. *Father must have gone for a walk or to gather firewood.* I try to convince myself. If it is indeed him, he will be furious with me in his wing of House Luz when he spent years telling me I was to stay away.

The knot in my throat prevents me from letting out a cry of terror as a strange animal limps onto the colorful rug at the foot of the bed. I glance at the door. The animal stands between me and the only exit. Well, the only exit that doesn't send me plummeting towards Stone.

A large nose, shiny against the moonlight, lifts into the air as it takes in the smell of me. This is no animal I've ever seen before. It licks its large yellow teeth, its tongue long and dark red. The stench that comes off its labored breathing is foul.

I'm frozen. This time, it's my own fear that keeps me in place, not the darkness that seems to hold me at the door. *Coward.* That can't be my last thought, but too weak and too scared to get away, a coward is what I am. The beast lets out a low growl and readies its feet to pounce in a motion that I have seen many times before when an animal strikes its prey.

Finally, my voice cracks with a scream. *Doesn't matter,* I say to myself. No one is here to help me, I've been left behind.

The beast lunges at me. I dodge the attack but hit the floor with a thud, a stabbing pain in the wrist that I used to soften my fall. When I turn over, I prop myself up, practically dragging my legs across the floor as I clumsily try to distance myself from the animal. My back hits a chair, which I use to pull myself up, but when I look back at the animal it is no longer pursuing me.

Instead, it falls to the floor after me, unmoving, a small whimper escapes it as it hits the hard wood. I do not take my eyes off the creature. I look to the door, and I'm ready to make a run for it, but the beast lets out a shallow breath. Instead, I take two slow steps toward the beast, peering over the top of it. It's wounded badly, a trail of blood in its wake.

It's not a dog, man, or boar but a mix of all three. As it lies in a pool of moonlight, I can see half of its ugly face clearly.

I blink away the blur of tears as I try to make sense of what is in front of me. I dare another step. a small glint of metal catches the white light that comes through the window. "No, no, no," I whisper as I recognize a copper pendant, a yellow stone set at its center, the official gem of House Luz tied by a leather string around its neck.

Hansel Luz, my Father, lay before me in the shape of a beast, unrecognizable had I not seen him wear that pendant every day for the last 18 years of my life. I reach for it, holding it in the palm of my hand. It's covered in a sticky black substance, blood, his blood.

He is heavy, but I push him onto his back and find the source. He shudders a breath in pain when his weight shifts but does not wake. A broken arrow runs through his ribs and sticks out his side. Small whines escape the beast with every heave of Father's chest.

For a moment, I just stare, waiting. Maybe for his chest to stop the rise and fall that signals life. My hands shake, I look towards the door. There is nothing stopping me, this is a dead man, just as my sisters said, I could leave him here. But that would make me no better than my sisters.

Quickly I get to my feet, grab a blanket off the bed and wrap it around Father. There is half-burnt wood in the fireplace. I start it just as Lupita taught me.

Next, I find strips of fabric and a healing salve in the bathroom meant for minor wounds. I can make them work. I begin to heat water over the flames.

Father's limp came from a large gash just above the knee. I once saw my Father wrap Cedric's leg after a fall from his horse. I made sure to memorize the technique as I hid in the corner stall of the stables. *Always hiding*.

Once the arrow is removed, I throw the yellow feathers from the fletching into the flames and begin wrapping Father's torso. With each sound he makes, I flinch slightly, ready to run if he wakes.

When I finally finish, my hands are coated in red. I sit on the wingback chair near the fire, counting the seconds between the beasts' breaths. Throughout the night I check Fathers' dressings and stoke the fire that is soon to run out of fuel.

I don't let myself close my eyes and even though the Shadows have not spoken, I still feel like eyes are on me. The feeling is not new. I hug my knees to my chest. His breathing is becoming more even now, and the healing salve seems to have eased some of the pain because the beast's face is no longer contorted.

Father sleeps well into the day. I fuss with his dressings once more, then bring a pillow from the bed to place under his head. The morning birds sing a melody. *Perhaps they would not sing such a happy tune if they saw the bloody mess in here.*

When Father stirs, I jump to my feet, but he only lifts his head and shifts his weight to face the floor. His fur lined back faces me, his skin is thin, and his bones protrude from his spine like a jagged mountain. Adriel's mangled arm comes to my mind's eye. I lean back into the chair and close my eyes. I don't let myself drift from consciousness as I think of this secret that my sisters have kept from me all these years. How much did they know?

Cedric has always avoided me. He being the oldest and I the youngest, we did not have much in common. My sisters used to play with me, more like a doll than a human. Adriel would braid my hair and dress me up in her old gowns. Medla loved playing house, of course it was just an excuse to boss us around and treat us as her children, which was nice, after all, I never had a mother.

Cedric and Medla had many years with Mother before she died. Adriel lost her when she was only 5. Because of me.

For a few years, things were good. Father did his best to raise four children with the help of nursemaids and servants.

One day, sometime after my 10th birthday, Father came home in a state of upset. He poured himself a drink, then another, then another. He looked like he had just seen a ghost and was trying to chase away its spirit with booze. He drank all night, crying out for Mother, listing the ways in which she had wronged him, starting with her obsession with magic and ending with me—her worst mistake.

More memories come flooding in of that day.

Letters were etched into Father's arms, but he paid no attention to the drops of blood that traveled down his elbow, bent as he tipped his drink to the sky, savoring every last drop. Medla chased after him, following him through the castle with a damp cloth, wiping the red from the floorboards in fear it might stain.

Adriel later told me he went to visit a woman who claimed to talk to the dead. He smelled of incense, a familiar scent that I smelled at church just a few days before. Of course that was the last time I attended. I did not understand why he could not look at me. Why he made sure that I was not within his sight.

And out of sight, I remained, avoiding him at all costs.

Slowly, my siblings forgot about me. Cedric was already used to ignoring me, and Medla wasn't much better. Sweet Adriel had no plans of following. She would sneak to my room or find me outside, and if the day was warm enough in the summer, she'd even swim with me. Soon, the visits became fewer, and eventually, they stopped altogether.

I should have known that if I was still for this long, if I gave myself a chance to remember, the images of Father's blood-soaked hands would soon creep up.

I learned the best way to keep them at bay is to busy my hands. After only taking a slight glance at Father's sleeping body once more, I leave. Not until I am out the door, far from Father, do I notice that my knees are quaking, and my hands feel like ice.

As I dress, I remind myself of all the freedom that Father's neglect has given me, I enjoy the simplicity of it all. Doing as I please, as long as no one is bothered. I can't imagine what madness I would descend into if I were to be kept where the Shadows could easily reach me. Or to have all eyes on me as they were on my sisters, their every move determining their status. The loneliness, the solitude, helped me protect my secret and I mustn't forget that.

Both Medla and Adriel's coming of age was painfully dull. Men were lined up at the door for no other reason than to sit in the library, which I was not allowed to be in, and stare at my sisters while they chatted of Gods know what. They would eat small sandwiches, which I was not allowed to have. Then, afterward, my sisters would exchange their likes and dislikes in a discussion I was not allowed to participate in.

Then, off to parties and balls held by wealthy men. Of course I was never to attend such places. So instead, I spent my time watching, and I even learned a thing or two, but never from the women.

I was uninterested in posh gowns and feathered hats. Did not much need the gossip that spread from one ear to the other, I had no one to pass it on to anyhow.

On the other hand, the men would line up outside, just past the garden in an open field. Under the window in which they knew my sisters and other women could see them from.

They stood in front of targets, aiming bows with arrows, I saw what worked for some and what didn't work for others. Finally, when no one was looking, I took a bow for myself, practicing on a tree stump hidden near the garden.

Soon I had a whole arsenal: a sword, a dagger, and a slingshot to add to my bow. Keeping them hidden from Cedric. Not only would he have punished me for keeping them, but I know what my brother did with his weapons, and it was nothing short of disgusting.

Wounded animals left to rot in the forest, rabbits caught in traps by their legs for days on end, foxes and deer found with arrows through their sides. I suppose it is Cedric who gave me the practice of bandaging the wounded, setting broken bones, and placing splints correctly. Father was fortunate to have raised such a disappointing son, as I was mending his wounds in the same fashion as the animals in which Cedric left to die.

Chapter 3

After spending most of the day in the garden, I venture back to the west wing as night approaches. Ignoring the Shadows as I ascend the long stairwell, they reach for me, but I do not let them latch. I haven't slept a wink, and my tired mind plays tricks on me. When I reach Father's grand door I knock with as much confidence as I can muster. There is no answer. I start to think he might very well be on the floor, still wrapped in a blanket, taken by death. *At least I did as much as I could.*

Slowly I turn the knob, terrified of what I might see. When I peek my head in, it's hard to decipher what is what in the darkness. The curtains have been drawn and there is a chill to the air, the fire long gone from early this morning. I enter fully and take a candle from the stand near the door. When the room becomes visible, no one is in sight, just as last night.

The blanket that was wrapped around Father is on the ground near the window where I left him. The curtains fly up as a breeze gets sucked in from outside. I part the curtains and peer down towards the trees below. The moon shines brightly, casting a white glow across the lake. The trees sway gently in the wind, a view that I am not afforded from my window. I look beyond our lands to the mountains. *It would not be so bad. If Father never comes back?* Maybe, like many wounded animals do, he will find a comfortable spot to die. I take in the view one last time before locking the window with a tight turn of the brass lock at its base.

Maybe I was right because Father has not come back, and the last few days have been calm. I tend to the garden and even tag a rabbit for dinner with my slingshot. I jump at every noise that makes its way through the castle, mistaking the settling for footsteps or the wind for voices.

Ignoring the sounds and Shadows and sometimes humming away the silences, I climb into the tub and use Adriel's mixes of soap for skin and hair that I gathered from her room. The soap fills the air with a lavender scent, the scent of my sisters, the one that made it so easy to avoid them. I scrub away dried blood from my hands—the rabbit's, but mixed with Father's under my nails, I'm sure.

Sinking down into the water, I hold my breath. I've taught myself to hold it for a long while. I've spent countless hours in the lake doing just this during the summer. Under the water, there are only the sounds of my heartbeat and the rhythmic back-and-forth as it hits the shore, my only true escape from the darkness.

I think only of what I should do next as I lather the soap into my skin. The water turns a brownish color by the time I am done. *I need answers. I deserve answers.* The only place for the kind of answers I require is Thorn Row. I must make the same journey that Father took all that time ago.

The horses are all gone, taken by my siblings, so I'm in for a long walk to town. I take a canteen of water and tuck my dagger into the sheath around my ankle, concealed by my boot but easy to grab. The last time I was in Thorn Row, I was a child.

Rumors have, of course, spread their way around to the lords and their ladies, but the people that frequent the part of Thorn Row that I intend to go to will never have seen me, or at least they will not recognize me after all these years.

Fathers' sickness cut short Medla and Adriel's coming out. *Not soon enough.* Cedric made his own rumors in the town long before that. He spent every allowance Father gave him on women and booze.

If Cedric is still here, doing what he has always done, I do not want to see him. I promise myself to keep my hood up and my head down as I search for a woman who claims to talk to the dead.

It's just as I remembered it, although it was long ago, and I know that the markets have grown double in size since then. Vendors come from all over Stone. They made sure it was the mecca of trading.

Thorn Row is the center of everything. The path to every other city and village in all of Stone. The northern and southern expanses of the city stretch endlessly, with rows of houses, workshops, and businesses. Only cut off by the ocean in the south and the mountain range in The North, which coined the name Shadow Gate by the people who survived the war. Past that, there are the Uncharted Territories, nestled just below the part of Shadow Gate that hosted the war. Made solely of villagers who refused to follow the King after his victory. Or at least that is what I heard through the door of Medla and Adriel's tutoring session.

The population of northern Thorn Row grows in the summer and shrinks in the winter, due to harsh winters. Some even travel to Flora to the left of Thorn Row and Fauna to the right.

The streets are meticulously planned, forming a labyrinthine network. Towering structures and elegant architecture characterize the skyline. My Father's design. Father also knew what he was doing when he built his own home on the upper east side of Thorn Row, outside the walls that hold the chaos within. Somewhere, he could truly be himself without the eyes of others. And when eyes *were* on him, he placed a mask over his face. One that hid his true self.

These gates are the main entry points, heavily fortified and equipped with mechanisms to raise and lower massive doors, securing the city from potential threats. Guards inspect those who wish to enter.

I hand my papers to the man at the gate. He looks over every detail. He takes extra notice of the column labeled *"Last Visit."* No stamps with the date in the last eight years.

He raises an eyebrow that has my heart thumping with concern. *He is going to turn me away,* I think to myself. Then, "Luz, huh?" I nod my head nervously. "Would that be Hanzel Luz?" he questions.

"Yes." My voice cracks when I answer.

"Go on then." He dismisses me with a hand after shoving the paper back into me.

People mill about the street, perusing wares and making offers. I had forgotten what a busy place it was here until I entered the markets. Men and women reach their hands out, trying to entice you to their booths with promises of "Something you've never seen before."

The noise from the markets blends into one muddled melody of people's voices, dogs barking, and wooden boxes clanging together as they are thrown into the back of carts. A whistle filled the air meant for a woman in a long light blue dress, her waist cinched tightly by a corset, and her hair in perfect unnatural waves of blonde. *What a strange way to get someone's attention.* The woman scoffs and continues, ignoring the man who threw the whistle her way. I keep my head straight, pulling the hood down around my face.

Behind the colors and the sounds of the city, behind the bartering and singing and pleading, there is darkness. It calls to me, even pulls me towards a side street, and when I look to where it wants me to go, there stands a robed woman. Her beauty maimed by a tattoo of an eye on her face, centered in the middle of her forehead. I know I have found what I'm looking for.

Today I am not in need of fruits or vegetables or exotic animal furs, instead I am here for one thing and one thing only, answers.

Before I can even begin to make my way to the woman a man pushes past me, knocking me with his shoulder, forcing me to look away from her, he looks me up and down before his eyebrows raise and he laughs in a disgusted snort. He nudges his friend as they continue, the other man looks over his shoulder and laughs as well.

My attire is not the fashion of women in Thorn Row, perhaps not even in all of Stone. They wear dresses, or skirts, with a tight corset, the same kind that Medla tried to dress me in. *I have vowed never to wear one again.* Women's waists are meant to be as small as possible, and their busts are to be on the verge of spilling out of their clothing. Looking down, I see that those things are not true of my body. I wear a lifeless white shirt tucked into trousers that are clearly not my own, paired with a long jacket that does nothing but hide my figure.

Besides, my body is missing some of the assets, unlike my sisters, who are big in all the right places and small where needed. I couldn't help the muscles that built on my arms and legs from long hikes, secret rides on Adriel's horse, trees that I learned to climb without having to look at the branches above, and the long swims that helped me escape the heat of the summer season.

Ignoring the men's sneers, I continue. When my eyes find the woman again, I see the flutter of her golden robe as she moves swiftly through a crowd. She turns towards me as she catches the attention of a man who passes by. A medallion hangs from her neck, with a picture of a woman, a Goddess, in its middle.

The noise of the markets fades slightly as I approach, observing as she grabs the hand of a red-haired beauty, pulling her in close. The robed woman smiles as she talks, like what she says is sweeter than honey. Dark brown curls swing wildly around her face when the wind picks up. The red-haired woman who looks to be wealthy tucks her hair behind her ear and looks down at her other hand, examining her palm along with the robed woman, her jaw falls slightly in awe.

Hiding myself behind the crumbling brick of a building I try to make sense of what the women are doing. The red-haired woman lets out giddy laughter, clearly pleased by what the robed woman has said. *Oh, I see.* She is no conduit to the other side, no witch at all, but instead, just a good businesswoman, telling all her customers just what they want to hear and collecting her coin.

My footsteps slow as the red haired woman walks away with a grin and her hand clutched to her chest. I think better of my decision. A con woman is not what I came here to find, I turn quickly back towards the markets. "You won't find answers there, child." a woman's raspy voice says behind me.

"How do you know that I'm here for answers?" I ask without turning towards her.

"You are," she says as a matter of fact. "You all are." My long black braid whips around as I face her, landing on my back with a light smack. Her eyes go wide as she studies my features. I lower my head to avoid the strange feeling I get when she looks between my eyes.

"You." her hand wraps around my forearm. "What are you hiding?" I look at her in shock before trying to pull away, but her hand only tightens. When I reach for my dagger, it's not there. Her other hand comes around from behind her, a flash of silver in her grip. She flips my dagger through her slender fingers with ease. She searches my face again, her eyebrows bunched together in confusion. "You have something that doesn't belong to you." Her breath hits my face, sweet, like she had just sucked on a sugar cube.

"I have nothing." I laugh, because it really is funny, everything I have is not mine, my clothes, my boots, the dagger that is in her hand. I really do have nothing. I've stolen everything, something that does not belong to me, she's going to need to be more specific.

"The Connection." She tells me releasing my arm and using her free hand to point to the tattoo that adorns her forehead. "Don't worry, I will not tell of your gift." She takes a step back, and the dagger refracts the light, blinding me for a second. Her words make no sense to me. *The Connection? And what gift does she speak of?*

My face must give away my confusion because she studies me for a moment before speaking again. "Magic, girl." She looks down at me, waiting for me to confirm her suspicions, but I can't. Magic explains Father's illness, but I never thought it would explain away my own.

"Can you get rid of it?" I ask her, maybe this woman is not a con. I would give anything to live a day where I do not fear the Shadows. If there is a way to get rid of the darkness, maybe there is a way to get rid of Father's sickness as well.

"Ah, but I did not give it to you." she lifts her chin, and the wind picks up once more, sending the smell of incense into my nose. The same smell that was on Father the night that he decided I was an abomination. It sticks to me, making me sick to my stomach. Overwhelming panic takes over me, sending me back to that day. I place my hand on my chest and take a step back. Forget finding the truth about Father. He is most likely dead anyway. Forget everything. I need to get out of here. I'm not sure I should have come in the first place.

"Give me back my dagger," I tell her, holding out my hand. She glances down at my palm, similar to the way she did to the woman before me. A smirk tugs at the corners of her mouth.

"You're going to need it," she says as she gently places the dagger into my hand. I take it and turn swiftly, walking away. The pounding starts in my chest and carries to my ears, urging me to run, so I do.

Glad that I took the time to memorize some of the city from maps hanging in Father's office, I take the side streets. I stop at the Center Square: A huge garden of dahlia roses, this time of year they are in full bloom, turning the whole Square a bright red. The reason for its name, Thorn Row.

My legs wobble as I bend them to sit on a bench facing the field of flowers. I would have thought them to be beautiful if it weren't for the state that I find myself in. It's hard to stop and smell the roses when my lungs are barely functioning, and my legs are on fire. My head feels heavy with new information, and my stomach has not yet settled. This is what I came here for. This is what I wanted, I remind myself. But those are not the answers I came for. Those are answers to questions that I did not even ask.

Falling forward, I place my elbows on my knees and put my head in my hands, blocking out the sunlight. Taking a moment to gather myself. *What do I do now?* Not my imagination after all, not madness, not insanity. *Magic. Fucking magic.*

"Rough day?" A low, and in a much too chipper voice for the information I just learned, asks. He stands in front of me, I squint up at his face, the sun just behind him, darkening his features. He's so close I could reach out and touch him. *Too close.* This time, I keep the whereabouts of my dagger in mind so that the events from earlier do not repeat themselves.

"I'm sorry. Do I know you?" I can't hide the annoyance from my voice.

"Well, I'm not sure. But I know you." He takes a seat, again too close to me. I slide away before looking over at him suspiciously, not taking his bait. He holds a knowing smile. "I've seen you before, at House Luz." He finally says when I do not reply.

No one saw me at House Luz. I made sure I was not seen or heard. "I believe you are mistaken." I try to convince him.

"Hmm, let's see, The Grand Masquerade, I believe your sisters called it." He sees right through my lie. Almost every family in Thorn Row was invited, so it doesn't narrow it down. How could he have seen me there? I think back to that night, my sisters drunk on wine, the men switching masks so that they may take a turn dancing with Medla under the disguise of one of her lovers. That night, I stole my first bow.

As usual, I wasn't allowed to attend the party, so I spent hours outside near the garden. No one goes to that side of the castle at night, especially during a party.

Don't tell me. I stole this man's bow, and he's clearly still upset about it. I do not let it show. "You're mistaken." I try again. This time with more confidence.

But he ignores me. "Ah yes, I do believe I went looking for my missing bow and Julian's missing arrows." *I knew it.* Julian, that's a familiar name, one of Cedric's wicked friends. Which makes this man a friend of Cedric's as well, which makes him no friend of mine. I let no indication of truth cross my face.

He looks at me with a grin that I want to smack from his mouth. He leans against the back of the bench comfortably. "Oh, come on, admit it." He looks down at my trousers. The white shirt I tucked into them now feels constricting under his gaze. "You look... different." He smiles. Leaving me unsure whether it's a compliment or a dig at my appearance.

There is something about this man, something that draws you in, makes you want to give him exactly what he asks for. I do not, will not.

My general distrust for men and all-around lack of knowledge when it comes to how they operate factor into that. Adriel would have blushed when flashed that smile and maybe that's how I should act too, but I can't bring myself to it.

He waits for a response, which infuriates me, but it is of no use. I give him the confirmation he seeks. "If you lost your bow that night, you should have taken it up with Father." He can't now, of course. Asking a beast about a bow would not end well—if he is still alive, that is.

He is still looking at me, his smile impossibly larger than a moment ago. He holds out his hand, "Kirian Bear." I do not extend my hand to him after his introduction.

"I have to go," I tell him as I stand.

"I'll take you." He stands as well. It is getting harder to hide the annoyance from my face. "Maybe I should ask your Father about that bow, maybe it's turned up somewhere. I really should get that back," he says in an I know something you don't know kind of way that makes my blood boil.

"My Father is sick, bed ridden. If I find your bow, I will return it to you." I lie.

"Let me take you back anyhow, I saw you arrive here on foot." *Stalker.* "House Luz is far. My carriage is parked outside the third gate, east wall." He waits, and his persistence, paired with his obviously purposeful, sultry voice, almost makes me want to take that ride, but I'm not going anywhere with this man.

I suspect he already knows my answer because after a short silence he tips his hat before saying "Miss Katsia Luz, it was a pleasure seeing you again." My full name, I have not heard it used in a long time. I am almost startled at his words, but I keep my composure and begin to walk past him. I do not look at him, but I can tell that he has not looked away. "You may keep the bow, although if you haven't improved your aim, I'm not so sure you have much use for it." I peek at him over my shoulder. He winks, giving me a knowing smile, and nods before turning away. Again, I keep the surprise from rising to my face. *What else does he know?*

Chapter 4

My body aches the next morning. It's easier to get to Thorn Row than to get back. The distance was long, mostly uphill, and the heat of the day was almost unbearable, but what's worse was the time it gave me to think.

I have so much to do. To understand. I start in Father's personal library, finding mostly blueprints of buildings and layouts of soon-to-be new land developed in Thorn Row.

I suppose if Father really is dead then his business would go to Cedric. *It will be run straight to the ground.* On to Father's bedroom next, perhaps he has gathered something of importance and has hidden it away since he was the one to go searching for answers from my dead Mother in the first place.

Father would be cruel enough to know the answers I seek and refuse to tell me. A long 18 years of paranoia and fear of the dark, exactly the way he intended it. My punishment for taking his wife, perhaps. I try not to think of that, of the way that Father and my siblings looked at me throughout the years. *Murderer.* Medla's voice floods my head.

I shove the useless books onto the shelves and head for the western hallway. Back to Father's room, I do my best to ignore the fear that grows with each step in that direction.

The steady clacking of hooves on brick stops me dead in my tracks, one hand on the railing of the stairs. I listen carefully, and sure enough, the sound of the gate. An alarm sounds in my head from years of hearing its hinges. One that has me running for the servants' quarters as I have always done. I walk through the garden to get a look at the visitor unnoticed. *Why would anyone come all the way out here?*

The Shadows appear in the corner of my vision, pulsing with the pounding of my scared heart. The visitor knocks again. *There will be no answer.* I think to myself. I peer over the bushes to see who stands at the door. A large saddled black horse is tied to the post at our front gate, now wide open.

The sound of boots hitting the steps makes me retreat into the shrubs, and my heart begins to calm. Whoever they are, they must be leaving. It's suddenly very quiet, but I don't dare move, hoping that they have decided to be on their way.

The horse kicks up some dirt, creating a cloud of brownish red at its feet, waiting impatiently for its owner. They do not come. Our visitor must still be waiting in hopes that someone will return soon. It is an awfully long trip to make twice. The horse whinnies with excitement, I lean forward to get a good look at him. His beautiful black coat shines in the sun, and his mane and tail have been braided. I've seen this done before, on the horses of The Guard, when I was younger.

I've always had a love for horses. I did spend a lot of time around them, riding Adriel's horse whenever I could get it past Cedric. She begged Father for years for that horse, but as soon as the mare bucked her off, she didn't dare ride another time.

The mare might have been bought for my sister but belonged to me. It was sad to see her go that day with Adriel. Perhaps more upsetting to me than it is that Medla left the same day.

As I push myself out of the shrubs, the footsteps begin again. Before I can stop myself, my head collides with something hard, I stumble back a few steps in search of balance. I push my hands up to my temples to ensure my head is still attached to my body.

Hands catch me at the waist, and I quickly reposition myself, distancing myself from the touch. "I'm sorry, I-" for *what reason is he sorry? Touching a woman without permission or for almost taking off my head?* "Are you okay?" Kirian, the man I met in Thorn Row. *Gods, he really is a stalker.*

"Why are *you* here?" I ask through clenched teeth without answering his question because, no, I'm not okay. Not to mention there is a strange man in my garden. I have to tilt my head up to look at him. His blonde hair is almost white in the sun, and his eyes shine the same blueish green as the lake. He wears a full sand-colored Guard uniform.

Kirian holds an envelope in his large hand, cradled to his chest. His other hand holds a hat, his knuckles turn white with how tightly he grips. His tanned skin is rough and dry from hard labor, and the calluses on his hands are the same as Father's, maybe years of swinging an axe or a hammer. I flush with embarrassment when he catches me staring.

I force myself to properly meet his eyes as he pushes out the envelope. "This is a search warrant for your western forest. There's been an animal attack," he says, pointing west. "Most likely a wolf." I try to hide the absolute gut-wrenching feeling that takes over me. A wolf, that's unlikely. They are not usually spotted this far south. Wolves stay close to the mountain. It's much worse than a wolf I am afraid.

He peers over my shoulder past the garden and to the lake you cannot see from here, where worn targets lay against the tree line. I don't turn around, pretending I do not see where his gaze lands.

He saw me that night, and it was the last time he saw his bow as well. It was quite some time ago. I had almost forgotten about it until

I saw him yesterday. The thought of him watching me fail to use the weapon is an embarrassment.

My cheeks heat again at the memory. I am not the girl he saw that night anymore. No, I have had lots of time to perfect my aim.

I pull myself from the thought. "I haven't seen anything." Another lie. You can search the land as long as you need. I will tell Father." I hope that sounded convincing. When he doesn't say anything for a while, I begin to busy my hands by adjusting my trousers and straightening the tangled braid that lays over my shoulder. I twirl the split ends around my finger twice.

When I think about it, I can't help it as relief washes over me. One of my problems would be fixed if Father were to be found by Kirian. I would feign ignorance as to what happened to him, whereas if Father never came back, I would have a hard time explaining his disappearance.

I give Kirian a polite smile as I usher him back to his horse. "You better get going. That's a long trip on horseback," I tell him.

He chuckles as we walk. "You mean the trip you took on foot yesterday to Thorn Row and back?" He unravels the knot he tied with the reins. I look the magnificent steed in the eye. Without thinking I reach my hand out to pet him. I can feel Kirian's stare, I ignore it. "Goose" Kirian says.

"What a peculiar name for a horse." I half-whisper and then suppress a laugh when Goose nudges Kirian, almost knocking him over.

"That's the response I usually get." He says as he rebalances himself. His white teeth shine when he flashes a wide smile. His eyes scrunch up, and a dimple appears on his left cheek. He places a foot into the stirrup and mounts Goose with ease. "Bright and early." He looks down at the papers in my hand.

I nervously look at the castle I call home. From the outside, it's beautiful, unkempt, but still grand. The inside, however, has fallen into disrepair since our servants left. There can't be people in my home. I'd have to start right now and clean all night for it to be ready for guests. Medla would say it's improper not to invite them in and...

"It will just be a few of my men. We will stick to the forest." I snap my head back towards him at the words, like he read my mind.

"Thank you," I say with a nod of my head. Kirian pulls the reins to his side. Goose obeys the command.

"It was nice to see you again, Katsia Luz," Kirian says over his shoulder.

Chapter 5

Kirian was right. They arrive bright and early in search of a wolf that they will never find. I watch through the library window as Goose and Kirian, followed by two others, make their way to the gate just as they did yesterday. I see Kirian search the area as they slow, first looking towards the garden.

His uniform lay neatly over his broad shoulders, tailored to fit him perfectly, no doubt. When the sun hits the metal pins on his left side, they flash golden light. As he approaches, his eyes scan over the entrance before searching the windows. I drop to the ground, hitting the hard surface with a thud. Then, crawl to the side to remain unseen, grateful for the empty hallways and vacant rooms.

As I stand wiping the dust from my shirt and straightening my suspenders, I think of all the ways this day could go wrong. I prepare myself, ignoring the Shadows that peer at me from beneath the cracked banister, and walk to the door to greet Kirian. I'm grateful that he is too far away to see inside. I take the precaution of opening the door only enough to squeeze through before closing it quickly behind me.

I start to understand why my sisters would have the servants clean for hours on end before guests arrived. As I stand on the steps before me, about to take the first, I realize that it's been a very long time since I've used my own front door.

"May we use your stables, Miss Katsia Luz?" he says over the short distance. Hearing him use my full name unsettles me, perhaps because I did not hear it often by others.

Lupita called me Kat, mostly, and my sisters and brother were not fond of me using their last name since my Father was not biologically mine.

I'm still getting used to how people communicate, having only heard conversations from a distance.

Does he address everyone that way? I wonder, my eyebrows involuntarily scrunching together at the thought. The same smile from yesterday when I laughed at the name of his horse takes up his whole face—the kind of smile that makes you want to smile too, but I don't.

"Yes, of course." I point to the stables and walk with him while he leads the horses. Although the walk is not far, it feels like an eternity in our silence.

Unaware of Kirian's watchful eyes, I throw a small bale of hay from the corner into the stall. Then, I give Goose a good scratch under the chin. When I finally look at Kirian, he has a curious look on his face. He glances between me and the hay that Goose and the other horses now enjoy before shoving his hands in his pockets and averting his eyes.

For a moment, his actions confuse me, then I begin to understand as I dust off my dirty hands. Women are probably not meant to throw hay in such a manner. My face becomes warm, and I remind myself to be careful of my actions around strangers. I guess I got so used to it, doing everything myself, there were no men to throw hay for me, nor did I want there to be. I've never wanted to appear pretty or act as though I am weaker than I really am for the sake of being ladylike, the concept lost on me until now.

Gaining an understanding of my sisters' choices as I stand in front of Kirian, I feel shame for not learning the ways in which to be a lady around men. This feeling is foreign as if I don't belong in my own skin. I suddenly want to get far away from Kirian, fearing he will learn about just how little I know, and I can't bear it. The look, the one that people gave to Father and my siblings when they would tell of Mother's death.

Kirian checks the structure of the lock, giving the gate a good shake. He looks at me and nods as he turns to leave. *Now is your chance. Tell him the truth.*

"Kirian," I say. He stops, turning towards me on his heels. "I have to-," I start to say again, but it comes out too quiet, then not all, as the words get caught in my throat. *I have to tell you that the wolf you're looking for doesn't exist.* The words are right there. I just can't make myself say them.

All my confidence in the decision to tell Kirian everything is disappearing rapidly. He still stands there patiently as he waits for me to continue. I play with a strand of my hair nervously. I could tell him everything, right now. *I'm afraid. I've always been afraid, and this time, it's no different. He wouldn't believe me anyway.* Still, I try once more, "I—"but the words do not come.

"Is everything okay?" he asks, but his voice seems so far away, like a dream.

"Yes. It's nothing." I swallow the knot in my throat, and when I open my mouth to speak once more, to tell Kirian to be on his way, to search for the wolf that doesn't exist, just when I was about to let another lie fall from my mouth, another voice from behind Kirian speaks instead.

"The youngest Bear. Kirian, it's nice to see you again." My jaw feels like it might fall from my face as Kirian spins around. He sticks his arm into the air straight, the proper gentleman, as he greets my Father with a handshake. Father's face is hidden from me as I stand behind the soldier, and I almost prefer to stay that way. Kirian is large enough that I cannot see around him without leaning to the side. I can barely look Father in the eye as I brave a few steps to stand at Kirian's side, hoping he doesn't notice the surprised look on my face or the fact that I am shaking.

My Father looks well, better than he did even all those years ago before he slowly became what I would refer to as skeletal. Hunched over and dragging his feet as he barely got one foot in front of the other. *He must be on a healthy diet of lamb.*

His cheeks are no longer hollow, and although he limps slightly, he can obviously get around fine. His hair grays at the sides, his thin lips and white stubble surrounding them make it obvious that he has not been taking care of himself, a job that I am assuming went to Adriel.

Around Thorn Row Father is known as a kind man, a man of his word, trustworthy even. All the things that I would use to describe the *opposite* of my Father.

Father leans against a cane as he shifts his eyes to meet mine, disgusted by my presence. Not only is this the first time that I'm seeing Father after his crippled animal body collapsed at my feet. It's also the first time I've seen Father in almost eight years, truly seeing him up close. I was not allowed in his part of the castle, and when I did see him, it was from a distance. His back turned or his figure on a horse as he disappeared down the road.

He would often retire early in a drunken stupor after one of Medla and Adriel's parties. That's when I would have my fun, walking freely through the castle, knowing I could not be caught. One thing is for sure, wherever he was, I was not.

It wasn't until a few years later, just when I had mastered elusiveness within the castle, did Father fall ill. That made things much easier until now.

"Katsia told me you were searching the West Forest." Father bellows. I certainly did not tell him that. "You know, all kinds of wild things are running around these woods lately." Father runs his eyes over me, from ill-fitting boots to unruly black hair. He's, of course, talking about me.

I feel nauseated, my head feels light, and the air seems to be thinning again. Kirian glances in my direction from the corner of his eye. Standing before Father and Kirian, I feel small. Like Stone will soon open up, and I will be swallowed by the dirt itself.

Kirian takes a step towards Father and pulls him away from the stables—away from me. My body still shakes, and my feet seem stuck to the ground, unmoving. I watch the two men walk out of sight, exchanging meaningless conversation about the weather. *Move,* I shout within the confines of my own head. *Move, you idiot.*

My ears ring, and the Shadows seem to be reaching for me as if I may fall without them there as a crutch to hold me up. I finally manage to turn towards Goose, who meets my eyes with what I can only assume is understanding. Then, I take one more proper look behind me to ensure they have truly left.

Were they there at all? My mind plays tricks on me, but no, this is all too real. I wish it weren't. I wish it wasn't magic, and it actually was an illness of mine, one that would explain away the beast and Father and the woman with a third eye.

There is a tug at my sleeve. It pulls me, beckoning me, I snatch my arm up to my chest to get away from its grip. All the Shadows that occupied the dark corners of these stables no longer cling to the walls. They do not speak but move in a way that begs me to follow them.

Not now, please, not now. Pushing my way through the ever-growing Shadows, I take large strides and head for a clearing in the east, leaving them behind, all of them, the Shadows, the men, the horses, all their eyes on me at all times.

The run leaves me breathless.

When I fall to my knees, dread takes over, my mind and body. My stomach begins to stir. I can't keep it in anymore. I heave up my breakfast. Then, when there is nothing left, I continue, heaving until my throat dries, my middle becomes sore, and my head pounds.

Here I stay until day turns to night and the stars appear above. The cool of night dances on my skin as the sun falls over the mountain. I've spent many nights in this exact spot. Those nights were much warmer, so I hold my knees to my chest to keep the heat.

The Shadows must have taken the hint because even as darkness surrounds me, they remain silent and unmoving.

I do not need to be there to know what will happen. Kirian will not find his wolf, and Father will not give him any reason to believe that he is anything but a man on the mend from a terrible illness. Father has always been good at deceit. A loving father, a grieving widower, a grand businessman, sober. I let every thought in, every memory. How could I be so dumb to think that I could ever stay here, that my freedom would last? What's worse is that I'm more afraid of what's past these lands that I've so easily made my own.

Thanks to my Father and his children, no home, no garden, no lake or trees, no money or status.

Chapter 6

The sun has not risen, but the morning birds wake me with song. *Shut up.* I want to say to them. As I walk back towards the castle, my back and shoulders ache from a nearly sleepless night on the hard ground. When it comes into view, I can't bear to enter for fear of what or who I will find. So, I find anything to fill my time. I check the stables, cleaning out the stalls in almost darkness. When I finish, I wipe the sweat from my brow as the sun rises, sending its beams down to warm my face.

It is no surprise that the men do not give up their search. I'm glad when it's not Kirian who comes riding down the hill, Goose and the other horses in tow. Still, I make myself scarce. I watch from the northern gate as a man fills a bucket from the well, letting the horses drink, then takes a drink for himself before walking back to join the search party. His head swiveling back and forth as a well-trained soldier should.

Looking down at myself, I notice that my shirt is muddied, and my boots have hay and manure stuck to the bottoms from this morning's activity. My black hair cascades down my back, and when I try to run my hands through it, they catch on to the pieces that have grown together. I glance towards the castle, but there is no way I'm going there. Instead, I head for the lake.

I peel my clothes and rinse them in the water. Knowing that the guards only have access to the western forest, I feel rather safe as I hang my clothes on the branch of an elm near the shallow part of the lake where I have bathed many times.

Even though it's ice cold, I much prefer this to being anywhere near Father. Besides, the cold relaxes my aching muscles.

I begin to scrub my scalp, using a nearby yucca plant and lathering its soapy interior to cleanse my long hair—a routine that I have done many times when I did not want to bother the servants or boil my own water for a bath.

The task becomes therapeutic, slowing the racing thoughts of what might happen to Father and what might happen to me for not telling Kirian what I know. Or the thought that I can't seem to shake, the one that I might actually be okay with, the one where Father is caught and killed, and I am rejoicing, relieved.

What's wrong with me? I almost say out loud as I scrub the dirt behind my ears.

"I waited for you." My hands instinctively go to my chest, concealing myself under the water. Slowly, I kick my feet to turn myself around to where a man stands, the water barely missing his boots as it laps onto shore.

Kirian holds another envelope in his hands, the same color and shape as the last, another search warrant.

He inspects the leg of my trousers as they hang upon the branch, touching them lightly with the back of his hand. I scan the horizon, searching for anyone who may be nearby. "You didn't come back. You would rather stay out in the cold all night rather than-"he cuts himself off, his attention still on the clothes that occupy the branch. Then, he thinks of what to say next. "Surely you could have found a way to avoid him without doing that." He looks at me expectantly, but I have no answer. After all, I am naked and trapped. These two things occupy my mind entirely, making it impossible to think of anything else. He seems unbothered.

When I work up the courage to respond, it comes out strained. "What do you want?" I call out so that he can hear me.

His shoulders move up and down with a laugh I cannot hear from here. Then he looks around at our surroundings before his eyes land upon me again. "Your father said you were peculiar." He smiles at me. *Peculiar? Father chose his words carefully not to raise suspicion. What he really wanted to say was an abomination, murderer, disgusting, just as he said to me that night.*

I do not reply. He can think of whatever he wants. The people of Thorn Row do not care about truth or lies, instead they merely believe whatever people tell them without a second thought. "Do you know where he is, by the way?" he asks. His eyes never leave mine, and I wonder if he is trying to make me feel uncomfortable on purpose. I shake my head in answer, sinking further into the water until it rests just below my nose.

My body shivers as I look at him, pleading with my eyes. Looking between him and my clothes dangling in the wind, they seem so far away under the eyes of Kirian Bear.

Someone whistles from a distance. Kirian's shoulders straighten, but his attention does not waiver from his target, me. He stands perfectly still. Even the water seems to settle as he pins me under his gaze as if he can't look away. I'll make him look away, make him leave, but I only have one place to go, down.

I suck in as much air into my lungs as I can. I, too, can play this game and might even win. A flash of light reflects off the whites of his eyes, and that's the last thing I see before I go under.

Water displaces as I push myself further and further until my backside hits something solid. At least twelve feet under by now, it's darker and colder but tolerable.

I count to sixty. Again. And again. Starting my count over, I get to forty-five before returning to the surface. Victory is mine. He is nowhere in sight.

On the way back to House Luz, I throw my hair into a braid as I walk. I look down at Kirian's tracks, where his weight has left indents in the dirt in the shape of his boots. I have to stretch out my stride to match his, and in some places, I leap from one to the other. They lead me to the stables, stopping at Goose before continuing.

I do not follow any longer. Instead, I lay on the hay bales and tip my head back until it rests against the post behind me. My eyes close as I listen to the steady in and out of Goose's massive chest, to the pulling of grass that one of the horses has discovered between the gaps of oak, and to the shifts of weight beneath their hooves. These are sounds that are not Shadow or man, sounds that distract me from my thoughts as I drift from consciousness.

My head falls forward, jolting me from sleep. I only drifted into a dream for a moment. I can't recall its contents. Goose and his friends warn me as someone approaches. I'm to my feet in an instant as Kirian opens the stalls and readies the horses for departure. "Did I interrupt your nap?" he side-eyes me as he heads towards the stall. Thankfully, he looks away as embarrassment warms my cheeks.

"No, I was just here to see Goose." I look between him and the large animal with a polite smile. I must have slept longer than I thought.

"I'm sure he enjoys the company." He brushes some dirt from Goose's back. *Leave.* The Shadows whisper into my ear. I ignore them. "Do you ride?" he asks, turning his attention to me.

"Not really," I say. *Any more I should have added.*

"I saw your sisters pass through Thorn Row. They had the horses and, if I'm not mistaken, took one of your Fathers' carriages. The other one is always parked outside of Gale's, your brother, I assume." Gale's is a place that employs beautiful, expensive women. That's what Adriel told me anyway.

"Yes." is all I can say.

"Do you miss them?" I bite my lip as I think of a response. *The horses, yes. My siblings, no. Not really.*

"Yes" I decide to say, he doesn't have to know what I mean.

"That was a lie." He pushes his brows together slightly. I'm sure my face is nothing less than shocked at his observation. Fibbing here and there is nothing new to me, but lately, the amount of truth that leaves my lips has become fewer and fewer. Life is easier with lies—or perhaps easier when the only person I was lying to was myself.

"No, I don't miss them. They left us." *They left me*. My fists tighten at my sides.

He shakes his head to acknowledge my candor before changing the subject. "Stay inside at night, Katsia." He says as he takes a few steps, closing the distance between us. He reaches into the inside of his coat and pulls out the envelope from earlier. The image of him staring me down at the lake pops into my head, I push it out quickly, but my face is already red, I'm sure.

He holds out the paper for me to take. *He's too close*, I think to myself. I cringe as we accidentally graze each other in the exchange. His thumb rough against my own. I practically snatch my hand away with the envelope. Silently praying that he did not notice the action.

"For the north," I say aloud as I read its contents, he looks down at the search warrant in my hand.

"More animals have been found dead, and we found tracks leading that way. Get inside at night, I mean it." he lets out a breath. "Listen,

I've seen the damage. It's like no wolf I've seen before." My eyes do not leave the papers in my hand. *The damage?* I shudder as my imagination gets the best of me. I picture Father tearing animals limb from limb.

"Yeah." I almost whisper my agreement. "I won't," I assure him, but going back into the castle is where the real danger is. Sleeping in the den of the beast, if only he knew. But if I say anything now, it may mean my life if Father were to figure out it was me who turned him in.

He loved Adriel, and look what he did to her. Imagine what he would do to someone he cares so little for. I swallow the lump that has formed in my throat.

Kirian takes his hat off and runs his hands through the blonde strands. "Let me teach you how to use that bow of mine." He says coolly. I convinced myself long ago that the weapons left behind were meant to be mine if the men never came searching for them. And no one ever did, the bow included.

He clocks the half-smile I stupidly let creep to my face and gives his signature wide grin in return. "Or that dagger you tuck into the side of your boot." He points down at my feet. "Did you steal that too?" he continues, mocking me.

"I don't steal." I lie again. "Besides, you never asked for it back," I add.

"Well, if that's the case..." he holds his hand outright, palm up. "I'll be taking it back now." I almost jump back from the sudden movement.

I hate to admit that I've grown attached to the bow, and I won't be giving it back anytime soon. Besides, it's my only one. *I guess they learned their lesson after the first one disappeared.* "I'll challenge you for it," I blurt. This will allow me to keep the bow if I win, that is. And

I don't plan on losing. I watched all of Cedric's friends fail miserably at their silly competitions. Kirian can't be much better.

Shocked, he steps back, crossing his arm in front of him as he contemplates. "Hmm." He coos, pretending like he hasn't already made up his mind. I have to keep myself from rolling my eyes. "Deal." He finally says.

The next day, Kirian arrives back at the castle early before his men, leaving them to search without him. "First, I'll give you an easy one." He says, placing a target a few feet away. The horses watch us from the stables. "Nearest to the middle wins round one." I've already won round one, the lake. The second win was when he agreed to the challenge. This, here, is the third round, but he doesn't know that.

"You first," I say timidly. All part of the plan, of course.

Without argument, he marks a line on the ground with the toe of his boot. Then, he straightens his back, knocks an arrow, and draws his bow. His large chest widens with the intake of air, and on the exhale, he releases. Bullseye. Kirian gives me a cocky side-long glance as he pulls the bow down from his chin. I suspected he was good, and he should be anyway. Being trained in weaponry is a requirement for The Guard. I pay him no attention as I step to the line.

He only takes a few steps away, but not far enough. He stands behind me as I take my stance—*too close again*. Over my shoulder, I push my chin out in a silent gesture for him to move back. He puts his hands up in surrender and takes a few backward steps. *There, now I can concentrate.*

Needing him to think he has the upper hand, I pull the arrow back with ease, the way I have done hundreds of times, but this time, I make sure to aim just slightly lower than the red circle, just beneath Kirian's arrow. He can win this battle because I'm about to win the war.

"Too bad," he says as he inspects the two arrows. "Just a little low." I give him my best look of disappointment. He grins, pulls them from the target, and walks them back to me. "1-0," he points between us.

He holds out my arrow to me. Kirian gives me a strange look as I take it, one I can't quite place, then he shakes his head and walks past me into the trees, giving me no choice but to follow.

He explains the next challenge as we go. "This one will be a distance shot" he takes a left towards the lake. My heart skips a beat, but I keep his pace. "I saw something that caught my eye at the lake yesterday." He says over his shoulder at me. *Caught his eye?* What is he playing at? *I* was at the lake, naked, in the water. He must be teasing me, getting in my head, but I will not let him.

"Yeah?" I decided to play along. "What did you see?" no hint of jest in my voice. He laughs anyway. His large shoulders bouncing up and down as we reach the shoreline.

"I'm glad you asked." He stops abruptly, almost sending me crashing into his backside. My last collision with Kirian Bear resulted in a headache that lasted me all day. Stepping to the side to avoid him, I look up at him with the twist of my head. *So tall.* I follow his eyes. There on the other side, just past the little cove where I bathed just yesterday, is a scrap of fabric. A lighter green than the muted colors of the coming fall. The tail end of the fabric lifts slightly as a gentle breeze drifts by it.

"Me first?" he asks, but he is already lining up the shot before I can answer. He takes the same breath and releases it when he fires. The arrow zooms over the water, nearly hitting a small wave before gliding upwards again, headed straight for its target, but he miscalculated.

The wind is not as strong as he thought, causing him to narrowly miss to the right. The fabric gets pushed to the side when the feathers attached at the end of the arrow hit the weeds on which it was caught.

Green waves of fabric float through the sky, the wind carrying it to the field nearby.

Without a second thought, I reach behind me, pulling an arrow from my quiver. I knock it, darkness blurs the outside of my vision, allowing me to narrow in on the target. The Shadows make their presence known *"now,"* one of them says. I loosen my fingers. I hear the click of my arrow releasing from the weapon. My arrow grabs the fabric, sending it further into the field. Before descending, the red fletching sticking out from the ground towards the sky, the fabric now pinned to Stone.

"I saw your arms drop," Kirian says from behind me, taking my attention away from the arrow. *What?* That's not the response I was hoping to get, I look back at Kirian, confused. My arms are still up, my hands clutching the grip. "You purposely aimed below my arrow." He looks towards the castle, where we aimed at a target only a few minutes ago. I lower my arms slowly. I've been caught.

"You, you hustled me!" he says excitedly. *Why is he happy? He lost.*

"What does that mean?" I ask him, a little embarrassed that I do not know. His smile does not fade, but he runs his hands through his hair in frustration not aimed at me.

"It means you tricked me. I was suspicious after the first shot. Thought I was just imagining things." He chuckles. "You win." He looks at the arrow once more in the field and shakes his head. "Keep it." He throws his arm in the air in defeat.

We walk back in a strange sort of calm silence. I make sure to walk behind him so that he doesn't leave my eyesight. He stops right at the tree line. I take a step further as I peer over his shoulder, wondering why we have stopped. I look down at the stables that are still full. *His men should be back by now.* Kirian leans up against a tree and takes a long look at me, I shrug my shoulders and push past him. He grabs my arm, and a very serious look takes over his face. *Shit. I know that look.*

"Why were you talking to Claire?" he asks. I have never heard that name in my life.

"Who is Claire?" I pull away from his grip and take a step away from him. I don't like serious conversations. They never end in my favor. Medla telling me how important it is not to be seen. Adriel sitting me down to explain the importance of reputation. They all end with a rule. *So many rules to follow.*

"The woman that you ran from in Thorn Row, the seer," he tells me. I look down at his hand, which stays firmly on my wrist. That's what the robed woman, Claire, was doing for that woman. Can she really see the future? There is no time to think of what she might have seen in my own. No, I'm much too furious.

"You saw me come into town, you followed me to that woman, Claire. Then you stalked me to Center Square. Now you're *here*?" I ask him. Coincidence or just following orders, either way he has an agenda.

"Yes," he says innocently.

"And what *are* you doing here?" I finally ask.

"My job."

"What is your job exactly?" I put a bitter twist on my words. He looks towards the castle. He can't even look at me. I'm so stupid. Why didn't I notice earlier? This was all a trick. It's always a trick, people don't befriend me, they hardly even notice me. Just when I thought I had won.

Kirian looks past the castle to the North. "What do you suppose is past the Uncharted?" he asks nonchalantly, ignoring my question.

I don't give a fuck about the Uncharted Territories right now, I'm becoming impatient. *Just get to the point.* "Answer my question," I order.

"No one dares the journey to Shadow Gate. Do you know why that is?" he continues as if I didn't speak. The answer to his question is *no*. My sister always told me it was rough terrain after the war, that most of the fighting happened in the North, destroying most of the roads. Maps are almost useless when it comes to navigating the old cities.

"Rough terrain," I humor him. Hoping to end this conversation quickly.

He huffs a laugh, making me feel so small, inferior without that knowledge that he so clearly possesses. "That's one reason I suppose. Would you like to know the other reason?" he asks. I remain silent. The castle cast a shadow over us as the sun dips down behind it. Kirian's men still have not come to gather their horses. Where are they? "Villagers in the Uncharted Territories have been complaining of barren crops this season, creatures that steal their babies, and beasts that eat their livestock." He finally takes his eyes from the mountain and directs them at me, accusation in his words.

The look has me seething. "What does that have to do with me?" I spit, making sure I give nothing away.

"That woman, Claire, she's part of an organization. The Spent. They are regulated magic users, commissioned by the King himself."

"Why are you telling me this?" I shake my head, pulling at my bound wrists, but it's no use.

"So that you will tell me the truth. Why were you there that day?" Just as the words leave his mouth, a whistle comes from the direction of the castle, the same one that sounded at the lake. A wordless command, I turn my head to the noise, Kirian does not. "You don't seem like the type to go asking about future lovers." He speaks, but it sounds far away as all the pieces come together.

I know now that I have not won at all. Kirian has been keeping me from the castle on purpose. He found me in the lake to keep an eye on me. Pretended to go head-to-head with me for the bow, leading me back into the forest to kill time. I take a step towards the castle, but he stops me once more, his hand still on my wrist. "It's best now if you just tell the truth." He tries again.

For a moment, I think about telling him everything—oh, how I want to get it off my chest. But I say nothing as I slip from his loosened grip with an angry pull of my arm. Instead, I take my defeat, walking in stride with Kirian as he leads me to the castle. When we step out of the treeline, Kirian's men have come out of their hiding places.

By the time we get to the stables the horses are saddled and ready to go. I look around for Father, almost expecting him to be chained up somewhere so that they can take him too, but he is nowhere in sight, and I don't dare ask about him. Who knows what he told Kirian, for all I know he is the reason that I'm currently being read my rights.

Kirian ties my hand in front with rope before lifting me onto Goose easily then climbs up behind me. There is no distance between Kirian and I as we ride together, his thighs press up against my own. Instinctively, I try to pull away, but soon, sitting up straight becomes tiresome, and my back aches from leaning forward. When I lean back to relieve the pain, I try not to think about how much our bodies touch. I cringe at the feeling of his chest against my back. "You don't have to fear me, I know it doesn't seem like it now, but I am on your side," he whispers before leaning back to give me more room, as much room as he can anyway. *On my side?*

He deceived me, but I suppose I shouldn't have been so naïve. On the other side of the coin, I do believe in justice, and I might not have killed those animals, but I didn't stop it either. Didn't think of the consequences when patching the wounds of a beast.

By the time we get close to Thorn Row, the sky turns from blue to the orange color it takes on before the sun sets. The houses become less spread out as we enter the city. They basically live on top of each other here, something I noticed during my last trip. It's too dark to see the roses, but I can see where Center Square sits as we pass by. There is a void of light in that spot, far from the candles or lamps that occupy people's homes.

Kirian and his men ride in circles before ending at the jail. If it was meant to confuse me, it was a failed plan. It's evident that the jail was built in the times before Thorn Row grew to what it is now. This part of the city that The Guard tried to keep me from recognizing was easily spotted when I saw the surrounding buildings, years of reading through Fathers' old documents, and books on new and old architecture. I know exactly where we are.

Chapter 7

Father's company built most of the new homes and businesses in Thorn Row. It even helped with the blueprints for the layout of its latest industry, the markets.

Travelers and merchants were already passing through the town. It's at the center of Stone, and every road passes through it. The only way to get from Flora to Fauna is through this city. The noble families made sure they would make money from its travelers. Now, Thorn Row is the largest city in Stone. Its largest export, dahlia roses, a peace offering from Flora. Its largest import, the coins from travelers' pockets.

Unfortunately, the markets are taxed so they make just enough to stick around, and the rich, like my family and families alike, profit.

They escort me down a dark set of stone stairs. The air becomes heavy and stale, mixed with the smell of old alcohol.

Kirian takes me by the arm, one of his men takes the other. My hands are still bound, and my wrists burn with every pull.

The men lead me to the farthest corner in the dim maze of cells, close enough to the door but not down one of the corridors I see that lead to God's know where.

There are thick walls on each side and a barred door at the front. Offering both isolation and a constant reminder of the presence of others. Every noise echoes off the brick.

I make sure to glance through the bars of every cell we pass, looking for Father. There are only men snoring on their cots or huddled over buckets as they release the booze from their stomachs after a drunken night.

Amidst the groans and snores, my eyes met hollow gazes and vacant stares, along with hungry smiles as if I am a piece of meat when they realize that I was a sheep in wolf's clothing, a woman amongst men.

Kirian releases me and takes a few steps back. He did not so much as make a noise as we walked before criminals and drunks. He continues his silence as one of his men shoves me into the cell, making me trip over myself without the balance of my bound hands. Unable to catch my fall, I crash to the ground, my hands outstretched but crushed beneath the weight of my body. Kirian only clears his throat before closing the door behind me and locking it with a large set of jingling keys.

The other man instructs me to stand. He pulls out a curved knife and motions for me to come closer. Kirian still doesn't look at me. He keeps his eyes forward, a statue. But I watch him. As the man taps the metal, motioning for me to set my hands between the bars, I do not flinch as he sloppily cuts the rope. Neither does Kirian. He is emotionless. I only look away from him to rub at the angry crimson welts that now occupy the skin around my wrists.

Then, they walk away. The sound of their boots slowly becomes quieter with the distance before they are cut off by the closing of a large wooden door, its hinges squealing before slamming shut.

Time escapes me, no doubt why they make sure the cells are located underground, no light.

One man yells at the guards for more blankets, and I feel the drop in temperature. I believe it's well past midnight now. The man continues to complain about the cold, but the guards do not open the door or even give him an answer. Soon the man's pleas become less and less until finally they stop altogether.

No one is across the way from me, granting me a sliver of privacy. Perhaps it was meant as kindness, although it doesn't feel like it. The other cell is empty, just dark enough for eyes and teeth to appear any minute now. I slide to the end of the cot and place my head on my hands, resting my elbows on my knees.

Refusing to fall asleep, I stare at the empty cell for a long time, waiting. Soon, just when I think the Shadows will not make an appearance, they become tangible, moving and grasping at the empty spaces around them.

I fall backward, letting my legs dangle over the edge. As time passes, I let the cold spread over my body. I don't pull the blanket over myself or pull my legs to my chest for warmth.

The Shadows whisper to me, I open my ears to them but do not let them know I pay them attention. Not much of it makes sense, all but one word that is. *Come*, they say from beyond the bars. I roll over onto my side and close my eyes, listening to the in and out of my breathing and not their demands. Soon they stop, replaced by the shuffling of men and dripping of water somewhere far off.

A few meals come and go, all brought to me by a woman, a servant. She wears a uniform of royal blue and a white bonnet that keeps her blond hair off her face. I am reminded of Lupita as I look at the notch missing from her ear. *Oh, how disappointed in me she would be.* I try talking to the woman as she slides a meal between two horizontal slats in the bars. She does not answer, adding to the loneliness of confinement.

As she walks off, I follow her with my eyes. She smiles once at my neighbor before putting her head down and walking quickly to the door.

When the door opens for her, I try to get a glimpse at the soldier on the other side. Still, I run out of room at the end of my cell, only able to see a muscular arm as they pull the heavy door closed after her.

My food grows cold as I pick through the stew and take a bite of very stale bread before discarding it on the floor to be retrieved next mealtime.

I lose count of the meals brought to me, leaving me unsure of how many days have passed. I pull the thin pillow around my ears so I do not have to listen to the scrape of wood on metal as the woman exchanges one plate for the other. I disregard the food altogether. Leaving it to either be eaten by mice or picked up by the woman. My belly growls with hunger, but my appetite is not there. I feel only a knot in my stomach as I think about what will happen next.

When all I can hear are the snoring of men and the same incessant plop of water on brick, I assume it's night again. My eyes feel heavy, but I do not sleep for long. When I do, my dreams are filled with terrifying portrayals of monsters and men who find me no matter where I hide.

As I lay on the bed, humming away my thoughts, I listen as the door opens and then shuts. This happens often. Sometimes, the guards check on us, walking back and forth. Some inmates mumble under their breath at the soldier with the task of interrupting their sleep. At first, I searched each of their faces. Hoping that one would eventually be Kirian. Then I could ask him *why* I am here, *what* I'm here for. Although I'm not certain I will like the answer.

A memory pops into my head. One where Lupita spoke of those who suffer from this particular affliction. The one that has plagued me my whole life. Little did she know that I suffered the same ailments she spoke of. A woman who had gone mad and started to see things that were not there. I promised never to reveal myself to her or anyone after hearing of what happens. Magic or not, it is enough to be put away for life or worse.

This time, when footsteps stop at the end of the hallway, and I do not hear their usual retreat back to the door, I am surprised when it is Kirian. He stands behind the bars, waiting. I immediately stand and go to him, ignoring the lightheadedness that almost makes me reach for the wall. The drumming in my chest settles as I near him for reasons I cannot explain.

The bars are cold, and I hold two between each hand. Kirian keeps his distance on the other side. "Why are you here?" I whisper weakly when he does not say anything.

Kirian seems to be contemplating his following words. "I need to ask you a few questions." His voice is low. I remain silent as I wait for him to continue. "Why were you talking to The Spent?" He pushes his eyebrows together as he tries to make sense of it.

I share his confusion. He already asked me about Claire. I didn't go there wanting to talk to what Kirian refers to as The Spent. I don't even know who The Spent are. I was looking for answers, and she was the first person I came across. *House of Hades*, I didn't even want to speak to her. She stopped *me*.

"Father's illness, it was a last resort. I was searching for a magical healer." I give him a half-lie. I really was looking for answers about Father. I admit, I was not all that interested in a healer. It was a selfish trip meant to tell me more about my Mother and his sickness was second on the list.

"Don't lie. Please don't lie to me. I am trying to help you, Katsia." His voice is low so as not to wake anyone, but it's still a scolding. I snap my head up at his words, prepared to say something. What? I do not know. So, I close my mouth and wrap my arms around my stomach. I take a few backward steps back until my legs hit the metal. I sit down slowly, afraid that my legs will give out from under me if I do not rest them immediately.

He looks at me expectantly, but I shake my head at him, letting him know that I have nothing more to say. *"I'm on your side,"* he said to me before, but I don't believe it, he brought me here. He tricked me. He is not on my side.

His gaze softens before he continues, "Claire. Did she provide any magical services for you?"

"Like what?" I lift my head and realize that my body is shaking. This feeling is overwhelming, and unfortunately, I have been experiencing it far too often.

"An incantation." He pinches the bridge of his nose. "Did she give you anything, anything at all?" he asks quietly, strained even.

"She read my palm. I think. I've never had it done before." I tell him truthfully.

"Well, that's just the surface of her abilities." He scoffs in frustration before moving on. "If you know where your Father is, I suggest you tell me." *My Father? He's not here already?* I assumed they had already arrested him. My face contorts in confusion as he continues. "Tell me, Katsia. The next man will not be so gentle with getting the truth." I stand at his threat, barely avoiding the crushing weight of my own body. He just looks at me like a wounded, helpless animal. I hate it, but as I look down, I see the reality of what I am. Caged and scared.

"If I knew where he was, I would tell you." It comes out louder than intended. As I take one more step I let my forehead rest against a rusted bar, my breath comes out strangled before I speak the following words "I don't know where he is." I plead. *Please believe me.* I just want this to be over with. When I look up at him, he steps forward and crosses his arms in front of his large body. Contemplation on his face as we hold each other's gaze for a few long seconds "Fuck." he says under his breath, shaking his head.

Does he think that I knew and was just not saying anything? He wants me to trust him, but he just *now* came to the conclusion that I might actually be telling the truth?

"What did he do?" I ask softly as he uncrosses his arms to run his hands through his hair, a habit I have noticed he often does.

He looks to the right, down the corridor of cells, back the way he came. His jaw clenches before he starts in that direction. "Just tell me why I am here" I try when he takes another step.

Without looking at me, he stops. "What your Father did..." he thinks of his response more before continuing. "He'll be hung for his crimes. If we can find him, that is." He lets out a heavy breath, still keeping his eyes on the door. "As for you," he sighs, "Suspicion of unregulated magic." My heart sinks. *This disgusting thing that others are calling magic.* The darkness grows around me as I think of it, I ignore them.

"Look at me," I beg. Kirian does not so much as move an inch. I close my eyes to keep the tears at bay. "I- I've never- "The words do not come out. They were all going to be lies anyway.

The pain in my stomach almost makes me double over. I grip the bars with all my strength to hold myself up. I wait for him to move again, but he doesn't. He stays. I wish he would. I wish for a lot of things. I wish he had never seen me with his bow in the garden that day. I wish I never went to Thorn Row in search of answers. *I wish I were dead.*

"Why did you stay there? In that castle? I saw it. It was"— he thinks of what to say next. "I'm sorry you had to do that." Pity, pity, pity. I can't do this anymore. I don't want to deal with this, confinement, Kirian, everything.

"Don't." I choke out as my eyes open to land upon Kirian's. He is now studying me, his arms still crossed and his body angled for the door. He doesn't say anything as he leaves. Something in me breaks as I watch him go. My eyes sting with the promise of tears, and my chest begins to pound so loudly that it drowns out every sound, including my own thoughts.

I give in, collapsing to my knees. The walls seem to close in on me. I crawl to the bucket in the corner, using my elbows to balance myself upon it. Then I retch, hoping that it would get rid of the knot that pulls at my insides, but the pain is still there. Not until I begin to shiver from the cold does that feeling go away.

Chapter 8

Time passes once more. I am unable to keep track of the days as I have ignored most of my meals and slept away the hunger instead.

This time, the scraping of wood on the bars signaling mealtime stirs me from sleep. As the servant brings me a slop of what can only be porridge with sausage, she pushes it between the bars, nearly spilling it over as the tray hits the ground. This gets my attention. I sit up from the cot, propping myself up on my arms as I watch the woman's body tremble as she takes sight of me.

Her startled eyes meet mine before she leaves as fast as her small legs will carry her, mumbling under her breath, a prayer. "May evil be swept from my veins," She whispers to herself. I watch her as she basically sprints to the end of the hall. She then gestures with her left hand, two fingers held to the bottom of her chin. She slides them out, extending her arm. An ending to her prayer.

I hum away the silence because when the world grows quiet, the Shadows appear. Some prisoners join in on my song, and some curse at us to stop.

Men are released, and others fill their spots. When the melodies are done and the room grows cold once more, we all settle in for bed. Again, footsteps make their way towards my cell.

If I am not mistaken, those footsteps belong to Kirian. They are heavier than the guards that usually stalk the hallway. I sit up and brace myself for another line of questioning. But when I stand and take a tentative step towards the sound. Nothing. No one is there, but the footsteps continue. They come right towards me, the sound right at my feet, on the other side of the metal bars.

This place is starting to play tricks on me. The confinement. I haven't seen the sun in so long. I've never let myself be still for this amount of time for fear of the darkness consuming me. I suppose it's finally happening.

Almost falling backward, I desperately pull the thin blanket from the cot around my shoulders to conceal myself from the weight of someone's eyes on my neck. I rock myself back and forth, head resting on my knees as I pull myself close.

What I see and hear cannot be trusted, I do not know of the things that my mind can create when pushed to the edge. *It's all in your head.* If it's not, at least if I die in here, no one will have found out that the madness was starting to take hold, I'll never have to go crazy or get those same looks that I received from Kirian, no one will have to feel bad for me that I was never able to be normal, like them.

The Shadows sneak into the cracks and crevices of the flimsy blanket. Their whispers make their way to my ears, just as they did that night before I found Father. They took me there, somewhere I did not want to go. This time I will not let them.

I pull and twist, ripping the blanket from their grip as they try to pull it from my body. "Leave me alone," I tell them. They do not listen. "Get off me," I whisper to them. They whisper back sweet promises of escape and the sun on my skin. The voices are slow and soft, as if they are talking through honey.

The Shadows soon grow long black arms, their fingers pick at my clothes and blanket, pulling me along with them, but I cannot go in every which way they take me. The feeling of weightlessness starts in my chest. Then, my body feels like it will melt, turning me into the liquid along with them.

I swing my feet over the side of the bed to anchor myself to the ground. When I look down, my feet are in a puddle of black. I nearly scream as I try to pull them out. They do not let me go.

There, on the other side of the bars, where the footsteps stopped, but there was no person to occupy the sound, lay another puddle, the same dark circle of black that pools around my feet. *Come*, they say again, so close that it's getting hard to decipher their voices from my own.

"I will not go with you," I say as I finally yank the blankets from their clutches. My knees nearly hit my chest when they release me. "Leave me alone," I say again.

The Shadows are mine. Therefore, they should yield to my command. Although it has not worked so far. The demand comes out louder than I intended. The man next to me stirs, grumbling to himself.

"Shh." The springs beneath him let out a squeal. When I hear his nearing footsteps end, his fists are pounding against the wall. "We are trying to sleep, dammit." The Shadow's arms shrink, and their teeth are no longer bare.

Finally, they slither back into the shape of the things around me. I push my face into the pillow, covering the sounds of my sobs until I fall into sleep.

My sleep is full of lulling voices and invitations into the abyss. I dream of a beast, one with the eyes of Father. Its long-pointed teeth nearly touch me as it snarls and growls. Something warm drips from my forehead and onto my white dress that flows to the ground.

My skirt whips violently in the wind, along with the tangled braids in my hair. I wipe at the liquid that has now seeped into my eyes. My fingertips come away coated in red, blood, my blood. It stains the beautiful silken fabric in patches of red.

The beast circles me before lying at my feet. Beyond his body is a door, I go towards it stepping over its rancid decaying body. The silk covers the beast like a sheet over a corpse, the hem of my dress only growing as I walk so as not to uncover its body.

When I finally turn around, there is only a long hallway of white silk with red stains. The beast's whimpers and whines are distant. I do not turn around. I do not feel bad for it this time. I do not uncover its body to mend its wounds or warm its body with a fire.

The further I walk, the less I can hear its snarl or smell its foul odor.

White sheets cover me, blocking out the light from the lanterns. I shove them off of my body with all my strength, still in a daze from the nightmare, thinking that I had somehow become the one trapped beneath the fabric. My stomach again threatens to expel its contents as I sit up. The thundering of my chest becomes steady once I take in my surroundings. Still in the jail, men shuffle around, and the familiar hum of my neighbor fills my ears. The melody stops when the springs beneath me squeak at the shift of my weight. "Your nightmares keep me awake at night." His voice is barely above a whisper.

"I'm sorry," I say breathlessly. Sometimes, my neighbor and I hum somewhat of a duet. But aside from that and his late-night complaints, he has never tried to speak to me before.

His humming continues but is soon cut off by the banging of an opening door which echoes through the room. Mealtime. I look down at yesterday's dinner as it still sits on the floor, some of it eaten by mice or other critters that live in these walls.

When the jingling of keys and the shuffling of feet make their way past the prisoners, they begin shouting.

The clinking of wooden bowls and the slosh of porridge hit the ground. One of the empty bowls rolls over in front of my cell. "Daimon!" someone shouts at the guards. "May evil be swept from our veins," they tell each other, reciting the same prayer as the servant as she left my cell. I make my way to the bars and peer out at the chaos. The prisoners bang on the walls, and my neighbor hits our shared wall at the same tempo as the footsteps on the ground.

"Settle down," the soldier commands as they approach. One looks at me. He smiles with rotting teeth and a crooked grin.

This causes an uproar, the shouts grow louder, the pounding more intense. The only one who does not curse at them is the man next to me. He must have grown bored of the commotion. He continues his humming as the guards come stand in front of me, the cell that was once empty across from mine opens with a heavy turn of its lock. When the guard slides it open the men seem to settle back into their spaces.

Two soldiers hold a bloodied, skinny man up by his shoulders. They release him with a shove, and the man falls face-first onto the cold floor. He doesn't even try to catch himself. I can't see his face, but a yellow glint shines from his neck when he rolls over with a groan.

My mind goes blank. I stand there for a moment longer, in shock.

Not beast, hardly even man, he seems to have decayed since I last saw him. It wasn't all that long ago, mere days in fact, that I had seen him standing there with Kirian, his face full of color, his cheeks filled and his eyes bright. Now he is gray, dying. His blood-soaked shirt sticks to his small body so much so that I can count every rib on his side. I take a few steps back on wobbly legs. *No, this can't be happening.*

There is no way that he could get to me, and I know that. Still, I retreat into the cell, pushing myself into the corner so that there is no way he could see me. Father lets out a groan of pain. I hear the squeak of springs as he finds the bed.

Then, the guard with crooked teeth takes another peek at me, sticking his head between the bars. He finds my eyes as I sit on the floor, cradling myself, trying to calm the wild thoughts by rocking back and forth on my tailbone. "Family reunion," he laughs before walking away with the others.

Every rattle of chains, every turn of bodies on beds and whispers between inmates sends me into a paranoid frenzy. I cover my ears, remaining in the corner, the smallest that I can make myself.

Tonight, I will be getting no sleep, something that Father does not seem to struggle with. His heavy breathing rhythmic with the sound of slumber since he lay on the bed this morning.

If their intention is to break me, they have done it. What was once a hairline fracture is now split, entirely down the middle, unrepairable. Sobs escape my body, ones that had been stuck in my throat since the day that my sisters left me. I wish for a way out. *Please, please, please.* I ask the air around me.

As if on command, the Shadows make their appearance. They lean close to me, cutting off the little light this place has. They once again continue their incessant pulling and prodding at my clothing. I no longer have the energy to swat them away. When I do not acknowledge their touch, they give up but do not disappear. Instead, they lay a blanket of black around my shoulders, and its heat radiates through me. I didn't realize I was shaking so severely until my body relaxes as my temperature rises. My temple hits the wall. I thank the Shadows quietly before I am lulled to sleep.

When I awake, I forget where I am, nearly tripping over my own legs in an attempt to stand. For a split second, I thought that the Shadows had taken me away somewhere.

No, the walls become familiar as I remember the events that unfolded the night before. My stomach aches and growls with hunger.

Flattening myself against the wall, I begin to walk towards the bars. I am able to hear the sounds of my humming neighbor as I move. He is in a good mood, unlike the rest of us.

A disagreement between a guard and the man who occupies the first cell has me moving even slower. Their argument ends with the slam of a door. There is no winning when you're in here. My neighbor's rumble of song gets louder as I slide closer to the hall, making sure that Father cannot see me. When I reach the corner, I take a few deep breaths to prepare myself for what I might see.

When I reach the bars, I'm startled as a warm hand grips my wrist around the wall I share with my neighbor. I nearly scream, but if Father wasn't awake, he surely would be if I did, so instead, I pull away, but the man is stronger than me. His song cuts off abruptly as he pulls me towards him. I use my other hand to claw at his flesh, but he does not budge.

"No one is there." The man's grip strengthens with his words. *Father is not here? How could that be?* Unsuccessfully fighting my way out of his grip, I stick my neck out slightly to see if my neighbor's words are true.

It's empty.

My shoulders fall instinctively, and the man must feel it because he uses the opportunity to pull me once more.

When I look down at his hand, there is a tattoo on the inside of his wrist—an eye—not just any eye, the same one that was on Claire.

"You're one of them. Let me go." My frail voice does not deter him.

"Ah, yes, and I know who you are as well." He tells me.

"And who is that?" I spit in anger, my voice course from heaving. I know the answer. A witch.

"What all of Stone has been waiting for." That's not what I was expecting.

I think carefully about what to say next. "What exactly have you all been waiting for?" I ask him as politely as I can with his hand still wrapped around my wrist.

"Not I." he lets out a huff that I think is a laugh.

"Then who?"

He pauses momentarily before the door opens again, letting out a long squeal from its hinges. "Choose your side carefully." He releases my arm, sending me falling backward. Then, he begins his song again.

I rub at the red mark he has left on me. "You're mistaken. I am not who you think. I am no one." the words come out breathy, desperate. The humming continues as the guards pass his cell and go straight to mine. They unlock the door. Two push their way into the space.

I look between them before they grab each of my arms and haul me out. I look over at the man in his cell, who leans against our shared wall, ready for my gaze. His gray hair is disheveled. His once broad shoulders sag as his body rolls forward as everyone's does with enough time. He gives me a nod of his head before disappearing from my view.

Chapter 9

The guards force me into a small, poorly lit room. They shove me forward so hard that I fall onto the hard floor. I try to catch myself, but not before my face hits the ground. My nose burns with pain, and when I reach up to touch it, my fingers come away red. *How many times are they going to do that?*

In front of me is a round table with two chairs facing each other on each side. I have never been interrogated before, but if I had to guess what the rooms look like that would hold such an activity, it would be this. I crawl to my feet and sit opposite the door, just as they want me to do. I suppose I have no choice but to play along.

Dirt and Gods know what else covers the scratches on my palms, I wipe my hands down my pant legs to get rid of the debris. The door clicks from the other side before slowly opening.

Blonde hair and green eyes, his uniform so put together, the seams of his guard's jacket lined up perfectly. His pins spaced accordingly and straight as an arrow. But something is off about this Kirian. His eyes look sunken into his skull, and his facial hair has grown around his jaw and neck. Sleepless nights must be popular around here. Kirian takes the seat in front of me and lets out a sigh. "This won't be fun for either of us." He whispers. He can't be bothered to hide the annoyance from his voice.

My hands begin to shake, so I rest them under the table on my lap so he does not see.

Turning my face from scared to brave as I swallow the knot in my throat. "Why am I here?" I ask boldly, my voice unwavering, but my hands still fidget with anxiety out of his sight. I ignore the look of surprise that takes up his face. If I am to be sentenced for witchcraft or spend the rest of my years locked away, I want to know.

"You're here for committing crimes against Stone." He says, almost bored.

"I've done nothing," I tell him. He told me he believed me. Why is he doing this? His sigh sends a puff of air moving my hair from my face, reminding me of how uncomfortably close we sit. I remember his words, "*The next man will not be so gentle with getting the truth.*" He is the next man. Does he plan to torture me for information that I do not have?

He changes his demeanor, leans forward and the already small distance between us becomes mere inches, as much as I want to retreat I do not. His face becomes more sinister as he stares me down. "Do you know Emily Blain?" he asks. I hide the surprise that takes over me well, what an odd question.

Yes, I do, she was friends with my sisters, they attended her boring parties. She ran off with some lower-class man from Flora, Adriel told me her family disowned her. I'm unsure of why any of that matters now though.

"Yes," I say keeping it short, not telling him of her elopement.

"Then you know that she no longer lives in Thorn Row." He states.

"Yes"

"You were friends?" he asks, his eyes still on mine. This is not the Kirian who challenged me for his bow or the one who visited me in that cell. So, who is this arrogant man who sits in front of me now?

"No"

"Hansel Luz knows her, did you know that?" he dips his chin down, looking at me through his lashes. This time, the surprise creeps to my face, and Kirian can tell because he, too, lets the corner of his mouth rise. I had no idea that Father kept in contact with Emily or *why* he would do such a thing.

"No," I say truthfully.

"We are going to need more than one-word answers, Katsia." Hearing my name on his lips makes me jump a little. My confident mask falls for just a moment. "See, I think you knew her much more than you're letting on." He growls. I don't know Emily, I don't know anyone, not truly, only names and faces, getting to know someone would require me to spend time with them, which I was not allowed to do. But I do not tell him this. "You knew her well. You know why your Father sought her out, don't you?" his voice is getting louder by the second.

"No." I shake my head.

"No?" Kirian laughs a little, it's not light and airy like the ones I've heard him use before. He is scaring me, but that's what he wants, for me to be scared. And I am, I always am.

"I was not allowed to leave the property. That day you found me in Thorn Row was the first time I had left in eight years." I try to explain but he does that menacing laugh once more.

Anger starts to get the best of me, this is no laughing matter, this is my life, I'm beginning to think there is no life left, this is the end of my journey. Still, my face warms with rage as I continue. "So, I don't know anyone or what company my family chose to surround themselves with," I say through gritted teeth, trying to convince him of the truth. But what's worse than his laughter is what I see underneath, what I see in his eyes at my confession.

"Do not pity me." I spit at him. Tears rise to the surface, stinging my eyes. I squeeze my hands together under the table. "I have done nothing, and why the fuck does it matter?" I'm past angry. I'm seething, barely able to keep my composure. The Shadows show themselves like the time at the lake when I sent the arrow before it tore the fabric from the air and sent it plummeting to the ground. Black blurs the outside of my vision before locking in on my target, Kirian Bear.

His eyes widen, but he does not see them, does not hear their promises of torture and death. "Where do you think Emily Blair is now?" he asks, louder now but still calm, almost joking, as he repositions his mouth into that awful smirk. How does he do that? Turn himself into something wicked in a matter of seconds.

"Hopefully somewhere far away from men like you!" *men like Cedric, men like Father* is what I want to say. That would only further the pity that sprouted in his eyes moments ago.

His mouth opens slightly, and his head tilts to the side. My comment has gotten under his skin. Regret floods my mind, sending the Shadows skittering back to their dark corners. But I should not care about being unkind to the man that has tricked me, lied to me, and thrown me in jail.

"No, Katsia, she is dead." He states matter of fact.

I stare at him like it does not affect me, and it doesn't, not in the way it should, maybe, but I did not know Emily aside from through my sisters. "Your Father was the last to see her, and now she is dead." He pushes back into the chair and crosses his arms. "Do you know what that means?" he half shouts. I do not reply to this. He wants me to say what we all know, Father killed Emily Blair, but I won't give that to him.

I can't bear to look him in the eye, so I look to the ground instead. "Give me my sentence," I say instead, begging him to get on with it and end this.

"You need to be put through trial for a sentencing." He says to me like I'm a child. "Just tell me the truth. Your Father's illness, it's not of Stone, is it?" This gets my attention again. He knows of Father's illness, Father was here, he was in the cell, and it wasn't just my imagination. Kirian knows what Father is.

"No, it's not, but you already knew that," I tell him.

"Listen, we couldn't care less if you're a witch. You will be put to trial. You will be hung." He states the facts. I suck in a breath to keep myself from collapsing at his words. "What we care about now is how your Father came across this... illness," he says the word sarcastically.

"I don't know." I plead with him, adjusting myself in the chair uncomfortably.

"You don't know?" he shouts before pounding his fists on the table, creating a vibration that rattles the small room.

"I don't-" I begin, but I do not think he hears me.

"Who gifted you your magic, Katsia?" he continues, his voice so loud that my ears ring.

"Gifted?" I ask confused. I know nothing about how it works, how people get their magic. Knowledge that I never thought I needed, nor was it around for me to study. After my Mother's death, Father made a point to get rid of her books in the library on account that they contained stories of the occult. My only link to the outside world was the small bits of information I could get from Lupita or from conversations between my sisters that I was not supposed to hear.

"Don't play dumb. Gifters are hard to come by these days, coveted by the King. You would have been sent to Fauna, trained with The

Spent, if that were the case." He lets out an easy breath. Someone would *give* another this sickness?

"Where is my Father?" I decide to ask, not wanting to think about the intricacies of magic anymore.

"You're wasting my time, Katsia." He says harshly as he pushes his hands through his hair. Then he leans forward, all the space between us gone. I don't pull away, I don't move at all, I can't. My body is frozen with fear as his turquoise eyes move back and forth between my own. I hope he sees it as strength, like I won't back down, but I doubt it shows that way.

"Your Father abused you, Katsia. He hid you from the world. Kept you confined for 8 years. Only using your name when he bragged of his kindness and goodwill for keeping you as a child after finding out you weren't his own." He spaces out the last words so that it sticks in the air.

He doesn't wait for me to say anything, not that I would have spoken up anyway. "You found a way to get rid of him, didn't you? You finally had enough. You found someone to gift you magic so that you could curse him." He gets impossibly closer, I can smell his skin, the mint on his breath. I close my eyes. "That makes two." His whisper tickles the skin of my chin. *Two what?* I wonder. I don't have to wait long for the answer. "Your curse killed your Father. Congratulations, you got what you wanted. Emily Blair was just a casualty. Doesn't change the fact that her death was ultimately your fault."

This finally has me moving. I shake my head at all the false words that have left his mouth. Sweat drips down my back, and my body convulses as I hold back tears. My eyes fly open. "No, no, that's not true. Please, why are you doing this? I just saw him, he- he was here." The tears come now, falling down my face, warming my cheeks further. Finally, I push myself away from Kirian, hugging my body with my arms, ashamed that I let myself get to the breaking point that he so desperately wanted. *Weak.*

"Oh please, you knew what would happen. The curse fed from his body, he was near death when we brought him in. It was only a day before he passed." He says as he stands. "Just give me a name." He looks down at me.

Father's wounds appear in my mind, the smell of incense, the tang of alcohol on his breath. The shattering of glass rings in my ears, a memory. Followed by what can only be described as relief. Which I should not feel.

Sobs escape me so fast and heavy that my body catches on every breath. "I haven't left the castle in 8 years. I know nothing, I *am* nothing." I reiterate. "8 years." I am now wiping the wet from my cheeks so that I can stand, too, so that I can look at Kirian and tell him the truth.

Kirian still towers over me, making me smaller than I already feel. My knees buckle, and I have to lean against the wall for stability. My head feels light. The little food that may be in my stomach feels as if it could spill out any minute. When I tilt my head up to look at Kirian, more tears stream down my face and drip from my bloodied nose. *Pathetic.*

Fine, I give up. My truth has been told more truth than I have spat to myself in so many years.

I let my shoulders move up and down as I stand there, terrified of what happens next. Kirian leans in close so that his mouth is at my ear. I try to pull away, but he keeps going, taking a step closer. My back is completely flat against the wall now. His large hand moves to my face. Holding me in place by my jaw, I try to free myself from his grip, but he does not budge.

When I stop fighting against him, he whispers so that no one who stands outside the door can hear him. "You did good. Now scream." It takes me a minute to understand what he just said, but then he pushes me to the floor. I do as I was told. I let out a shriek of terror. Obeying him, yes, but also because I have wanted to scream since I got here, to the world, to myself. He flips the table on its side, then the chairs fall to the floor with a loud crash.

He then takes out a knife from the sheath at his thigh, leaning down before me. He slashes his palm in the center, wincing slightly at the pain. He lifts his hand once more, then he wipes his blood on the right side of my face and down my neck. I do not dare move. It's almost gentle, a caress, far from the terrifying man I just saw him become. Good or evil, I can't tell anymore, nor does it matter. Making sense of it will not make a difference. He said it himself. *Put to trial. Hung. That is my fate.*

New tears replace the old, and I can't stop shaking. Even as Kirian stands to leave, I keep my eyes on the floor. "She's useless." I hear before the door closes. I'm left there for what feels like hours, confused and curled into myself on the disgusting floor until guards gather me and take me back to my cell.

Kirian's blood marks the sheets in crimson, but I do not care. I bury my face into the thin pillow and weep once more.

When Kirian's words stop repeating themselves in my head, *that makes two,* and my body stops convulsing. Sleep takes me away. Even in slumber, I remain in the cell. My surroundings are the same, water-damaged walls, red-soaked sheets, the flutter of a torch nearby that makes the Shadows dance. All but one. The Shadow in the shape of a man stands beyond the bars, beckoning for me to come to him with a gesture of his hand.

I go ridged, unmoving from my spot on the bed.

Like one does in sleep, without permission, my body starts moving on its own. I glide over to the metal bars where the man stands. The Shadow's figure emerges from a pool of black made from the same liquid darkness as his body. My hand unwillingly grabs for him between the metal bars. Before my fingertips reach his blackened shoulder, he falls. Into the puddle like a drop of water. As he goes, he reaches out for me, grasping my hand.

I brace myself with my other as I wait for the pain of metal against flesh. My arm goes with the Shadow, and I'm thrust violently into the bars. Just as I thought, I can't get through. The Shadow man does not let go. My arm stays submerged from the elbow down, and I'm too weak to pull it out.

Wake up. I try to force myself back into consciousness. My eyes close as I plead the Gods that when I open them, I am no longer in this nightmare. It works, the tension on my arm releases and my body is no longer strained against the bars. I let out a breath of relief. The dream is over.

I open my eyes, but I am not in bed. I am not in the cell at all. I am where the Shadow was standing just moments ago. Outside of my cell looking in, I see myself sleeping, tossing and turning. *Wake up,* I tell myself with a deep inhale. The body I see on the bed, my body, also takes a breath. *Wake up.* The blanket slips, revealing nothing but the same liquid Shadow, molded into the shape of me.

Familiar humming comes from nearby. My head whips hard to the right to find the noise. Hunched over his knees, his hands folded, sits the old man. When he looks up at me from his hands, he becomes frightened at first but then, with a playful smile, says, "Now that's not fair." He half whispers. I can only cock my head to the side and look at him, confused, unsure of why he is in my dream. "Get out of here, girl. I'll keep your secret." He shakes his head in disbelief as he chuckles to himself. *What secret?* I wonder but cannot ask aloud. My dreams do not often let me speak.

This dream is nothing more than a wish for escape, the kind I so desperately crave when I am awake. Still, I take a tentative step toward the exit. Then another.

Just a taste of freedom, even if when I wake up, I am still buried beneath those stained sheets. When I pass by the old man's cell, it only takes a few seconds before he starts his song again.

Chapter 10

Others do not stir even as I open the large door. Guards stay passed out at their stations, snoring as I tiptoe by them. I search each face among them, but none belong to Kirian.

When I reach the top of the stairs, a set of glowing eyes are on me. A dog lies between where I stand and the exit. He lets out a low growl as the floor creaks. This stops me dead in my tracks as I wait for it to attack. The dog takes a look around the room in search of the noise, but its eyes do not find me, further evidence that this is just a dream. When its ears relax, and it lays its head back down on its large paw, I move again for the door. I try to pull the handle, but it does not open.

I inspect its brass lock before searching the walls for a key. There is nothing. The glow of city lights catches my eye. An office opposite the door. This door was closed when I arrived. Beyond it is a window, or more importantly, a key.

I squeeze through the space in the door without moving it so as to not rouse the dog. A man sits slumped in a wooden chair by the window. Cigarette butts litter the ashtray on his desk. When I cannot find a key, I head for the window. Thick metal bars line its interior. One is bent slightly, creating a hole just big enough that I am sure I can get through.

I stick my head out first. The drop is not far, no further than my favorite resting place above the lake in an old oak tree. The man shifts, and his head hits the wall behind him. My shoulders tense as I prepare for him to wake, but he does not. I make as little noise as possible as I shimmy through the bars.

My feet hit the ground with a thud. My ankle burns, but I pay no attention to it as I suck in as much cool, free air as I possibly can. My ankle twitches as I stand. *Pain.* Something I have never felt in a dream before. I felt it as I was being pulled through the cell and now as I walk on my injured foot.

My head feels light as if I might faint.

None of these feelings make sense, or maybe I am so exhausted that my dreams are becoming hallucinations. The wind blows my hair across my face. It sticks to my eyelashes. I pull the strands from my face, pulling all my hair together and tucking it into my shirt to be rid of it.

Empty, quiet streets. Stars speckle the sky. Dream, nightmare, or hallucination, I will take it.

Leave, never come back. So, I do. I run, not daring to glance behind me. I don't know where to go, but I know I cannot stay here.

Lamps begin to illuminate windows as I pass. My bare feet are beginning to blister as they rub against the dirt streets of Thorn Row. My head aches and a stitch stings at my side. I barely make it three blocks before I begin to slow.

Two men appear before me. They stand with their arms crossed, stepping from side to side so that I cannot pass. Playing with their food, I suppose. They smell of cheap beer and spirits, a smell I remember many times as Cedric stumbled through the castle in a drunken stupor after a long night out.

One of them burps as he bends down to inspect me. "Where are you off to, boy?" He asks. I tilt my head down to conceal my features.

I do not answer so as to not give myself away. Then, I try to proceed forward. He steps in front of me and inches even closer with his face.

He reaches a dirtied hand out and places the edge of his finger on my chin. When I meet his eyes, his face contorts with confusion as he looks me up and down carefully before stopping at my chest. "Well, well, look what we have here." He lets out a laugh from down in his fat belly, sending him back a step.

The other man is intrigued. I hear his heavy, drunken breathing as he walks up behind me. I shudder as he sends a large and slightly damp hand crashing down onto my shoulder. *Fuck.*

"You shouldn't be out this late, little lady." He hiccups, applying pressure to my shoulder. As he pushes a hand into his pocket, his jacket parts slightly, revealing a knife that hangs from his chest in its sheath. He retrieves a flask from his deep pocket and takes a swig of its contents. "I'd be happy to escort you-hic-back home." he laughs, and the men exchange looks. One that lets the other know that his offer means something else entirely.

I could snag his dagger, plunge it into the side of the smaller one's chest, then take off in hopes the big one is slow. "Which way?" he asks as he licks his cracked lips. I pull my eyes from the silver piece. It's so close, I just have to reach out and grab it. *Think.*

Pointing to a random group of houses, "Over there, only a few blocks down." I lie. They drunkenly follow my finger in that direction. With their heads turned, I spin sharply on my heels, sending a twinge of pain down my twisted ankle. Using the opportunity while their heads are turned to run. They curse at me as I go, I have no idea where I'm headed, my head pounds and my muscles do not propel me as fast as I would like.

I can see a woman carrying a lantern down a side street. If I can get to her, maybe she can help. She is there one second and gone the next as a large figure appears from a doorway. Just as big and stinky as the last two. Unable to stop fast enough, I hit him head on, his gut springs me backwards, I trip over my feet and into the arms of one of the others who pulls me back up by the hair. *So weak.* I tell myself as I shudder in pain.

"Going somewhere?" one asks from behind me, all three have now circled around me, blocking any chance of escape.

"Home." I say as confidently as I can while the man still has his hand wrapped in my hair. "My Mother is expecting me," I say in hopes that they will give up if they know that someone is waiting for me.

"Surely your mum can wait a little longer. Yeah?" he forces our faces together as he speaks. His breath stings my nostrils with the smell of liquor. If I held a match to his lips, it would ignite me with flames. "Come on, girl, the boys back at the pub are going to get a kick out of this." He picks at the collar of the jail's plain white shirt that I wear. "A pretty little thing like you, ha, dressed in men's clothing." He snorts. The others have no objections as the man releases my hair and ushers me into the alley behind the pub.

Men wander about, smoking and drinking outside the door. They watch as we pass in amusement. A man spits onto the ground as he watches us, a woman curled around his arm. She's dressed in a small skirt that hikes up to the hip and her brassiere makes her breast nearly touch her chin as she looks down. Her makeup is dark to match the circles under her eyes. Above her lip is a poorly covered bruise. The man then exchanges coins with the woman for reasons that I try not to think about before they walk inside. We follow behind them to enter, they take a left and head for a set of stairs. I look around the bar, curious eyes find mine as men mill around and a band plays an upbeat tune in the corner.

When the door slams behind us, I tense before gluing my eyes to the floor. Finally, I have my freedom from that jail cell, but this is somehow so much worse. *Disgusting pigs, all men are.* I should have known that, with Hansel Luz and Cedric, even Kirian. *No one is to be trusted.* The three men take me to a table where they pull out chairs for themselves.

One gestures to their knee, asking me to take a seat. I do not move. His disappointment is nearly palpable as he gives me another once over. He waves over a woman, Rosie, he calls her. "Let's get you into something more...ladylike," he says in a playful voice. She carries mugs on a platter with swishing brown liquid as she makes her way over, looking at me curiously before noticing that I am indeed a woman. The man does not ask this time as he grabs at my hips and places me squarely on his knee. I can feel his stomach on my backside, and my own stomach twists in knots.

"I see you boys are up to no good." Rosie says, her eyes never leave mine. "What can I get ya'." She asks the group.

"This one here is going to need a change of clothes." The man's words tickle the hairs on the back of my neck. The others nod their heads in agreement.

"I might have an extra uniform upstairs." She says, bored. Rosie's eyes snake their way down to my exposed toes. She ignores the 'help me' look I give her as she sets the beer down on the table for the men to grab before she leaves.

The larger of the three shoves a mug into my hand. "Drink up." He says with a smile, his teeth are gray, and his face looks to be infested with bugs, little white dots surrounded by red around his mouth.

I try to stand, but hands come crashing down once more, holding me in place as he leans forward. "We are just having a little fun is all." He whispers, his breath hot in my ear. Slowly, his hand strays from my hip to the inside of my thigh. I do all I can to keep the bile from rising to my throat.

Anger, disgust and embarrassment boil my blood. Liquid black drips from the dark corners of the room, threatening to kill the man that holds me. The words, more clear than anything I have ever heard them say before. He does not stop. His finger makes small circles that travel to the inside of my hip.

His mouth is still near my ear as he sits comfortably too close to me. Fight or flight, this is where I make my decision. Before his hand can travel further, I quickly turn my head towards him. My teeth sink into his ear, I bite down hard, and when he pushes me off of him, I do not let go. The warm drip of blood falls from the corner of my mouth. I gag before spitting the chunk of flesh to the floor.

My hands fly up as the men stand. I place my fists in front of me in a defense-like stance that I had seen Cedric take many times while sparring with his friends all while making sure to keep an eye on the other men as they look between us in surprise. The man whose ear I have tasted stands and takes a step towards me "you little-"he stops mid sentence, cupping his left ear as red gushes from between his fingers.

I take a step back to further myself from that look as if he wants to kill me. Let him, I would rather die than be subject to whatever plans they have for me tonight. My heart is beating faster than it should, but I don't dare turn away from them. The men all look up at the same time. One straightens his shoulders, and the other turns away as if he has just remembered that he has somewhere to be. I take one more step back, but I can move no further as my back hits something hard.

"These men bothering you, Miss?" a man says from behind me, above me. I almost laugh as I recognize the voice. Kirian. *Curse the Gods, how they play these cruel jokes on me.*

"We were just having some fun, boss. We swear, she came in here on her own, looked lost." He lies, the other two suddenly become very interested in their drinks. I almost can't help but roll my eyes at the chicken shit before me. *Boss?* Kirian must be their superior in The Guard. I tip my head back and squint up at him. He doesn't look at me. He keeps his eye on the man who had his hands on me.

I can feel the anger radiating off his skin, the same anger that I felt not that long ago upon that man's lap.

Kirian's face is of a furious storm, his eyes locked on the bloodied soldier. The men cower as Kirian steps towards them, his hand still firmly on my arm, but I plant my feet on the ground, pulling him in the opposite direction. I do not want to be anywhere near these men any longer.

"Funs over." Kirian growls. He pushes me in front of him as he turns. We walk quickly to the door.

He doesn't stop after we exit, we walk further but I notice it's not in the direction of the jail.

As the smell of smoke, strong perfume, and the shouts of drunken men fade away, he slows. His grip loosens on my arm as we approach a large building. I slip into step beside him, but he does not let me go. He does not say anything, but his jaw clenches tightly. I look down at our footsteps to avoid his burning rage.

We come to a halting stop. It's a different kind of fear I feel now than I felt on the lap of that man, a different kind of fear than when Father's beast limped into his room. *Put to trial. Hung.* The words ring in my ears again and again. My fate slowly creeping up on me no matter how hard I try to prevent it.

He drops his hand to my elbow before pulling me close to him violently. I see a flash of the same face, the one I saw when he held me against the wall in the integration room, anger, pity, and regret all in one. "What the fuck were you thinking?" he asks through his teeth. Almost off my feet, he takes my shoulders and holds me up to face him.

I haven't really been thinking at all, not past my escape anyways. My escape that was so dream-like I haven't had time to understand it.

"I wasn't – "I start, but he cuts me off.

"Do you know how stupid that was?" He's furious. He releases me and turns around. He places his hands atop his head, his large arms flexing as he curses under his breath. When he turns back to face me, I can't seem to hold his eyes.

"Those men? I would have gotten away," I say unconvincingly as I look in the direction of the pub. His piercing green eyes darken. I'm unsure of the emotions that they hold. It looks a lot like worry, a look Lupita would often give me but never voice her opinion on.

Kirian does not hold his tongue. "What did you think they were going to do after that little stunt? Release you?" he huffs out a frustrated laugh.

"Whatever." I barely get the word from my mouth before he erupts again in anger.

"You have no idea of the things that happen here. You have no idea how the real world works, Katsia!" he says my name in two syllables, like a curse.

His words hit me hard because I wish I *did* understand. All the books I read and all the maps I've studied were nothing compared to real world experience, but it was not my choice to be kept from this place. Even if I would have left with my sisters I would be in a different kind of confinement. I hunch over slightly as the pain in my stomach grows once more. I pull my arms in tight. I can't help the way I am, and that fills me with so much shame that it makes me sick.

We stand in silence for a moment. I make sure to keep my head down so that he can't see what must be written all over my face. "Take me back," I whisper. It's the only option, I know that. I stretch out my arms, tapping my wrists together, signaling that I am prepared for the same ties he placed on me at House Luz.

He huffs out a breath, sweet mint. "We aren't going back." He places his large hand on the two of mine, it covers them completely as he pushes them down. I rest them at my sides and look up at him as I try to make sense of what that means.

"What?" I ask.

"Three days, all you had to do was wait three days, Katsia." There it is again, my name, a curse on his lips. This time, he is mad for an entirely different reason.

"For what?" the words are hardly audible, even to me. Kirian doesn't say anything. He's still fuming, practically pacing back and forth as he thinks. "For what?" I nearly shout to get his attention. This has his head snapping back at me.

He looks around in search of listening ears. "Not here." He grabs me again. He begins to pull me further into darkness.

There is no word that describes my emotion as he drags me down the side street. Kirian has never given me any reason to trust him. *Run.* Everything in me tells me I should do so. I look down at the hand that holds mine. I stop.

Kirian turns when my feet are no longer moving. "Katsia, please," he begs.

"Why should I trust you?" I ask him sincerely.

He searches the street we are on, and I can tell that he grows impatient with every passing second. Then, he takes a step forward, forcing my back against the wall. The Shadows warn me, but it's not Kirian they fuss over. A patrol guard passes by, taking a long look down the street for a moment before continuing on his route.

Kirian's sternum is almost pressed against my face as if his body would have hidden me if the guard were to come this way. I am about to push him off of me, but he tips his head down to look at me, and as soon as the thought comes, it goes just as fast. He steps back but not nearly enough, only the amount needed to speak to me face to face. His hand is still firmly in my own. "You shouldn't." he warns me.

"I'm not going to run," I say as I yank my arm from him.

His face becomes soft as he looks down at me, only half of him illuminated by a streetlamp far away. "You're safe. You've always been safe." His words come in a calming lull. I tilt my head up to meet his eyes and I don't know why but I believe him, believe that I will be safe if I go with him, so I do.

He looks to his left, and soon, his feet follow. "I didn't know," I whisper as I take a step in his direction, suddenly guilty for my accidental escape.

"How could you have?" he says over his shoulder, his hand tensing at his side. I realize he isn't angry with me. He is angry with himself.

Kirian then seems to go into a deep state of thought. I can see it, the inner struggle. I don't dare say a word as he leads the way.

We take a few alleyways and push the branches of a larin tree to the side so that we cross a small garden area before he finally speaks his mind. "That first night when I questioned you, I just needed to make sure for myself." He takes another turn, taking us up a set of stairs. "That you really weren't a part of what your Father has done." He pauses for a moment, surveying the building's windows beside us. He gives me a sideways glance before we continue. "The other guards, it was their idea to put your Father in there with you. They were hoping you two would talk, but you didn't, you couldn't even look at him, that's when I knew for sure that you two were not working together. It was just a matter of making everyone else believe it, too." He seems relieved to get this information off his chest.

During the interrogation, he was forcing me to relive my past so that they would know just how much my Father hates me. "Most of them agreed that you were telling the truth." He looks down a narrow street with lots of trees in search of our next move. "I can tell you more, everything, if you are willing to trust me." He says, looking up at the sky. Its colors are turning from cool to warm. *Morning, the sun, how I've missed him.* I only give a nod in reply as I close my eyes and let the oncoming warmth from the day absorb into my skin.

"Follow me," he says urgently. With sunrise comes townspeople, and soon it will be known that a prisoner has escaped the jail.

Kirian becomes more careful. We walk down different alleyways and do not pass any businesses or homes where people might see us. We finally stop at the back of an old Inn. Vines grow up its sides, and the shudders seem to be holding on for dear life. 'The Charlie,' I read the script written on the back door, its wood splintering and the paint chipping away.

"Stay here, I'll get you a room, they can't see your face, or they might recognize you when The Guard inevitably comes through tomorrow asking questions of your whereabouts." He checks the door. Sure enough, as he knew it would be, it's unlocked. Kirian leaves it open a crack, but he does not go inside.

Instead, he pushes me back a little further into the dark wall of the building once again. This action startles me now that I can see his face clearly in the daylight. I flinch as I remember the moment that he pushed me to the ground before flipping the table and chairs at the jail.

He takes his hands back in retreat but continues. "When I tap on the window above," he points towards the sky, and I follow his finger, tipping my head all the way back to see the glass reflecting the purple sky. "Go in through that door and take a right, the second floor, second door, got it?" he speaks as if giving orders to his men.

"Yes." I nod. He moves the door once more. Kirian turns his head slightly back at me as if he wants to say something but changes his mind and disappears through the door of The Charlie.

I could leave, I could run, I could- moments later, I hear the taps of Kirian's knuckles against the glass and abandon my plan. Where would I go anyway? Besides, Kirian trusted me not to run. I make my way inside the Inn carefully, quietly, something that I have gotten very good at over the years. When I get to the second floor, second door, I do not knock. I just twist its old knob and enter.

Kirian stands there with a grin on his face as he releases a breath in relief. Perhaps the thought of me running crossed his mind as well. "Quiet as a mouse," he half whispers as I close the door behind me.

Chapter 11

"How did you know the back door was going to be unlocked?" I ask as I walk about the room. Inspecting the sheets on the bed that were once white but yellowed over time, along with the worn pillows.

Then, down to the large rug that covers the floor with frays at its ends. There is a round stain on the corner. I do not let myself think of the things that might have caused it. A table and chair sit in the corner, untouched. People do not come here to chat or do paperwork. The chair looks like it wouldn't hold the weight of a small child.

The other corner holds a rusted tub for washing. When I'm done with my inspection of the room, I notice Kirian's eyes piercing me through a mirror hung lopsidedly on the wall. I stop as if his stare pins me to the floor.

"It's no castle, I know." He says to my reflection, I rip my eyes from the mirror, to avoid him but also so that I don't have to see myself. I haven't forgotten that he hasn't answered my question.

He's right, though. It's no castle, but it's also no jail cell, either. Nervously, I sit on the edge of the bed, grateful to be off my feet, which now have more scratches and blisters than I can count and a bruise appearing on my left ankle. I begin to pick at the mud that weighs down my trousers. *Gods, I'm a mess.*

Suddenly, moans come from the opposite wall, I snap my head in the direction of the noise. Kirian clears his throat uncomfortably. "Uh, that's how I knew the back door would be unlocked. The Charlie has a...reputation." He says nervously as he walks in front of me. My mind wonders as I peer at his boots. How many women has he had in a room like this one? I knew it was common, especially for the men in The Guard to buy...lovers.

Kirian is handsome. I wouldn't think a man like him would have to pay for something like that. I lean back and prop myself up on my arms. I try to push the thought of Kirian entertaining women here, on this bed, out of my head. The noises from behind the wall continue forcing my mind to wonder once more. My subconscious pulls me from the bed, away from what it has seen. I now stand awkwardly at its edge, favoring my right leg.

"I've caught a few of my men here. I have never- I –"he stutters. "I've never stayed here." His cheeks turn red with embarrassment, and I give him a reassuring half-smile as he defends himself like a child. He quickly moves on. "So, uh, you'll have to stay here for a few nights. I'll bring you some food and a change of clothes." He is still stumbling over his words and avoiding eye contact.

Kirian turns as if he is done. Then he swings back to face me, his hand in his hair. "You've been requested to wear a dress." He says shyly at the end of his ramble. He finally looks up and scans me over me from head to toe, no doubt taking in the matted hair, bruised skin, dried blood, and Gods know what else.

I chuckle to myself, both my nerves bubbling over and at his statement. Like Hell, I'll be wearing a dress. I push my knotted hair over my shoulder. He laughs, too, but it's for an entirely different reason. He's laughing *at* me. His face is stretched into that smile that shows his dimple and all of his teeth. I look down at his boots again, embarrassed. "Oh, you're serious," I say when realization hits.

"Red or green?" he asks, and his smile grows impossibly larger. I remember the terrible red color that Medla dressed me in the day she and Adriel left. Red, the color of blood that ran down my face, both my own and Kirian's. Red, the color of being left behind.

"Green," I answer. "No corset," I say at the end, never again. "And a change of men's clothing as well." he tilts his head down, concealing his grin. I ignore him and continue. "I'm going to need a bath. I haven't had one since- "I let my words drift off when I remember that I haven't had one since he found me at the lake. When he was only keeping me away from the castle so they could search it. I took bird baths in the cell, and they brought us a change of clothes only once. My face warms and I look down at my trousers pretending to dust something off my knee.

Thankfully, Kirian is quick to fill the silence. "Anything else, princess? Furs or leathers? Jewels or gems?" Kirian takes the opportunity to tease me, so easily changing to the man who challenged me to his own bow and not the man who was in that small room tossing furniture and pushing me to tears.

"No," I say, still looking down. Not acknowledging his jest.

"Alright, done." He says, walking for the door, his right hand on the knob, the other squeezed tightly at his side. He twists his head over his shoulder. "Katsia." My name on his lips makes my heart quicken as if I am about to receive another bit of bad news. "Do not leave." He waits a moment, his words as serious as a strike to the heart, straight from Zeus. His eyes bore into me, and I swear heat radiates from his words. So, I nod.

"I will be back at dusk with food, then I'll ask the servants to bring hot water for your bath." He gives me a reassuring smile then leaves shutting the door behind him. His feet shadow the other side of the door, when I stand and click the lock into place, he leaves.

I curse at myself for not getting more information from him before he left and now, I will be alone all day, until dark, until Kirian returns. I pull the chair to the window and take a seat, looking out at Thorn Row, or the little of it that I can see anyway. It helps to have the distraction from my thoughts of Shadows and men that want me to occupy their laps. I push Claire's cryptic warning and Kirian's words that were said to get under my skin out of my mind.

As the sun warms my face, I retreat from the window so that no one will see me as I watch the city. We traveled far from the markets, but you can tell where they are from the faint glow in the sky when the sun was still coming up. The owners are most likely lighting lanterns and setting up their respective shops for the soon-to-be-busy day.

Finally, I strip from my dirty clothes, looking down at my body, noticing that my ribs now protrude from my torso and the bones of my hips jut out further than my stomach. I run my fingertips over the hills and valleys of bruised skin before climbing into the bed. Ignoring my thoughts of what has previously happened under these same sheets.

The midday sun spills into the space, warming the small room, making it hard to keep my eyes open. I watch as the light reveals more of the room's character. Torn curtains and cobwebs fill the corners. This bed is much more comfortable than the metal cots with broken springs under their thin mattresses at the jail, and for the first time in a long time, I fall right to sleep. No eyes or whispers, no nightmares, or pools of darkness, or the rattling of chains wake me.

Sleep does not last long. When I wake, I return to the window and think only of what the world would be like if I were in it, if I were the woman floating towards the markets with a basket in hand, if I had left House Luz long ago.

Father would not have had his reputation of generosity for taking me in. Cedric would not have had to seek me out for punishment for disrupting his wickedness. Adriel wouldn't have had to fake kindness or pretend she wanted to be near me. Who knows how Medla would have chosen to release her anger had I not been the target of her insults.

Basking in the diminishing light and listening to the sounds of the city and sometimes the sounds of satisfied men and women so used to the noise now that I am unbothered by it. I stay like that until there is a knock at the door.

Is that fresh bread I smell? The sweet scent that I often enjoyed as Lupita fussed over my hair or made me wash my face and hands before I could take a slice for myself.

I open the door a crack at first, just to be sure. When I see Kirian holding a bag from the markets, I open it all the way, letting a smile take over my face at the thought of a good meal. He sees me eyeing the bag and hands it to me immediately. I take it over to the small table that I have placed near the window as well and sit down on the chair that is surprisingly still in one piece. Kirian follows, sitting on the edge of the bed to face me. He is not in his uniform this time. Just black slacks, a white tunic, and a gray jacket adorned with brass buttons. Its fabric stretched to fit his massive shoulders.

"So, where am I to go?" I ask through a mouth full of bread and cheese. Kirian's eyes go wide as he watches me eat. I do not let it deter me as I continue. He laughs at me once more, and I've decided I'm okay with that. My siblings used to laugh at me, too.

I used to care, used to question Lupita about all the ways I could avoid their laughter, their judgment, or unnecessary comments. How to act and what to say. Until, no matter how many times I tried to win them over, they still went on about their lives without me.

So, I pay no attention as Kirian's eyes bounce from my tangled hair to my dirty hands and finally land on my nose, still sore to the touch. Which likely means that it's fractured. I ignore that unusual look that takes over his face for a second too long.

He clears his throat. "The Spent have questions. They will decide where you stand amongst those who have The Connection and most likely assign you a job within the organization." He watches as I wipe my hands off on my trousers. He takes out a handkerchief and places it on the table, I slowly reach for it and nod in appreciation.

It's almost laughable. How many questions had Kirian asked me about associating with The Spent, with Claire? Yet he is to deliver me straight to them. I make sure not to let the surprise leak to my face. If I wasn't so worried about death, the Shadows, and my Father, maybe I would have realized that The Spent is who he is working for. I should have picked up on the not-so-subtle accusations. He so clearly thinks that I had figured it out long ago.

So I let him believe I knew all along as I ask, "And if I don't want to work for them?" I pay no mind to his curious grin. I wipe the crumbs from the corners of my mouth with the orange fabric that Kirian pulled from his pocket, it smells like him.

His face goes from playful to serious. "You'll have no choice." He tells me. "For some reason, they care more now than ever about keeping those with The Connection alive. That's why you're not hanging from a tree somewhere." This turns my stomach in an awful way, only hours ago I was terrified that that was my fate. I do not ask more about the Spent. It's clear that Kirian will be handing me over to them whether I want him to or not.

"So, you've done this before?" I ask in hopes that the distraction will take my thoughts away from the image of me swinging back and forth, my neck in a noose.

"Yes." He says calmly as he stands. He leans against the wall, crossing one leg over the other. And the room grows unbearably quiet, so quiet that music can be heard from somewhere on the floors below.

"How did you know that I escaped?" I ask to fill the silence. Even though I have a million other questions.

"When I went to your cell to check on you, you weren't there." He pauses. Raises an eyebrow at me. "I wish I had noticed sooner." Kirian leans his head to the side to see the city below.

He wasn't there. When I passed those guards, he was not one of them. "Do you always check on the prisoners?" I ask without thinking.

"Only the ones I am assigned to watch" he lets that stupid smirk pull at his mouth again. I become suddenly interested in the crumbs I left behind on the table, pushing them around with a finger. How many times in the night did he come to see me in the fit of nightmares? My cheeks heat at the thought of him watching me sleep.

"You're turning red, Katsia." He says, but when I look up, he still looks at something outside. Not at me at all.

"I'm embarrassed. That I didn't notice."

"You were not meant to notice." He pulls a bag from his shoulder, just another thing that I had not been paying attention to and didn't see when he came in. But give me some slack, I was jailed and thought I was days from death, wished for it even.

He takes out a pair of trousers and a black shirt. Then a jacket with gold buttons. It is of high quality. I wonder if it cost him a lot, or if he had it from when he was a boy. There is no way I would be able to fit into something of his now.

Then, he pulls out a long, solid green dress and a white petticoat. I hate it. And my feelings are not well hidden because he chuckles as he lays them on the bed. "It's not that bad, is it?" he asks. He sets a pair of worn boots at the foot of the bed, my boots, I realize. I stare at the worn straps that hardly hold the leather together.

I look up at him, and his eyes were ready for mine, as he settles back into his comfortable stance against the wall. "Have you ever worn a dress?" Now it's his turn to turn a shade of red, but I just keep his eyes as I wait for an answer. And he steps up to the challenge.

"No Katsia, I have never worn a dress." He says, looking between my eyes wildly as he waits for me to speak.

"Well, count yourself lucky. Don't get me started on all the things you're not *allowed* to do in a dress. Not to mention the things you physically *cannot*." I shake my head as I speak. "You can't run or lift your arms above your head. You can't walk through tall grass, or the skirt will be filled with burweed. Even if you could do those things, you wouldn't be able to breathe while doing them. The damned thing is a death trap." I point to the fabric on the bed, peeling my eyes from his.

Kirian doubles over, a deep laugh fills the room.

My cheeks redden further, I only said what was true, I don't understand what is so funny.

"You're feral." He says after his fit of laughter. *Feral?* I use forks and knives when I have them. Reply to others with please and thank you. *That* is not feral, but no use to argue, I know that. I know what people see when they look at me.

"You've caught me at a bad time," I reply, turning back towards my crumbs to avoid his gaze.

"I haven't *caught* you Katsia. You cannot be caught. Why just yesterday you escaped me, remember?" He plays on my words. Then he walks over and squats in front of me, using the back of my chair to hold himself up, our heights even now. "It's more fun when it's not easy." He drawls. When I look over at him, he has wiped the smile from his face. "I'm sorry for what I had to do." I glance down at his hand to see if the cut remains on his palm. It's now scarred over slightly, pink but still there. He, too, is looking at the place on my neck where blood dripped down onto the white shirt.

It was kindness, what he did for me, his blood over my own. I see that now. I look at him, really look at him, to make sure that his apology rings true. While I have his face so close to mine, I catch myself studying his features. His jaw is sharp, and the blonde stubble along his chin gives him a look of a man.

When he is clean shaven his features turn more boyish, that's who I saw first, the man who sat next to me on that bench in Center Square, a boy. There are thin lines around his eyes and mouth, years of wearing that smile. My hand plays a foul trick on me, reaching out to touch one of those lines that surround his mouth. The same gentle caress that he afforded me.

He clears his throat, something I've noticed he does when he is uncomfortable. I don't want to make anyone feel like that. I snap my hand away quickly, just as he did when he guided me under the window, both of us ashamed of what we might have made the other feel. I turn my head, looking anywhere but at him.

My hair tickles my arm as he lets out a breath. "I'll get the servants to bring you hot water," he says before he stands and points to the tub that barely fits in the small room. It's rusted on the sides. I try not to think of the disgusting things men have done in that tub.

"T-thank you." my words barely make their way out. He stalks out the door, disappearing for a short while. When he comes back, he is disheveled, his hair is ruffled, and he has pulled a few buttons undone, baring his chest to me. I do not let myself look for long.

"Get into the bed, cover yourself with the blankets when the maids come in. Once they are done, you can bathe. Do not let them see you. I will be back." I nod my head but do not say anything. He walks out the door once again, running into a servant as he leaves. He pulls the door behind him so that they do not see me. "My wife is not decent. She needs a moment," I hear him say to one of them.

I leap to the bed, tucking myself under the blankets. When the door opens again, he gives them the okay before pushing past them. They filter in, I hear the buckets of water sloshing into the tub. They come in and out a few times before a woman's voice tells me the bath is ready. The door shuts again, and I get out of the bed to lock it before crawling into the clawfoot tub. I'm already warm from my interaction with Kirian, so the warmth from the tub does nothing to relieve me.

"My wife," I have to laugh to myself at his words. What kind of couple would choose to stay in a dump like this?

Kirian does come back that night. He places a bag on the table as I lay on the bed. He must have thought I didn't have my fill of food because my nose rejoices with the scent of something sweet as he passes me.

My black shirt clings to my body where my long hair has dampened the fabric still wet from the bath. My legs are only covered to just above the knee, which he scans over quickly before looking back at the table.

I pull the blanket over myself to hide from the emotion on Kirian's face that I cannot place. Hunger, I decide. He looks at me like he hasn't eaten in days. I prop myself up on my hands "Would you like to stay and eat with me?" I ask him.

His large hand pulls at the strands of blond at the top of his head. He seems to go into thought because his jaw clenches and his eyes wander the room but never make their way back to me. "No." he decides. Then, he walks back to the door, white knuckles the knob, before turning it and slamming it behind him. This time he does not wait for me to lock it. His boots are already heavy on the stairs, and I hear the back door of The Charlie slam into its frame as he closes it.

It was not hunger that I saw behind those green eyes. No, it had to have been anger. At me, for not staying in that damned cell, for being ignorant to the world, for forcing him to take care of me in this room for three days. I do not open the bag he left. I only strip off my damp clothes, lock the door, and lay in bed with my eyes open, wishing I knew how to correct the situation I put him in.

Chapter 12

Sharp nails dig into my arm, fingers wrap around my wrist, then my leg falls off the side of the bed, a desperate grip around my ankle. The sheets are pulled from my body, sending a chill down my spine.

My mind begins to clear the fog of slumber, but not soon enough. The Shadows pull me into their embrace as a blanket of black appears above me. I fall from the bed in my panic, pushing myself away from the black. Pain radiates through me as I catch myself on twisted ankle and sore palms. The Shadows voice their concerns, "*run,*" they say as I use the nightstand to pull myself up.

Men's voices fill the hallways, my head whips in that direction. It's not the regular customers that frequent the hallways in search of women willing to give them what they want. They pound on the doors below me. Objects clatter to the ground and a woman lets out a terrified shriek as a man shouts, "Everyone out, now."

I know what they search for, who. The Shadow above me dissipates and reforms on the floor. I shuffle backward, half expecting the same figure of a man to appear above it like before, to take me into the darkness, to take me to another beast. Perhaps one far worse than Father.

Think. I turn to look for my clothes, but the heavy footsteps make their way up the stairs, so instead, I pull the sheet from the bed and wrap it around myself as I search for an escape. The pool beckons me. The Shadows tell me that I will be safe, but I do not believe them. I fear what will happen if I step inside, as it seems I have no control of where it takes me.

The only way out is down. Heaving the window open, I peer at the street below, then to where Kirian and I stood when we entered through the back door of The Charlie. A man in a guard's uniform blocks the door, a sword strapped to his hip. I quickly dismiss the idea.

Facing the room again in search of an impossible escape, I see the pool of black move to under my feet, I try to step back, but it grows, giving me little room to avoid it. A door opens nearby, something hits the wall near me with a thud, then sinks down to the floorboards, a woman cries out in pain. "Look at me." One of the men says, she lets out another, more desperate scream.

There is silence for a moment, "It's not her," the men tell each other. Then the door slams shut, and footsteps start in my direction. My heart hammers in my chest. I can't think. The Shadows pull me in all directions again, gripping at me with their long fingers in a silent plea to move. To do anything but what I am doing now, which is nothing. I remain frozen, the pestering becomes urgent, violent.

I swat them away angrily. *Think*. But there is nothing, no escape. My body starts to shake, I blink away the blur of tears, and when I open them, I see the Shadow figure once more, its arms outstretched from the pool of darkness, my legs swallowed by its black grip as he drags me under once more, just like before.

The last thing I see is a guard's boot breaking through the wooden door frame as it's forced open, fracturing the lock. The sheet is ripped from my body as I fall. I take a deep breath as I plunge into the black liquid.

It's warm and weightless. My body convulses as I try to make sense of what's happening. I swing my arms the same as when I dive into the lake at House Luz, but I'm slowed by whatever substance surrounds me.

Minutes tick by. I can't hold my breath forever.

When my chest aches with the need for air, I breathe, surprised when I can inhale and exhale easily while I remain surrounded by what I thought was water.

I stretch my arms and legs out, searching for something, anything to grab onto, but nothing is there.

"It's empty." a voice says from above me, it's muffled, distant. I try to look in the direction of that voice, but there is just endless nothingness. It consumes me, when my stomach comes out of its knots and my chest stops aching, an alarm goes off in my head. *Get out.*

Kirian, he's going to come looking for me, but I won't be here. *Get out, get out, get out.* I thrash around in a desperate search once more. Tears leak from my eyes, but they do not fall, they are suspended in time, sticking to my face like mud. More voices come from above, below, all around me. I stay like that listening to the multiple conversations, the clattering of glass as it breaks, women's scrambling footsteps and men who are upset about the disruption of services.

Soon, the sounds stop, replaced by silence, the silence that comes from the city right before the sun rises. The in-between, the times when men and women are either asleep or sitting quietly in their warm homes before they start the day. The silence turns into the faint sounds of glass being pushed into dustpans and emptied nearby, the same servants who fetched me water for my bath whisper their complaints of the soldiers who trashed the rooms as they clean.

I drift in and out of consciousness, it's hard to know when I am asleep or awake, whether my eyes are opened or closed.

Sometimes I think I've had a dream but can't remember the details. I listen and wait. It's all I can do.

No more tears come, and soon, I no longer search for a way out. A sense of calm falls over me, like the abyss wants me to stay in it forever. Soon, I begin to think that's not such a bad idea. Nothing can hurt me here, no one expects anything from me. I curl my legs to my stomach. *Yes, I can stay here. It's not so bad.*

"Katsia," my name floats over the top of me. The voice, it's panicked, worried, angry even. "Katsia," the familiar voice calls again. It gets closer to me. I reach for it. Lifting my hand is hard, like wading through honey.

I push it above my head with all my strength, searching once more for something to grab hold of. I hear nothing, only the sound of boots on wood as they further from me. *Wait.* I force myself out of the calm and back into reality. I cannot stay here.

No, please don't go, don't leave me here. No words come out, but I scream anyway. It just rattles around in my head. *Kirian, I'm here.* I try again, unable to tell if the words are coming from my mouth or are only in my mind.

I will myself to reach again, stretching my arm impossibly further. *"Please"* I beg the Shadows. They are the ones who put me in here and they are the ones that can let me out.

Something solid hits my hand. I scratch at it, pain radiates from my fingernails up my arm. Again, I paw at the object until I wrap my hand around something solid. The object is cold compared to the warm abyss that I currently swim in. I follow the cold, hoisting myself up and into it, the world becomes tangible once more.

My nose sucks in the icy air, the smell of must fills my lungs, I try not to gag at its intensity. I continue to breathe in, ignoring the ripples of pain that make their way through my body and focusing on the faint scent of mint that Kirian must have left behind. My shoulder aches as I lay on the rotting floor. The cold air now has me shaking uncontrollably. *You do not belong here.*

I do not realize my eyes are squeezed shut until the light blinds me as I relax slightly. Even from behind my eyelids, the light seeps through, creating a burning sensation behind my eyes. I give myself little time to adjust before I force myself to open them all the way, I bite my lip to stop myself from crying in pain. I blink until the room comes into focus.

The mattress has been taken from its frame as it lays on the floor, and my dress is thrown to the other side of the room. The small dresser near the bed is missing its drawers and the oil lamp leaks from a crack at its side. This world seems gray, bleak and unbearable. I struggle to my hands and knees but that's as far as I can get.

My hair falls to the sides, the ends laying limply on the ground near my hands. Where it touches my arms, I feel heat—a stark contrast to the frigid air. My knees feel as if they lay on a pile of glass, and my hands feel as if they might shatter under my weight. This world is hurting me. Everywhere I touch, it stings.

Someone steps into the room. I do not look up. The movement would make me sick. Slowly, they shut the broken door behind them.

The person kneels before me, their breathing so loud, their own knees hitting the floor, bone and flesh on wood like thunder to my ears. They drape something warm across my back. I ignore the bite of the fabric, every stitch my skin mistakes for needles. I concentrate on the smell of mint that now surrounds me, the same way that the darkness surrounded me only moments ago. Kirian.

He stands, and picks me up with him, effortlessly. He places me on the mattress and wraps me in blankets, disgusting yellow splintering sheets that dig into my sides. I shiver violently, both from the cold and fear. He slides under the blanket as well, pulling me into him until my body relaxes as I become accustomed to the air once more. "You're safe" His words surround me, like they have their own aura. I believe him.

We stay like that for what could be hours or minutes, I am unsure. "I could hear you." He finally says into my hair. *Hear me?* When I called for him from the abyss, I did not speak at all, I only wished it inside my head.

Suddenly, I am very aware of my naked body pressed up against him. My eyes go wide as I slither out of his arms, making sure that I am covered in all the right places before I sit up. It takes everything in me to look at him, and when I do, he searches my eyes for answers that I do not have.

"I'm sorry." Is all I can say. Hot tears sting as they fall, this world has not had enough of hurting me, I guess. So, I wait for a moment before continuing, gathering myself and letting the pain subside. Kirian does not mind, or at least he does not show it as we sit in silence. "I was here, I think." I finally say. He shakes his head as he sits up so that we are eye to eye. "Here and not here at the same time." I clarify. I swallow hard, and I don't want to think of what just happened, how, or why.

And can't bear that look that he is now giving me, confusion and awe and God's dammit, the pity that has never truly left his face since that day at House Luz. I want to wipe it away.

"You don't have to-." He stops mid-sentence. "You're here now, that's all that matters, you're safe." He reassures me for the second time. *You're safe.* His words repeat in my head. *You're safe.* And I can really feel it. It sinks into me, I've never felt it before, *safe*.

I lift my chin at the realization and press a gentle kiss to Kirian's lips. It's almost out of my control.

My hand releases a part of the yellowed sheets so that I can place it on his face. He grabs my wrist, as we fall onto the plush mattress, now bare of its bedding. My legs part as I straddle him, my naked breasts push up against his muscular chest. The beat of his heart against my body sends a wave of heat rushing between my thighs.

I surprise myself by pushing further into him, never having felt the pressure of a man, never wanting to. I shudder out a breath before crashing my lips back down to his. A growl escapes from somewhere deep in his chest as his tongue circles my bottom lip before sucking it into his mouth, holding me in place with his teeth as his hands move down my back in a desperate need to touch as much of my skin as possible.

This is the first time I have kissed someone. The touch of others often prevents me from getting this close, but this feels right, good even. Maybe even amplified, just as the world had been moments ago when it pained me to exist in it.

It only lasts seconds before he pushes himself upright, leaning back onto his hands. This sends me flying backward. Embarrassment makes my cheeks flush. I lick away the saliva from my now swollen bottom lip as I prop up on my knees, straightening out my upper body, one leg on the hard floor and one on the mattress. I quickly grab the sheets and wrap them around my body once more.

Stupid, Katsia, so stupid. What have I done? Whatever emotion I let myself feel just seconds ago is gone, replaced with overwhelming guilt. Especially as I watch him stand quickly, pacing about the room before he looks down at me like he just made the biggest mistake of his life. My wide eyes find something, anything else to look at that is not him. He straightens out his shirt and grabs the discarded jacket from the ground. "You- "he starts as he throws the jacket over his body and begins to button it from top to bottom. When he turns back to me,

I see that he has only gotten halfway down. As if he can only do one thing at a time. "I- " he tries again but fails.

Embarrassment fades away and something else takes its place, rejection, a familiar feeling. *Feral* is what he called me. Why would he want to be with someone like that? He wouldn't. He deserves better, someone with etiquette and manners and not someone who spent her life afraid of the dark, afraid of everything besides the land and animals and the sun. *Stupid.* That's what I am, so stupid for thinking he would want me as much as I want him. "You don't have to explain." I half-whisper, still kneeling.

"Don't you dare." His voice low and demanding, my head snaps up to see the expression on his face. He takes one step towards me. He towers over me. When I make to look away, he reaches down and lifts my chin up to meet his face. I pinch my thighs together as the warmth presents itself again. I pull away quickly, embarrassed that even after his rejection he can still make me feel that way.

"I get it Kirian." I spit, my head still tilted up at him. Forcing myself to keep his eyes and wishing that the tears that I feel welling up again would disappear.

"You have no idea how much I want this, you." He sweeps his hands over his hair, slicking it back behind his ears. "It's not that simple, we can't do this. I *won't* do this. To you." *Do what?* I think to myself. "You haven't lived, you haven't had men *pine* after you, court you." He sighs and sits back on the bed beside me, leaning over onto his knees. "And trust me they will, fight over your affections, fight each other just to get one taste of you." He speaks to the ground. How can this large man look so small right now?

What do I do with that information? Nothing, and I don't. I ignore him as I slide off the bed and find my clothes tossed onto the table near the now-emptied bag of food lying on its side.

I pull my clothes on quickly, taking another glance at Kirian, whose internal struggle I will never understand.

He stands and continues buttoning his jacket. Then he comes over to me, I'm still trying to piece myself together to understand something that I've never felt before, I have no words for it. Kirian forces me to face him. He places his hands on the back of my head, pulling me to him. So hot and cold, but my body molds into him so easily, and I let him keep me there for just a moment longer. "Don't waste your affections on me, Katsia," he says my name again, so drawn out and lazy.

"I'm not wasting anything. I'm not a child. I knew what I was doing." A lie. I have no idea what I'm doing, I never have. I push myself away from him. It's not easy. It feels so good to be near that chest, near his heart.

Hurt molds his face as he takes a step back. He scrapes the palm of his hands against his jacket, straightening out the wrinkles as he corrects himself.

"Tomorrow morning, we will have to head out before the sun is up. They will be waiting for you. South-east gate three. Wear the dress." He speaks like is giving orders again. I wish *I* could switch so easily into a different person.

Then he walks over to the dress and lays it on the bed. It's green, so dark against the disheveled sheets. He makes his way to the door, placing his hat on his head and reaching for the knob. "I'll see you in the morning." He whispers.

I know he should go. I know I should hate him for making me feel this way, but what's worse than rejection is being alone. *Don't go, don't go.* All day by myself, all night, I can't do it, not after what happened. Who knows when the Shadows will present themselves, when they will take me to that place that I almost did not escape from?

Don't go. "Don't go," I finally say aloud. "Please," I add before taking a few shaky steps toward him. "Please" I say again to his back side as he still holds the door, so tightly that his knuckles turn white. "I don't want to be alone," I admit. "I don't care about my future, men fighting for my affections, or being courted. Right now is all I have, it's all I've ever had. For once I don't want to spend it alone."

He doesn't turn around.

Chapter 13

I spent the rest of the day in a daze. First, picking up the destruction left behind. Mostly, I watch the people of Thorn Row pass by outside. Nearest to the window where the light shines, keeping the Shadows at my back.

A young couple walks hand in hand. I think of what Kirian said about men who would do anything to get a taste. I think of the steps of courtship as I watch the man pull the woman behind a building, kissing her deeply before pulling away with a smile. Is that how it is supposed to be? Two people who are so happy together that they sneak away for secret moments like that. Perhaps I got it wrong this morning. Scratch that, I *know* I got it wrong.

I lay lazily on the now put-together bed or pace about the room. I hide when the servants come to replace the busted lock and ignore the growling of my stomach as I was not able to eat the food that Kirian left before the guards came through. Whatever kind of red fruit pastry was in the bag from the markets now has a boot print in its middle.

I almost considered picking at it, eating the bits and pieces unmarked by the muddied print. It wouldn't be the first time. Medla once made sure I was not allowed the food from Lupita's kitchen. Starving me was one of her favorite punishments. Often a failed one the older I got, when I would wait deep in the trees for a rabbit or squirrel to pass by.

Boots shadow the other side of the door. My chest tightens as someone slides a key into the brass. Quickly, I take a few silent steps to the tub and crouch behind it before watching as the door opens slowly. The Shadows send no warning. They do not recreate on the floor in an attempt to kidnap me.

When Kirian steps through the door, I understand why they didn't bother to hide me. I stand behind the tub, watching him as he scans the room before landing on me. "I didn't mean to frighten you," he says as the rest of him appears from behind the door. I was not frightened at all, only surprised, as I thought I wouldn't see him until the morning. I thought many things that made my head spin and my insides knot.

I give him a reassuring nod and head for the table when I see that he has brought another much larger bag from the markets. My stomach lets out an embarrassing rumble at the sight of it. No reaction from Kirian besides pulling the table so that we can both sit, him on the bed, me on the chair. He takes out bread, strawberries, and chicken breast that smells so good that my mouth waters. He places two napkins down along with silverware and plates. When he reaches in again, he grabs two glasses and a bottle of wine. I'm not sure what to do with most of the silverware but I arrange them around my plate in the same fashion he does. He pulls the cork from the wine and pours us both generous amounts. *He came back.* I let a smile creep to my face.

"You're smiling." He looks up from the chore at hand. I drop my face immediately like a child who has received a scolding. "That doesn't mean you should stop." He says, dropping his napkin into his lap, I mirror the movement. "I thought you would need something to eat after this morning."

"I didn't think you were coming back until tomorrow," I admit.

"What happened… between us- "

But I cut him off as soon as I look at the neatly placed table and notice his freshly shaven face and nice clothes. Medla and Adriel had many of these courtships. They would end in the bedroom for Medla. Adriel was never so brazen. "This is a courtship," I say plainly. He just smiles politely and nods his head with a low laugh that has my heart skipping a beat.

"Not a very good one." His head swivels as he takes in the old room, the tearing wallpaper and the holes that cover the ceiling, all things I've already noted, as I have had plenty of time to memorize the small room.

Carefully, I take a sip of wine. I can't stop myself from cringing at its bitter taste. I observe the red liquid swish back and forth, sticking to the sides of the glass. I was expecting it to be sweet. It always seemed like it would be when I would watch women gulp it down hastily, dancing and giggling. Sneaking back to have more.

He laughs a little, then grabs his glass as well and holds it out to me. I watched as my sisters would clink their glasses together. Peaking at them from afar so that I would not get in trouble for attending their parties when I was supposed to stay put in my room. When our glasses touch together, creating a satisfying clink, I set it down without taking a sip as Kirian does. I can't imagine why anyone would want to drink that.

The room grows silent, and I'm left with my thoughts once more. "I never forgot about you, you know." He peers up at me through his thick blond lashes. "That night, when I saw you with my bow, you looked so... determined, stubborn. Not much has changed." I can't tell if he means that in a good way or not. As we eat, I try my best not to shove large pieces in my mouth, chewing my food thoroughly before swallowing. It's exhausting, being this concentrated on something so trivial.

"I don't remember you," I say truthfully. I do remember the men that would practice on targets, none of them as tall or as broad shouldered as Kirian.

"I looked for you the next time your sisters held one of their... parties." He chooses his words carefully. He takes a bite of food, chews on it, then raises his eyebrows at me. "Could not find you." he shakes his head slightly.

Memories of the masquerade come flooding in. That night, after I hid the bow from the men, from Cedric, I went back to my room. I lit the candles. I laid in bed listening to the steady beat of the band from a distance. Suddenly, the grating of something on wood came from the hallway. In even measure, the sound got louder and louder.

Then, laughter came from outside my door, a man's deep laugh and the echo of a woman's directly after. I waited until the sound stopped and their footsteps faded away. When I went to open my door, it was no surprise to find something barring it from the other side.

It took me all night to work up the courage to climb out the window and scale the walls to another. The sun was peeking over the hillside, and the party was long since over when I landed face-first into an empty room.

I'll never forget the beating I received for breaking the window to get in. Cedric has always been heavy-handed. That was not the last time my siblings found inventive ways to keep me from their parties. They even made a game of it.

"I was not supposed to attend them," I tell him. To avoid conversation of my dreadfully boring set of rules that Medla gave me and to keep my mind from thinking of the open wound on my brow that I adorned for weeks after Cedric's punishment.

I decide to change the subject. "Why haven't you asked me how I escaped the jail?" I ask avoiding his eyes so that I cannot see if he has caught on to why I have abandoned the earlier conversation.

Kirian plays along, "I already know." He states as he sets his silverware down and dabs his mouth with the napkin from his lap. Then he places his hands together and rests his chin atop them. He is being cocky, I realize, he knows something I do not, and he can't help himself but to put on a show.

I try my best to copy his behavior. It's unconvincing, and I can tell by the smirk that pulls at the corner of his mouth. I stupidly let myself scan over him before moving my way up to the forest, reflecting back at me. I blink and find as much confidence as possible. "Tell me," I say. I, too, have set my silverware down on the sides of my plate, ignoring the hunger in my stomach for just a moment.

"The Connection. I've seen only one other with your gift." His eyes float about the room as if he is searching for something before he continues. "The ability to manipulate darkness. The King's right hand, Augustine Nero, Light Taker. He, too, has escaped many prisons, much worse than the one you were in." I now let the surprise creep to my face, *the ability to manipulate darkness*. I almost laugh at his description.

So far, the darkness has not been used *by* me but rather *through* me. The Shadows started as distant murmurs, like they were talking amongst themselves, filling the silence. Eyes that I felt on the back of my head. Then, they would reach for me. Speak to me. Nonsense at first, then words so clear and close that I thought they were in my head. Like when I shot the bow at the lake with Kirian and again when they warned me of the guards searching the rooms.

They are not manipulated at all because, just as they did this morning, they pull me into a puddle of thick nothingness. It's terrifying and completely against my will.

I'm unsure of so many things in this world, but what I am sure of is that I was not meant to have this *gift*, as he calls it. Somewhere along the threads of fate, a grave error occurred.

Wherever Kirian plans to have me go, I must know more about The Connection and how to get rid of it. My mind wanders as I begin to contemplate all the ways in which I could live my life free of the Shadows. *A seamstress, farmer, maybe even a nurse maid, taking care of small children—that wouldn't be so bad.*

I say nothing, but Kirian sees the curiosity blooming within for all the wrong reasons, as is evident when he says, "Yes, your Gifter was very generous indeed." He talks again as if I know more than I have let on. But I know nothing. I do not particularly care about how I got it, and I don't plan on keeping it long enough to find out. His curiosity will not be sated.

Kirian continues, "The Spent will give you a highly sought-after job with that kind of power. Just like Augustine. After you take The Vow of course." He says. *I will not be around long enough to take a job from The Spent.*

"What's that, The Vow?" I ask. Out of curiosity and because I realize that I have not spoken in a long while and have instead just let Kirian fill the silences.

"A ceremony where you vow to use your magic to serve only The Spent. It's the only way to legally use The Connection on Stone."

"What happens to people who do not? Take the Vow, I mean." I lean forward as I wait for a response, my elbows on each side of my plate. Kirian's smile spreads from one ear to the other. There it is again, the feeling that air seems to surround him. With a breath of it, I could be smiling, too. I don't.

"Oh, you will want to." His green eyes move back and forth between my black ones. "When you have completed your training, you'll realize how important the cause is. You will want to take The Vow and become a member of The Spent." He says it with such confidence like there is nothing more to say about the matter. Coming from his mouth it sounds nice, like he wants me to be a part of something. But getting your hopes up is for fools, and I am no fool.

The night is mostly filled with idle chit-chat, I narrowly avoid most questions that lead back to my siblings or Father, and the night begins to slip away.

Soon, Kirian pulls a small watch from his pocket. "It's well past the time that I was planning on leaving." He says with a grin.

When he stands, I also stand. Another important gesture I learned from my sisters. The men that they fancied would be walked to the door. Those men would inevitably bend over and place a kiss upon their cheek before their departure. Our door is merely steps away, giving us little time for the same sideways glances and accidental missteps that would lead to such a thing. Medla was a trickster, always coming up with ways to get close to the men without them even noticing she was doing it, but I saw her. I saw everything.

Kirian's face stretches into a yawn as he makes for the door. I happened to get a good look at that pocket watch as well, and if we are to leave by first light, it's only hours away. By the time he gets to the barracks and back, I am willing to bet he will only get a wink of sleep. Still, I let him slip on his boots and pull his jacket over his shirt. There is no pleading this time. I will not ask him to stay.

We take the few steps to the exit, just like I saw dozens of times with different men at my sisters' sides. And just as I suspected, Kirian bends down slowly and places a kiss on my cheek, a light, gentle kiss that lights my skin on fire and has my stomach flipping. This one is much different than the one we shared before. "Til' first light, Katsia," he lingers near my ear for a moment before straightening.

My breath hitches, but I manage to reply, "Goodnight, Kirian." The door closes, and I let out a long-held breath as his footsteps fade from earshot.

I don't let myself sleep. It is for no other reason than the fear that I will once again slip into the abyss, only this time, who knows if I will make my way out. So, I slip from my clothes and curl into the warm blankets, but I do not dare let my eyes close.

When the sun begins to rise, I rise with it.

With a lace bottom petticoat now over my head and the green dress atop it, I take a regretful look in the mirror, hating the body that looks back. Straightening the fabric unsuccessfully and fidgeting with the gold detail around my waist.

The dress does not fit my form. It hangs loosely around the collar as if it belonged to someone with a much larger chest. The dress is also much too short, showing off more of my boots than even my sisters would deem acceptable.

My hair falls to my waist. I run my hands through it and then throw it into a quick single braid. I look into the now broken mirror again, which seems to fit this dingy room better with a new wiry crack down its middle. Only looking long enough at myself to tuck away stray hairs.

As good as it gets, I guess. I'd much rather wear the clothes I had on before. Instead, I shove the shirt and trousers into the bag that Kirian left behind.

Then, I wait.

Chapter 14

We make our way slowly and well-hidden to the gate, not a word spoken between us. Not until I hear the slam of metal as it closes after us, Kirian slips a man a coin as we pass, and Thorn Row is behind us, do I realize it's too late to turn back. "What now?" I finally speak. Kirian doesn't answer, his attention caught on the seemingly empty hillside.

"Don't worry." He finally says. "You will be taken care of. These people will not harm you." He affirms, and I believe him. Suddenly from where Kirian's eyes were concentrated, five men on horseback appear from behind the hill. Followed by a carriage in the color of midnight. I notice there is no insignia or crest on it. The carriage stops in front of us, and Kirian greets the elderly man, who exits with a bow of his head. I take a step closer to Kirian, following his lead, tipping my head down in a silent bow. I rein in my fear as best I can, making sure to take shallow breaths so that the men around me do not see my chest heaving. I swallow multiple times to keep the contents of my stomach from rising, and my hands begin to sweat. *When will this stop happening?*

To distract myself, I memorize the man before me. He is covered in fine jewelry. Gold rings occupy every fragile, sun-spotted finger. The bracelets on his arms clink together as he moves, and his robe, the same color of deep blue, blends into the carriage behind him. Golden thread flashes as the wind takes the hem of the robe in its grasp. He holds a shaky hand out to Kirian, who kisses the largest Stone that adorns his middle finger. Then he turns to me and holds out his hand in the same fashion. I ,too, make to kiss the Stone, although I have no idea why. My body almost detests the touch, but I force my lips to the ring anyway. When he lifts his head in approval and looks up to Kirian once more, revealing the spot beneath his chin. A wrinkled tattoo of an eye centered over his Adam's Apple.

The men on horse's are now in a circle around us as Kirian exchanges pleasantries with the man. I quickly pull my hand to my side when I realize I'm nervously twirling my braid behind my back.

While they all have their attention on Kirian and the man in the robe that stands before us, my own attention goes to those who surround us. I squint into the sun, looking for something, anything to tell me who they are. These men are not in the same tan as the Soldiers here in Thorn Row. Their dark uniforms hold no distinguishing marks either. The less I find the more I know that they belong to The Spent. Suddenly, I have the urge to run, but as I am surrounded, where would I go?

I quickly talk myself down from the ledge. *I have to do this.* To end the torture, to rid myself of this. They would not be collecting magic users if they did not know more about it. Keeping Kirian's promise of safety in my mind, I have made the decision to let these people take me to The Spent. No matter how many times my legs tell me otherwise.

I slide my eyes along each man on their horses, watching them as they concentrate on the conversation between the two at my side. They eagerly await their next orders that must come from the wrinkled man, their leader, no doubt. All but one man, whose uniform is not the same fashion as the others, he lets his eyes wander. To the mountains I realize. His face bored as he adjusts on the saddle.

He does not notice as I take in his raven-colored hair, strands of it falling into his face. His jaw clenches and unclenches many times. *What is he looking at?* I follow his eyes to Shadow Gate, the blue mountains in the distance, ones that no one occupies anymore, not farther than the Uncharted Territories anyway. A sight to behold and one that is unique to the northern parts of Stone, while the other parts of Stone are filled with plains and rolling hills. Equal but different beauties.

I make to look away, but then I see his line of vision change. He now burns a hole in the back of Kirian's head, his eyes red as smoldering embers. The atmosphere changes then. I could have sworn it did as I beheld the man. I have half a mind to step to the side, placing myself between them, to protect Kirian from the fire behind the ravens' eyes. It will do no good. I'm tall, but not as tall as Kirian and much too small to cover any of his huge body with my own.

"Let us depart soon." The old man's voice makes my head snap to his attention once more. He takes a step back, holding out a hand as he gestures to the door. When I do not move, Kirian places a reassuring hand on my lower back and guides me forward. I look to the old man and then to Kirian, and his gentle eyes meet mine before I take a step inside. *Trapped*, I think to myself as I sit between the wooden walls of the carriage.

The men disperse on their horses, either making their way behind or in front as if they have assembled like this many times before. My thumbs twiddle on my lap as I watch them, nerves getting the best of me. *Run*, no.

The man with red eyes and raven-like features must have been ordered to guard the door. His horse is covered in braided black armor. They would be right in assuming that I need someone to keep the door, to make sure that I do not escape because everything in me is telling me to run all over again. I keep shoving the thought down, and it keeps reforming in the front of my mind.

Even the Shadows beckon for me from a distance. Past the red eyed man and his horse, they peek at me from behind trees and beneath the brush as if they fear coming closer. The world seems to hold its breath as I let myself really see them. Surprised when I see that they are...scared. Perhaps their fear and my own are one and the same.

When the robed man speaks again, I begrudgingly peel my eyes away from them. "I have many questions for Miss Luz." The man says. He speaks to Kirian as if I am not here. The robed man also takes a step into the wooden, too-small box on wheels with Kirian's helping hand.

"Of course, My Lord," Kirian says back, one hand on the door as he watches the robed man sit from the outside. "I hope you'll find her true of heart." All of the things unsaid, phrases that only insiders understand, makes my skin crawl. *Run.* As if Kirian can read my thoughts "Do not be afraid" he whispers, his words calm my pounding heart, but only slightly.

The thought of never seeing Kirian again did not cross my mind until right now. Of course, he can't come. He lives here. He has a family here. The thought seems to come to his mind, as well as he keeps my eyes, even as the door closes. The small window only allows me to see half of his face through a slit in the curtain.

There is something that takes over his features entirely, but I cannot tell what it is. Regret, pity, worry, they all look so identical to me.

His jaw clenches and he gives me a small nod as a man out of sight grunts and the horses begin to pull away. Kirian looks down at his feet and I too turn my attention elsewhere. And I regret not being able to look him in the eye, to show him how scared I truly am, because the last thing Kirian will ever see on my face is cowardice.

"Lord Andres." The man across from me introduces himself. "And I already know your name, Katsia." My name comes out as if spoken by a snake. His slithery words stick to me, making me nervous. I grab at the end of my braid and his gaze follows my hand as I twirl the black hair around my finger. "Are you afraid, child?" he asks.

Yes, but I would never admit it, especially to this stranger. One of the many rules, of course, I made for myself, so it is an easy one not to throw out: *Never admit you're afraid.* But the word comes from somewhere deep in my chest, pulled out of me without my consent. "Yes," I tell him. I am far too nervous. He is taking advantage of that fact.

"Ah, that is to be expected." He nods his head in understanding. "Tell me." his voice shaky with age. "How old were you when you were gifted?" he asks. The Connection, my magic, not a *gift* in the slightest.

"I do not know." Again, the words seem to spill without thought.

"Did your Mother or Father ever give you the name of your Gifter?" he then asks. *When will the questions stop?* I wonder. I have a feeling this old, wrinkled man plans to learn everything about me before we arrive at our destination. I will not give him the satisfaction. I cross my arms and lean back onto the wooden bench.

My mouth betrays me then, "No." I shift uncomfortably as the words escape. *Don't say another word.* I tell myself as panic begins to build in my throat, my chest. He remains unmoving, his legs crossed and his hands in his lap. His once blue eyes that have taken on a clouded silver haze with age concentrate on my lips, slowly moving down to my neck. *Curse this dress for exposing me.*

"I see." He lets his eyes flick to mine for only a moment. "Do you know who put the curse on your Father?" His words come quick like he has the questions lined up, one after the other. I've already been beaten, interrogated, every bit of information I know has been spilled. No doubt sent to the ears that sit before me now.

I decided that for the remainder of this very unnerving ride, I will remain silent. I especially do not wish to talk of Father. I purse my lips and turn for the window. The man coughs slightly in an attempt to regain my full attention. When I do not look at him, he speaks again. "Do not make me draw my own conclusions." At that, my head turns, and his eyes still do not meet mine. He seems to narrow them at my chest, but when I cover myself with my arms, he does not let it deter his stare as if he can see right through them. *Don't speak, don't say anything.*

Something inside me screams and the word is already on my tongue before I can stop it. "No." Something wants out, and it's going to get what it wants no matter what I do. *What is he doing to me?* His eyes never move from the spot between my collarbones. I look to the window on the left, then the right, where the man remains on his horse, in search of an escape that I know does not exist. My chest tightens further. There is not enough air to fill my lungs in this tiny carriage. There is not enough air in all of Stone.

My head goes light, and my vision blurs. The muscles in my throat tighten before I can no longer hold the words in. "I wish it was me. I wish I would have known how to put such a curse on my Father." I blurt out, and the pressure around my neck releases. My eyes grow wide, and my heart speeds up as the words keep flowing from me like an unyielding waterfall. "My Father was cruel, and he taught his son and daughters to be cruel, or perhaps it was in his blood what made them that way." I cover my mouth with my hands, but the words keep coming out. "I was not sired by Hansel Luz, thank the Gods." My words are muffled as I speak through my fingers.

The words feel like bile. They were not meant to leave my mouth. Those thoughts have only ever been said in my head, never aloud.

He just looks me over, pleased. He nods his head, "Tell me of your Mother."

No, no, no. Never speak of Mother. It was the biggest rule at House Luz and one that I did not mind abiding by. If I didn't think about her or talk about her or look into the mirror for too long, then I never had to feel the guilt of taking away the Mother that Cedric, Medla and Adriel had come to know, to love. Never had to remember the words that Medla never forgot to remind me of. *You're a murderer, Katsia.* The words in my head echo in Medla's voice. "I murdered her." I shake my head furiously as I hear my own words.

Tears begin to build, threatening to fall down my cheeks at any moment. Now I search for ways to get out of this damned carriage, no matter what it takes, no matter if the man outside takes my life. I can't be here anymore. I can't answer another unwanted question.

I reach for the door, but Lord Andres is quick for his age, he swats my fingers away before I can turn the wooden block which would release me. The man outside lets out a huff that I think is laughter at my attempt. *How much has he heard?* Now, my stomach churns for an entirely different and embarrassing reason.

"You don't want to do that, child. You would not make it." Lord Andres peeks over to the window. Before settling back onto me with that disconcerting habit of letting his eyes wander to my chest. *Disgusting.*

I take my eyes away from him long enough to see that we are going over a large bridge now, and far below, a river flows.

Lord Andres seems to be unaffected by my confession. "I do... want to." *Shut up.*

"Want to what?" Lord Andres asks plainly, but I know what he really asks.

I push my lips together as tight as I can until my cheeks hurt, and the words that seem to be inside will soon force their way out somehow. Either by ripping out my esophagus or rushing from my mouth. I chose the latter.

"Give up," I tell him. I will not win this fight. Death to a rushing river below would be better than living the way I always have- afraid, weak, and alone. And I can't say this is the first I've thought of it. Taking my own life.

Once, when I looked down from my window, where I was to scale the wall to the other room. I looked down and thought to myself, *"You are better off dead"*. The next time was upon the lap of the man whose ear I tasted. When, for a split second, I had accepted my fate. Death was the option that I was most okay with at the time. Before Kirian showed up.

"Ah," he says after a long moment as if he was letting me sit with the words as if he knows exactly what they mean. Andres just nods his head and readjusts in his seat. The air seems to be back to normal, and the panic dissipates. *What in the House of Hades was that?* I don't have to wait long for the answer, "My gift is truth." He points to the tattoo on his neck as an explanation. Claire had one on her forehead, and the man in the cell had one upon his wrist. I wonder if Kirian has one as well. For what I do not know, he never used The Connection around me. My brows involuntarily push together at the thought.

"You may very well be a murderer. Though you don't seem the type." I dare a peak at Lord Andres, but he is gazing out the window now, his eyes skipping back and forth as they latch on to different far-off objects. "I have lived a long life, Katsia, heard many truths." He relaxes into the seat before he turns back to me, his eyes finally meeting my own. "Some tell the truth, the facts, the absolutes." he blinks slowly at me. "Some tell only what *they* believe to be true."

The rest of our time together is eerily quiet, and as many questions as I have, I do not ask them. We both keep our attention at the windows on the opposite sides of the carriage. Stone becomes flat, and the buildings become sparse. I'm unsure of how long we travel, but where we are going must be far. As hard as I try to stay awake, I am soon drifting in and out of consciousness. And I can't help but think it is another trick that has my eyes heavy and my head bobbing.

When I wake in a panic for what has to be the sixth time, I notice a drastic change in climate. It's warm and muggy making me believe that we are headed into Fauna.

Many books have told me of its low level compared to the sea. This makes it difficult during some seasons. Large storms result in floods, devastating homes and businesses. Father was working with a man from Fauna to build houses that would withstand the weather. He sent Cedric to deal with it, but he did not come back for many days. His face was bruised, and he looked like he hadn't slept for days. There were no more discussions about it after that.

After a while, we make a stop. I can't see the city beyond the marsh and trees, but in the distance, I spy a sign with the words 'Fauna' and underneath 'Lest We Forget.'

Lord Andres pushes out the door, startling me. I watch as the guards attempt to help him onto horseback. He vigorously swats the man away as if it's against his dignity to need help. Painfully slow, Lord Adres lifts a leg and straddles the saddle. Before heading towards the front with the others, somewhere out of my eyesight. Finally, alone, I settled down into the seat, glad not to have the eyes of Lord Andres on me. I watch them pass the carriage window, positioning around me once more, three in front and two behind.

We are stopped for a few moments longer and I start to let myself relax. Letting myself take in the scenery that I never thought I would be able to visit. I lean my head against the door to see the road ahead of us. The trees almost make a tunnel with their long branches curved perfectly for the travelers that pass through them.

I am interrupted when someone whips open the door. I nearly hit the roof of the carriage with how high I jump. He practically pushes me to the side before slamming the door behind him. It doesn't take me long to notice who Lord Andres switched places with, the man with black hair and red eyes. I sit back down and wait for him to say something, but he does not. Instead, he falls back into the seat with a puff of air and crosses his arms as if he couldn't be bothered.

Dressed in a black uniform, the expensive looking fabric seems to meld with his form. His jaw tightens and his brows furrow, clearly uncomfortable. *That makes two of us.* The lines around his eyes make him look much older, although he can't be much older than Kirian. In his late twenties, the same as Cedric.

Every movement he makes is deliberate as he purposely focuses on whatever is furthest from me. I quickly look away as well, concentrating on the noises outside to distract me from his presence.

As the wheels move over Stone, a memory comes to my mind's eye, the day I hid in the grass during that summer as Cedric left, all his belongings crammed into the back of a carriage. Much like this one. I shake my head to clear the images behind my eyes but they take their time fading.

Little did I know that was only the beginning, and now I am here. It was so much easier, when all I had to do was avoid distant whispers in the shade and plan my days around my family. *Be in the right place at the right time, make sure no one sees you.* Words I have repeated to myself many times. This *is* the right place. This *is* where I have to be in order to achieve my goal, I remind myself.

During my time ignoring the new passenger I look out at the houses dispersed throughout the outer city. I have read many books on Fauna. They started as simple farmers, although now looking at all of the different types of animals, the flocks of sheep and all the cattle that graze their pastures, it doesn't look so simple anymore. All of Stone's meat, milk, eggs, and wool comes from Fauna, a fitting name for the city.

We come to a screeching halt that has me gripping the wooden bench beneath me. Still, I do not dare look up at the man. I hear dogs barking, the pounding of hooves as they near us, and the bleating of sheep. My heart races with anticipation. Soon all I can see outside of the small window are the large tan animals. Like clouds that block our view. Their baaing fills my ears. They follow each other in lines as they run from the dogs that tail them.

I move from one window to the next in awe as they scatter and then reform as a man whistles for his dogs once more. I have never seen sheep before, only sketches of them in books. I memorized their anatomy and the process of making their wool into clothing. Some would appear in my dreams, just like that, the flock of them surrounding me and then leaving. I would pretend I was above the clouds, but seeing it in person is so different, real.

Although I guess for people who see it every day it's not that interesting. Must get old to be stopped along your route by the many farmers trying to transport their animals. Still, to me it's *literally* a dream come true. I can't help myself but to stare as they go.

It's not until they are almost gone that I realize I had gotten too close to the dark-haired man across from me when he clears his throat. Even using the headrest behind him to balance myself as I still watch the last one make its way down the hill. I turn my head to the noise, our faces mere inches from one another, his eyes trail down to my chin and back up to my brows, annoyance apparent in his expression.

I retreat to the other side slowly, crouching down so that my head does not hit the top of the carriage. The driver pulls us forward with the same grunt once more and the motion slams me back into my seat. Making me hit the wooden bench with a hard *thud*, all the air leaves my lungs.

My cheeks flush and I nervously fold my hands as we continue, not daring another glance. Clearly, I am an inconvenience to the man before me. He doesn't even try to hide the irritation, and soon, the space between us becomes thick with tension. I hardly stop myself from rolling my eyes.

He does not speak to me, and I do not speak to him. He must have heard all he needed to know during my time with Lord Andres. The warmth that I feel in my cheek's spreads to my whole body. I usually do not care about what others think, but what this man heard was never to be said aloud, not to Lord Andres or strangers who listen in on private conversations.

There are no more disruptions, and as we drive through the city, I gawk at all of the beautiful buildings, putting the ones in Thorn Row to shame.

Thorn Row was built quickly after the war. The King was sure to make a profit off of the miserable citizens. Its houses are plain brick or wood, constructed quickly and with little to no embellishments, none as elaborate as those I see before me. All uniquely decorated, each a different color of the rainbow. The tops of them have balconies where women hang laundry across lines that are connected to the houses across the way. The same women swoon at the soldiers that surround us out of my sight.

The streets are busy as men and women walk about. Not in a hurry as I saw them do in Thorn Row from the window of The Charlie. Music plays from somewhere far off. The sound gets closer as we pass a man with a brass instrument paired with a woman who sings a melody. Children dance near the music and a man in a brown suit drops a silver coin in the hat at the woman's feet.

Her black braided hair falls perfectly behind her as she sways to the beat. I do not move from my seat as I did before, preventing another awkward encounter. Soon, the city is gone, and we are on a path between large golden trees.

The man shifts uncomfortably in his seat as we near a large gate with the letter 'A' on one side and 'O' on the other. Two guards dressed in the same dark uniform as the others open it from the other side. It's hard to see what is in front of us, but as the carriage circles around to the front, I find myself unable to look away from the huge white castle with stained glass windows and dark oak doors. Men scrabble around us, unable to see them, but I hear their footsteps on brick and the swish of leather as they unsaddle their horses.

Lord Andres comes into view. Two men help him off the horse, which he begrudgingly accepts. He faces the carriage, waiting for *us* I suppose. Men come from both sides and stand in a line, one of them opens the door. The others place their swords on their shoulders pointed at the sky as they await their next command.

The man across from me sucks in a deep breath before making his way out of the carriage and onto the red brick that lines the ground. He then holds out his hand and looks at me expectantly from behind his shoulder, his scowl doing nothing to calm my nerves. I swallow away the knot in my throat and look at the hand that now holds mine. A large scar peeks out from beneath his sleeve. I do not look at it long as the man catches me staring. My own hand is now shaking before I have even taken a step.

I make to take a step but stop, cursing under my breath as my dress gets caught on the wooden seat behind me. I rip it away with my other hand and step out, not caring about the tear in the fabric I've just created. Everyone stares as we emerge from the carriage. The man drops my hand when I am finally on Stone and takes a step. I follow.

My wobbly legs are obeying me for now, but at any minute, I feel as if I could collapse. We walk behind Lord Andres, who is excruciatingly slow. Sweat drips down my face and while the walk is unhurried, my heart seems to be going twice its normal pace. I place my hand upon my chest as if to slow its drumming, but it is no use.

I can't help but watch the faces as we go by them. They clearly see my nerves. One man even whispers something to the other, and another fails at hiding a smile from their face. *Pathetic.* That is what I am.

It's suddenly too much. There are too many people. That feeling that sometimes makes me purge my guts is now as present as ever. My mouth waters in preparation. I swallow over and over until my throat hurts. When I think I can no longer take it when my head goes light, and just as the Shadows seem to whisper from far off, the doors open, and the beauty that shows beyond them pulls my mind away from that dark place and into the present once more. I let go of the arm that I had not realized I had grabbed for balance. Not looking at the raven to make sure I avoid the hatred that I could feel the whole way here, radiating off of him.

Much like the castle I grew up in, there is a staircase that leads up onto a balcony. Servants stand there, awaiting orders as they look down at us. I flinch at the loud *thud* as the doors close behind me. *Fewer eyes, that's good.* The gnawing in my stomach subsides for now.

Lord Andres stays by my side as I take in the room. The lights above me flicker and when I look up, I realize that they are not lanterns or candles. They are suspended balls of light that fill the room. They seem to move on their own accord as they float, never letting a space fill with darkness. Dozens of roses, fill vases set on tables, and more go up the stairs and hang from the balcony.

The air also seems different. There is an aura to the whole place that I have not felt before. I breathe in, expecting the sweet aroma of flowers to fill my lungs, but the smell is not pleasant at all. What is that scent? Like the smell of blood or the metallic taste of copper.

I look about the giant room in search of its origin, Lord Andres and the man follow my eyes as I search for something that cannot be seen. I become fearful that the smell may actually be blood, and I was deceived once again, led to somewhere far worse than the jail, far worse than living with a beast that hunts animals and kills women.

My eyebrows scrunch together in confusion, then I look to Lord Andres for answers, but he does not seem to have any or even notice my discomfort. "Mana," a husky voice says from beside me. I spin to look at him, my breath catches as I look into his brown eyes. The color of honey now reflects the white light and not the yellow of the sun that sent them ablaze before. His face still in that permanent frown that I saw sitting across from me in the carriage.

I didn't realize I was staring until Lord Andres stepped closer to us, he clears his throat before saying. "I will take my leave." Then he drifts past, through a door to the left of us.

"It's mana, it's in the air." The raven reiterates as he removes his jacket and throws it onto a nearby chair. "The whole place runs on it. Spartus heats itself in the winter and cools itself in the summer." He looks at me, but I do not say anything. I can't, it seems, the words are lost in my mind. *Spartus*, I repeat in my head. Then I just nod to let him know that I understand.

Then he looks down at my legs, and when I follow his line of sight, I see what catches his attention. The tear in my dress from when I pulled it free before I stepped out of the carriage. Without thinking I pull up my skirt slightly to see the damage up close. His eyes drift from the dangling piece of fabric to my bare legs that I now have on display. He inspects my knees, dried blood and bruises from Gods knows what.

The last few days have left my body in disrepair, my nose still swollen, and bruises on my chin and arms to match those on my knees. Even my hands have healed over scratches on the palms and buildup under my nails that my bath at The Charlie failed to clean. I must look absolutely appalling. It's embarrassing, really.

When I realize I still have my dress bundled into my hand, I drop it immediately, my thoughts distracting me. He just huffs his annoyance at me once more. Confirming what I already knew, that he does in fact find me disgusting, as he should.

He turns away from me and calls down the servants with the wave of a hand. "Take Miss Luz to her room." At his words, the women who occupy the balcony scurry down the stairs to gather me. They circle around me, and one takes my arm gently. I look over at her and down to her touch, reminding myself not to pull my arm from her grasp.

"You will need a trim," one says, holding out my long braid and inspecting the ends.

"And these callouses," another exclaims, before she lifts my hand to show the group, I squeeze it shut tightly and place my hands at my sides as we walk.

"First a bath." The leader of the group says, her mousy brown hair and harsh features paired with her gravelly voice give her a more masculine appearance. This silences the servants until we get to the top of the stairs when she leaves to fetch something from a room. That's when they look me over, obviously noting all the unsightly things that need to be fixed before putting a hand to their mouths to hide what they say to each other in hushed voices.

I keep my mouth shut. I'm drained from the day and don't have the energy to fight, nor do I care what the women say about me. It's all been said before by my sisters, this time I don't have the luxury of hiding away where no one will see me. They take me down a hallway with many doors. I think I hear one of them open nearby, but the woman scolds the person behind it and not another one opens again. The room is quaint, with a bed and washing basin, a three-drawer dresser, and a vanity with a mirror. The red curtains and matching bedding make the room feel very uniform. I don't get to stay long before I'm dragged away again. "We have lots of work to do," one of them says.

Chapter 15

The servants spent the night fretting over me like a child, the same way that Adriel did when I was young. The gruff woman whose name I've come to learn is Agnus, oversees the servants of the house. She made sure the ladies didn't skip even the smallest of details when preparing me— from my hair down to my toes. And I let them, it was a cleaning I desperately needed.

A clear liquid that smelled of citrus was added to my bath. At first, it stung around my wounds, but when I awoke this morning, all my cuts were healed over, now only pink lines remain. My hair is shiny, and a floral scent fills my nose when it falls into my face.

I promptly pulled it from the tight pins that they set in my hair last night. I couldn't sleep on the damned things, not that I slept well anyway.

Maybe it's this place, the room was too quiet and the bed too soft. Something was off, missing even. While my days in the jail all rushed together, night and day becoming one, last night felt like it went on forever. For the last few days, weeks, or however long I was held in that cell, I felt like there was danger slowly creeping its long fingers closer to my neck.

Last night all I felt was calm. Soon the reason that I couldn't sleep was not the bed or the pins that stabbed at my scalp, it was the thought that things around me had become too easy. That I was too comfortable. The Shadows have seemingly disappeared without the threat of danger. Which had me thinking of all the things that could go wrong.

Agnus now stands behind me at the vanity. I try not to look into the mirror except to apologize after she scolds me for ruining my hair. *Always look your elders in the eye.* She then braids it into a single plait, which she secures tightly around my head. It almost wraps around twice, even with the inches that the servants were so anxious to cut off. "Remember how I do this girl. You'll do it this way from now on." She says roughly as she places the last pin.

"Yes, ma'am," I say. She raises one brow and shakes her head in disapproval, but I'm not sure at what.

She pulls from the nearby drawer a midnight blue pleated skirt and button-down white shirt. "These are the women's uniforms. You'll wear this for your studies," then she opens another drawer and pulls out a sleeved shirt, the same color of blue. Along with trousers that are reinforced at the knees. "These are for training." She tells me as she sets them both neatly on the bed.

"Training?" I ask the ground for fear of catching a glimpse of myself in the mirror. "For what?"

"Every student must learn simple defense and weaponry." Agnus places her hand on her hip and uses the other to point to the clothes that remain on the bed. "Every morning, you will study in the library, and every evening, you will join the others in the arena." I turn away from my reflection altogether to see her move her finger back and forth between the two outfits as she speaks.

When I stand, she steps to the door, and one of the other servants hands her dark brown leather boots with black laces. Noise from the hallway catches my attention, but I cannot see past the two women before me. Agnus sets the new boots on the floor. "And wear these." She says as she pinches the collar of my old boots between her fingers and picks them up, most likely to discard them. They are not only covered in layers of mud but also falling apart. A large hole on the left one's heel would often result in a wet sock on rainy days. They served me well enough.

"Yes, ma'am," I say, still eyeing the worn leather laces that dangle to the floor.

"Agnus." She corrects me, which has me blinking up at her pointed features as the look of disapproval takes over her face. She does not see me nod before she shuts the door to allow me to dress.

The skirt hangs down to just above my ankles. The white shirt has pleats down its middle and it smells of clean linen, not like the yucca soap I use to clean my own clothes. It hangs loosely around my neck and arms. I pull at the loose fabric, but I won't bother Agnus with finding a smaller one.

This library is very different from the ones at home. Father's office library was mostly filled with his personal drawings, city layouts, and import and export documents. My sister's library had many romance novels that I did not care much for, as well as textbooks from their private study lessons. Those of which I would steal away at night for reading. After Medla found me with her arithmetic book, which I did not understand anyway, she made sure to hide the rest away or tear the pages out so that I had nothing to read anymore.

I would not let that deter me. I would often push my ear against the door to listen to their sessions with a private tutor. The tutor was male first, a tall man with spindly fingers who would often entertain my sisters on the piano. Then, for some reason, only women were allowed to teach my sisters.

The library before me is filled with not only readings of the occult but also many books from the history of Stone. There are so many books that I so desperately want to read, but I am afraid I may not be allowed to take all of them, so I settle for only one. A thin brown book with leather bindings. I take it from its spot and tuck it under my arm, taking note that it's from the very small fiction section of the ginormous library. Fables were easy to get a hold of at House Luz, all but forgotten by my siblings after they grew out of their stories. I have never heard of this one before.

I become so distracted by not only the books but the artifacts that are dispersed throughout the library that I almost didn't notice that there are others also milling about and pulling their own books from the shelves. It would be very easy to be in this library and never see another person, I am not so lucky. I shift around the room as far away from those around me as possible.

The long room seems to go on forever, and the vaulted ceilings hold artwork in detailed paintings or upon stained glass between the beams that hold the room together. The colorful glass above the shelves casts different colored lights onto the porcelain woman who stands at the center, her hands raised and her feet bound. There is much more to see in this vast room, with more knowledge than I have ever had access to, but I will have to see the rest of it at a different time, with fewer eyes.

I watch a few for a moment from behind a statue's feet. The people disappear down the different rows as they find what they are looking for. They all look like they belong here, tracking down books and scribbling their findings on paper. They begin to take their seats at tables nearby. This part of the library is boring, only the mage lights and plain white chairs, not the beautiful colors behind us.

As they find their seats, I follow, nervously looking around for a seat myself. There are no more empty tables and almost no empty chairs. A few curious glances are sent my way before they look back down at their hands or whisper to the nearest person. It's not hard to tell who they speak of.

Soon, a petite girl catches my attention, waving me over and pointing to a seat next to her. There are no other choices, and she is the only one who offered. So, when I make my way to the table, I try a small smile "Ava." She holds out her hand. More side-long glances and words that will never reach my ears.

"Katsia." I reach out and shake her hand, telling myself today that I will be on my best behavior, use all my manners, and act accordingly. Not at all feral. That's what I will be, *tame*. I take the seat next to her and cross my legs as she does, even pulling the skirt over my knees in the same fashion. Ava tucks her chin-length shiny blonde hair behind her ear, which reminds me of Adriel's in the summer.

She gives me a kind smile that makes her round face and delicate features look like a child's. Of course, she is rather young, perhaps even younger than me. I look between her blue eyes but do not return her smile.

An older woman in a dark robe, similar to the one I saw Lord Andres wear but with a rope tied around her waist and a pendant swinging from her neck, comes from behind a shelf and snaps a wooden cane across her palm. *Crack*. I try not to associate the sound with similar sounds that have come from wood on flesh in my mind.

Ava and I watch as a few more bodies appear from different parts of the library and take their seats at the noise.

"You may call me Sofie." The older woman says from her position at the front of the tables, she looks only at me as she continues, suggesting that the others have already heard this speech before. "You will be here, in these chairs, every day for the next three months." Some of the students turn to look at me. "You do not have to learn. You do not have to listen, but you will be here, understood?" I nod my head, hoping that the heat that I feel rise to the surface of my cheeks is not noticeable.

For the next few hours, Sofie talks about her life as she gathers books and places them on the table. Often disappearing from sight, her voice echoes off the shelves until she makes her way back with another book in hand. Sofie has led an interesting life, from her time in the military to her searches in The North with The Spent. You can tell she was a soldier, the way she speaks, how she holds herself is much like the way that Kirian holds himself.

As she sets the last book down, she tells us to read and exchange them with each other until we have completed all of them. The table is now filled with stacks of ginormous books, and I'm not sure I will be able to keep up with the others.

When class is over, I decide to return the fable that I grabbed before. I don't think I will have time to read it along with all the others.

But as I slip from the group and make my way back to the section where I took it from, "Keep that one." Sofie's withered voice says from behind me, causing my spine to straighten. I turn around, looking past her wiry, dull red hair, to see that others are already picking through the pile, some with two or three in their hands before shuffling out of the room. Ava holds two books in her hands and looks at me impatiently, holding them up for me to see.

"A-alright," I say, tucking it back into my arm. She gives a nod and then walks away, leaning on her cane for balance. There, on the back of her head, where the hairline meets the neck, the mark of an eye. I should not be so surprised to see it.

Ava grabs my arm and leads me to the hallway. "Let's eat together" she says taking my hand and pulling me along with her, I almost immediately release hers but still walk by her side. I have not eaten in so long, my stomach growls at the thought of fresh bread.

She leads me to the dining hall. I already knew where it was from when Agnus and the others toured me around the castle. The castle, I soon come to find out, is actually a school and the doors next to mine belong to the other students, Ava included. Still, I let her point in the direction of the student section where we are supposed to eat, and listen as she explains mealtimes and curfew. Nodding like it's the first time I am hearing it.

Ava finds an empty table after grabbing plates of bland looking food. Years of Lupita's cooking has spoiled me to what most would consider regular meals. Although, I am nothing close to picky and grateful that I no longer am served the slop the jail so kindly dished out to its inmates. I grab the silverware and remind myself of manners before beginning.

It might be my imagination, but I do feel like the other students stare as we sit. Some even whisper to one another, and when I turn towards them, they stop. I try to ignore it as best as I can. Ava seems to have not even noticed the chatter surrounding us as she shovels food into her mouth. She even begins to read her book as bits of meat fall off her fork before it gets to her mouth. Manners be damned.

Her small hand is barely able to hold the book open, but that doesn't stop her from reading it. I feel bad for whoever gets the book next, most likely me. I can't help but laugh as she continues. I slowly scoop the food to my mouth, wishing that I was devouring the food before me the same as Ava.

Soon after finishing our meal, Ava begs me to meet her here for breakfast. I don't usually eat in the morning, but fitting in might prove more helpful than not, so I agree. We walk to our rooms to change into our training uniforms. Her room is almost on the opposite side of the hallway to mine. When I finally get to my own room, I hardly have time to change before she is already standing at the door waiting for me. This is going to take some getting used to.

She keeps a smile as we walk to the training grounds, but it fades when we enter the arena. "I'm not much good at training," she admits.

Soft grass lays around the edges of a square that's roped off. There's a circular dirt patch in the middle, where a woman in similar clothing as ours stands. She introduces herself as Christoph, Madam Christoph. Although she is small you can't miss the muscles under her long sleeve that she has hiked up to the elbow. The pads on her knees and the front of her shirt are dirtied like she has been doing her own training before we arrived.

Her wild, almost black hair, chopped at seemingly random lengths, paired with wild eyes and a mischievous grin, leads me to believe that the woman is out of her mind.

When Madam Christoph sees that everyone has gathered, she separates us into pairs. Ava with a boy that looks just as frail as she does, with brown hair and square glasses that he keeps pushing further onto his nose. I end up with a girl about the same height as me and of similar build. Her long brown hair and blue eyes make her a beauty to look at, but when her lips curl into a wicked smirk as she glances at her friend behind her, I see just how ugly she truly is. "She thinks she's so special. I'll see about that," she remarks to no one in particular. There is nothing special about me at all. In fact, Adriel often said I was quite mundane. My brows push together as I try to make sense of what she means.

Madam Christoph grabs a student and demonstrates a basic defense maneuver, pulling my attention away from the girl.

We then disperse along the arena in our pairs. "I'll be the attacker." The girl says, that smirk sneaking back to her lips.

She gives me little time to refuse before she braces her hands on my neck the same way that was demonstrated. Unlike Madam Christoph, she digs her nails into the back of my skull and squeezes with what I can assume from her pinched face is all her strength. The fast movement takes me by surprise, and instead of doing as was shown and lifting my dominant arm to come across hers that are now held out to choke me, I grip at her fingers, unsuccessfully peeling them back.

When she does not remove her hands or even loosen her grip, I feel my blood begin to boil with anger before lifting my knee, which meets with her middle, sending her falling backward as she tries to catch her breath. I place my hands across my burning neck to rub away the pain, and when they come away, they are covered in blood as she ripped through my skin in her retreat.

Everyone gathers around us. Ava pulls at my arm, but I take it back, ripping it from her hand. I take in as much air as possible to avoid the unwelcome feeling that threatens to take over. The girls' companions comfort her as she lay on the ground sobbing, I didn't think I hit her that hard. I just wanted her *off* me. "She's fucking crazy." She spits. All eyes turn to me.

"Everyone thinks you're crazy. You have no idea what Father has told them. If you try to tell anyone about this, they won't believe you." Cedric's voice filters through my head.

Without a second thought, I push my hands back up to cover my bloodied neck, then I turn and walk away. To my surprise, Madam Christoph does not stop me. Everyone watches as I go, their jaws open and their mouths ready to speak ill of me. I don't stop until I've rounded the corner, unknowing of where I am headed. I think I hear Ava's soft voice call my name through the ringing in my ears, but I'm already gone.

When I reach a fountain surrounded in lush, perfectly cut grass, so manicured that it's almost as if from a painting, I sit at the edge of the water and use it to clean the blood from my neck, then splash my face, but it does nothing to soothe the anger that boils under my skin. I peer at the reflection of the sky above me in the water, near cloudless, casting its bright blue upon the rippling water. That tight feeling in my chest comes to the surface when black eyes, my Mother's eyes, look back at me. I splash the water so that she no longer exists.

My head swivels when I feel the weight of eyes on me. An eerie feeling settles over me as I try to trace where it is coming from, but it's no use, not with all the windows reflecting the sun and the thick green surrounding the area. They could be anywhere. Especially when light footsteps sound behind me distracting me from the task.

"Don't worry about Cora, she's broken. We all are." Ava's small voice says from over my shoulder. She approaches the fountain and sits timidly beside me, skimming the water with her own fingers.

"What do you mean?" I ask without turning my head to her.

"My family didn't want to tell anyone. About my connection." She takes a large breath before continuing. "I worked for King Aron. I was a servant. Tended the gardens with my brother." She tucks her hair behind her ear. There is a missing square of flesh, something that I missed before. Much like Lupita's circle that adorned her ear, those who work in Fauna must have a different shape to their mark. She swallows hard as if she doesn't actually want the words to come out.

I turn to her to let her know that it's safe to speak. "A man once visited the King. Told me I was a beauty. He loved me, Katsia. He even asked for my hand." She fidgets uncomfortably, like it hurts to be reminded of the past. "My Brother was not fond of the idea, and neither was my Mother. Gordon was his name. He told me he could improve my status so that we could marry. That's when he gifted me magic." Before I can speak, she places her hand atop mine. This time I force myself not to take it back as she continues. "My brother took me North, in search of someone to reverse the gift but we were arrested, and after a while I was sent here, my brother however-"her words get caught in her throat "they killed him." a tear drops from her cheek.

"I'm sorry" is all I can say, and I know I should feel worse for her, but my mind wanders to what could be in The North that could possibly reverse this so-called gift. Who was her brother searching for?

Much like me she was arrested and transferred here. I wonder if Cora and the others were also brought here in such a manner. This has me questioning everything, why they would do such a thing and why those with The Connection have been spared, but I do not share my thoughts with Ava while she is obviously in such a depressed state. "What gift do you possess?" I ask instead to change the subject and save myself from not knowing what to do when someone cries in my presence.

Ava takes her hand away from mine and bends down so that her chest touches her knees. She puts her hand to the ground flat. And from all around her small fingers that I now recognize as a gardener's hands with all the lines and calluses of her labor, sprouts new grass. It grows so tall that it almost brushes her nose before she straightens. The once perfectly manicured and oh-so-green lawn now has a patch of unruly brown with seeds at its ends growing from its center. I cannot hide my awe as I stroke the tops of the newly grown grass. "That's amazing, Ava." I half-whisper.

When I finally look away from her work, I see that she has no more tears in her eyes and an almost smile upon her face. "My magic seems to have disappeared." I say as I stand. Ava follows. We head in the direction of the arena. I do not say more about my magic, and Ava does not ask. She knows that I do not wish to tell more of my story like she has told me.

When we get back, everyone but Madam Christoph has left. She sits cross-legged in the middle of the arena with her hands on her knees. She appears to be deep in meditation, but as we approach, she opens one eye. "Get some rest tonight, you'll all pay for your sins tomorrow." She tells us that, and nothing more before she resumes her meditation. We look at each other and shrug at her strange choice of words. We turn and silently make our way back to the rooms. I leave Ava and now I must walk past all the other rooms, one, two, three, I count twenty-four in total.

When I open my door what lay before me is a complete disaster, things thrown to the ground and the drawers ripped open, emptied of their contents, reminding me of the way that the guards searched the rooms at the Inn. It doesn't take me long to know who could have done this.

Of course, I came here with nothing of my own, so it doesn't affect me much when I see Kirian's jacket and the ugly torn green dress in a pile on the floor. I do not repair the room. Instead, I grab the book of fables from the floor and plop on the bed to read it.

Chapter 16

Stone was once rampant with magic, those with the proclivity to it were often seen as Gods and Goddesses and one, beloved amongst all, Hecate. Her beauty was beyond our world and her magic was just as such. The ability to gift others magic.

Queen of Witches, she was known to her people and soon to be a Queen in more ways than one, as the King had been inclined to make her his wife. King Meron was known for his decisive nature and swift actions when it came to pursuing his desires. It was not long before they were wed before the courts.

After their union, Hecate became reclusive as she studied her magic. No heirs were born, and not even the King's mages could break the ward she placed around herself. After all, it was only a fragment of her own magic that they possessed.

It was no surprise when Hecate fled from the Kingdom and traveled north, making her way to Shadow Gate. To an abandoned city that once held treasures beyond the mind's imagination, in the days before magic was plentiful on Stone, the days of the Old Gods. Before the sun and moon, before the mountains pushed up from the ground. Long before the rivers flowed, and the ocean's water seeped up from the center of Stone.

When word spread that Hecate had become ruler of a realm made from her own hands. Merchants, Nobility, and peasants alike wished to see the city that Hecate created. Hecate's secret path through the mountain was only apparent to those who were worthy, those whom Hecate deemed acceptable. Those whose hearts were true. And those who were not worthy, those who traveled into the mountain with hopes of finding the city to conquer it, to strip it from Hecate's hands, quickly went insane. Returning home with voices in their heads.

King Meron had many questions, and rightfully so. For he did not believe Hecate to be so powerful as to create her own realm. When he found proof of her betrayal, proof that her lover aided her in the creation of Understone, he became enraged, for it was forbidden to use such magic. Magic that belonged to the Old Gods. It's dark and mysterious, turning good men into beasts and beautiful women into crones.

He planned to go to the city and claim his wife, to save her from the evil that was soon to take hold of her. The word was spread to those who were entering the city that the King wished to speak to his wife.

King Meron was welcomed into the city by Hecate and her lover. A man, a trickster, Hades. King Meron was no fool. He knew the man to be a God of darkness. He tried to warn the people of their new ruler, but the city was under a spell and, therefore, peaceful, so the people stayed. Ignoring King, Merons pleaded for them to flee. That's when the King knew he had to do whatever it took to save his Kingdom from such a monster.

An army was led to The North. No men were spared. Those who were capable fought a long and arduous battle against Hades. But Hades was prepared, destroying villages and ravaging cities with ugly beasts and men with wings. The King did not let up. He fought for many years. There was no end in sight. When he could no longer afford to continue, he called a meeting with Hecate, and her lover Hades once more.

There, they declared the war over. There would be no more destruction. Hecate was still displeased with the King, angry at his wrong doings to her and her people.

When the King left Understone, he made his way down the mountain, seeing all the destruction that the army had caused. When he got back to his castle in Fauna, a strange calm fell over his Kingdom, the kind that comes when something is missing, something important.

The doors to Understone had disappeared, along with a great deal of magic that once occupied Stone. They were now devoid of the abundance of magic that once existed in their realm. With the majority of magic gone, the people of Stone had to adapt to a world with limited magical capabilities. They relied on the few individuals who still possessed magical gifts from Hecate, who became highly revered and sought after. These individuals became the last practitioners of magic in Stone, responsible for preserving and passing on the dwindling magical traditions to future generations.

The memory of Hecate, King Meron, and the enchanting city of Understone live on as legends, reminding the people of their rich magical history and the consequences of tampering with forbidden powers.

Chapter 17

I hardly pay attention to Sofie's lectures during our next visit to the library. Fearing what comes at training. Our punishment for my so-called outburst. Whispers trail me in the hallways of students calling it by that name. *Let them say what they want. Nothing I do will change their opinions now.*

Although I will say, it was hardly a fight and more of an ambush, one that left marks from the claws that tore through my neck. I reach up and rub at them with the palm of my hand. Almost gone, thanks to the elixir that Agnus dropped at my door last night.

Ava walks me to the arena after mealtime. I have a feeling she will be meeting me here every day, looping her arm around mine as she does now. We all stand around a very calm Madam Christoph as we wait for her to deal us our punishment, her hands once again on her knees as she sits in meditation. This is more sinister in some way, void of emotion, never letting us know her next move. Her stillness gives me time to study her face. One that, when rested, could be almost pretty. Until she opens her wild eyes and her lips curl into that mischievous grin that shows all her perfect, almost sharp-looking teeth.

Once we have all assembled, she scans us from left to right. Just when I think she is going to say something, she silently gets up and walks away, leaving us. No one says a word, one person even sits down as if the day is done. The small woman saunters off, she never turns her head or looks down at her feet, she only walks out into the trees as if she has walked the path a million times before.

This is enough to pique my curiosity. Just like I used to follow my sisters to their secret lovers and Cedric to where he left injured animals, I grab Ava by the elbow and pull her in the direction of Madam Christoph. I watch the woman disappear behind the large trunk of a sarro tree, its long, spindly branches almost touching the ground in a cascade of light green. I push them to the side, to see where she emerges again.

Ava and I trail her from afar, footsteps sound behind us and I turn to see the rest of class has followed us as well. Cora pretends to be uninterested but follows anyway. Soon, past all the trees, damp leaves the size of my head and grass that comes up to our knees, the ground evens out.

The sound of water lapping onto shore catches my attention first, but I get distracted by the large wooden structures in front of us, overrun by vines and weeds like it has not been used in a very long time. Dirty water has washed up from the lake and pools under the splintered oak of an old obstacle course.

Beyond the course, the lake's edges are thick with cattails and rocky at the start. Not the soft sand that I am used to. At its center, a red flag, and a blue flag, atop a platform that floats in the middle, marking the end of the course. It is not a short distance. If you aren't a skilled swimmer, it will be hard to reach.

I'm already planning my route when Madam Christoph shouts from somewhere above us. I scold myself for taking my eyes off of her. "Split into two teams." She sits upon a perch that overlooks the course, the perfect place to see all the action below. Everyone begins to move around me, I notice that all Cora's friends stand closer to her and the only person who stands near me is Ava.

There's already a full team at Cora's side before I can even take a step. As we walk to the group that needs two more to fill their team, they cross their arms but do not protest. They do not look at me though, they are all looking at Ava. One even teases her, a large boy with pointed features and freckles that cover the entirety of his face. "Don't try to fly again, little bird." He says to her, holding out his arms to mimic wings.

I have no time to ask her about what that means before Madam Christoph's voice echoes above us once more. "Above the high beams and below the low ones, under the vines, across the planks, and up the wall, swim to the platform and raise the flag. Easy." She smirks as she sits back in her chair. Easy is right, too easy. There is a catch. I just don't know what it is yet.

We stand in two lines, the red team on the left, the blue team, my team on the right. Cora purposely positions herself fourth in line, the same as me. An arrogant dark-haired boy that always finds a way to strip out of his shirt stands first at the front of our line. He looks over to the girl with long black braids and deep brown skin as she stands first on the opposite team and gives her a wink. To which she just rolls her eyes and crouches down in preparation. You can tell that her physical strength is nothing to underestimate.

Ava is third. She stands in front of me, her shoulders shake and her hands fidget at her sides, but she doesn't turn around. I want to ask her what's wrong, what the meaning behind those words meant but she clearly doesn't want to talk about it, nor do we have time. My heart pounds and I swear I can hear Ava's steadily growing heartbeat coming from her own chest.

A loud whistle comes from above us, where Madam Christoph sits. The girl wastes no time as she hurls herself forward. She is strong. You can see the muscles in her arms and legs as she jumps from the last high beam and is on the ground, crawling with ease underneath the vines, her small figure giving her plenty of room between the sharp thorns and her back. I make sure to peek at Madam Christoph, who seems almost uninterested in the race before her. Even yawning as she crosses her legs lazily.

The boy also makes the beams look easy, but the hard part comes when his large body barely fits beneath the latter and the thorns scrape at his flesh. He doesn't so much as flinch or slow down. Instead, he continues, pulling himself up out of the mud at the end and immediately going into a dead sprint towards a large wall. Red lines of blood fall down his back, mixed with sweat and dirty water, I cringe thinking of the pain that will eventually come later after the adrenaline leaves his body.

The girl's long hair swings back and forth as she, too, runs for the wall and grabs hold of the rope that falls from the top. They both begin to pull themselves up.

The boy, *Ezra,* his friends shout, has a head start up the rope. He turns to look at his competition. He holds his hand out to the girl with a huge, toothy smile. He's quite handsome if it were not for the cocky aura that surrounds him. She reaches for him, but at the last second, he pulls his hand away, sending her crashing to the ground onto her back. She curses loudly after retrieving the air that was forced from her lungs.

When I look up at Madam Christoph her face is curled into a cat-like grin, as if she is enjoying the pain that the fall must have caused the girl, this makes my stomach flip. *Something is wrong.* I think to myself.

Cora laughs, her team follows suit. Christoph's smile drops and her eyes shift from Cora back to the course. "All members of your assigned teams must make it to the platform. We will do the exercise every day until you do." Madam Christoph informs us in a bored, no-nonsense sort of mocking voice. Like she is using all her strength not to roll her eyes as she changes the rules to fit her game, letting us know that she can and will.

"Grab the rope, girl," Cora shouts, her laughter now gone as she realized the consequence. As the girl pulls herself up, another whistle blows, sending the next person in each line plummeting toward the wooden forms. Their start is not so smooth. They have a different reaction to the beams. One girl stands atop one for a long time, her shoulder falling and rising in heavy breaths before letting out a horrifying scream. She lowers herself down onto the beam and holds on for dear life, her arms and legs wrapped around the wood as she hangs from it like a child.

The other girl who went for our team makes it to the horizontal ladder of thorns and dives underneath but stops as she hits the water. She lay there, paralyzed for a moment, her eyes wide and unmoving. Just when I think she isn't going to move, she flails her arms wildly as she swats at the air and water around her, her hands getting caught in the vines. She wiggles her way out through a narrow spot on the side of the ladder, taking the thorns that are now embedded into her skin with her. When she pulls out a silver knife that she seems to have stolen from the dining hall and begins to cut at the vines around her in a frenzy, I look up at Madam Christoph, who sits with her hand on her chin, concealing a laugh at the mayhem before her.

What in the House of Hades is going on? The next whistle blows. Ezra is now running back towards us, confusion and pain, and fear written all over his face. Only wet up to waist from trying to make it to the platform. His face white as a ghost. "There's something in the water," he says between breaths.

Ava looks at him in disbelief and her already shaking shoulders are moving up and down in sobs now. She is supposed to be running, the whistle was blown, she needs to move. Ava's opponent has already made it to the first obstacle. I push her to the side and send her to the back of the line heading into the chaos myself. Cora curses as she watches me leave without her.

The first few obstacles are easy but when my concentration goes from my own steps to the person in front of me to see how close I've gotten, things seem to shift. The beam I was about to jump down from has grown in size. The ground looks the same as when I peered off of the edge of a small waterfall that only leaks from the mountains in mid-summer near House Luz. My chest heaves as I look at the now impossible height to drop from. My mind can't make sense of it. I climbed up here just moments ago, a short distance to the top. A distance that I had climbed many times before in my lifetime.

Behind me, someone shouts a command for me to keep moving, but I can't, won't, not without a broken leg or worse. I twist my head to look at the line behind me. Cora shouts something indistinguishable, but I pay no mind to her. My head feels heavy. Horrified faces look back at me.

The girl that went first is now in the fetal position, her hair slung over her face, soaking wet from the lake, being comforted by her teammates. Minus Cora, who only looks at me as I stand atop the beam, my arms outstretched as I balance myself against the breeze. *Something's not right.* I tell myself words that I already knew.

My eyes go from the crowd of terrified students to Madam Christoph, who pins me with wild eyes, and a curled grin spreads across her face. She raises her hand without taking her eyes from me, sticks her thumb and pointer finger up to her lips, and lets out another whistle that I hardly hear over what's going on inside my head.

As her attention wavered, the illusions dissipate, revealing the truth surrounding me. My perspective changes once more, and the fog that once surrounded my thoughts clears. I look down, and there is the ground, only mere feet below me. I jump down with ease, but do not move forward as I collect my thoughts. *Mind tricks.* I conclude. Her new target, pinned beneath the gaze of our instructor, now lies helpless on the ground. *But I'm fine. And the boy gaining distance on me has no look of fear in his eyes. Mind tricks.* I almost say out loud.

If I'm going to beat Madam Christoph, I need to make sure that her concentration is elsewhere. To prove my theory, I listen to whistle after whistle. Watching her shift her attention to a different person.

Just like the distance to the ground changed when she took her eyes away from me and onto the girl holding her knees to her chest, fear blossomed on her face and Madam Christoph looks away again, satisfied. *It's not a race.*

So, there I stand, frozen, but of my own free will this time. I let the next pair go ahead of me and I take my time through the course, they all stop at different places as their own minds see a false reality. Slowly I make my way over each obstacle, not caring about my speed. I find myself at a giant wall at the end, listening to the lake's water rushing onto shore just beyond.

There I wait for my next opponent to come to the wall first so that I may climb with ease. No one comes, not a single person, whistle after whistle, no one moves. Madam Christoph looks bored, her legs apart and her back resting against the wood, she is no longer paying attention to us at all. All around me, sobs, shrieks of terror, frenzy, chaos. But her, she is calm, her job is done.

"Get off the course, Katsia," Ava shrieks from the long distance. *All members of your assigned team must make it to the platform.* Madam Christoph's voice sounds in my head. It's no use to continue if no one else will. We need a plan. They need to understand that there are no real dangers, only dangers of the mind. The students who made no effort to move from their spot in line most likely have almost no idea of what has happened.

The ones who have made it back to the start have hardly recovered from their panic to be able to tell them of the horrors that they endured.

Cora tends to those who were injured, nothing serious, but the scrapes and bruises that were once on their bodies are gone with the wave of her hand. *Interesting*. She tries to hide the exhaustion on her face after she is done with her mending, but her body sags and her brows pinch together as if she has given herself a headache. Her gift could be useful for what I'm sure we are about to endure for the next few days, maybe even weeks, if we all can't work together. Although I doubt I will be getting much attention from the healer.

Between sparring and basic defense, Madam Christoph ends the day at the course. Mealtime is when we talk of strategies, to get us to the platform, all of us. The days turn into weeks, and even though we are getting closer, it's still not a victory, and I'm not sure if it ever will be. I'm beginning to think that Madam Christoph knows very well that it's impossible. Cat and mouse, Ava and I call it, she's playing with her food. It's just a matter of time before she eats us, right?

Everyone uses some part of their gift to help us along the way. Ava has pulled the thorns away from our bodies and Cora helps with minor wounds. Others have found ways in which to incorporate their gifts, some of them help and others only slow us down.

Ezra has a high tolerance for pain. Now I understand why he didn't flinch as blood was falling down his back after an entanglement with the vines. A girl named Jane is almost undetectable if you are not looking right at her, making me wonder how many times she has been standing right next to me that I have not noticed. She rarely gets caught by Madam Christoph's mind tricks, lucky her.

Others have gifts that are best suited for the classroom. The boy with glasses, Will, his memory is so good that he can recite a whole history book without looking at the pages. He hardly opens his books during class, most likely because he already knows the material. Besides, he is too busy counting the strands of hair that lay upon Ava's head. Or at least it seems like it with the amount of time he spends staring at her. Ava is, as usual, unaware.

One girl who sits alone. Her name starts with an M, but I cannot remember what it is. She sits with her head down and her eyes closed. Her stringy brown hair could use a washing, and her daily punishment for wrinkled clothes seems not to have taken.

Ava swears she can hear our thoughts. Something about her never having said her job for King Aron was in the gardens, but that is pure paranoia. Ava never stops talking. No matter who is around, I wouldn't be surprised if the girl- Mira? Mia? just overheard her blabber.

The elements are what make magic possible in the first place. Sofies teachings are starting to make sense as one boy swirls wind with the movement of his arms. Just as Ava has been blessed with the gift of Stone. *These gifts are said to come directly from the Gods. While other gifts are only a mutation of the four elements.*

Late at night, I stay awake to think of all these gifts surrounding me, ones that do not claw and scratch at you. Ones that do not whisk you away without permission. *What kind of fucked up mutation are the Shadows?* I think as I stare at the ceiling of my room. It does not matter, they are gone. Not a whisper or a wink from them. Not since I arrived.

I kick the covers from my legs and swing them over the bed. The hallways are usually calm at night, maybe a person or two tiptoeing to another room in a not-so-secret romance, or at least not a secret to me. It's where I distract myself from the thoughts that plague my mind at night.

Wandering is what I have always done while others are in bed. At House Luz, it was easy to avoid the guests that stayed for the parties that went on late into the night. They were always too drunk or pre-occupied to be bothered by me. Asleep in their beds or lazily drinking the remainder of their wine while having boring, run-on conversations with the man or lady of their choice. In hopes that they would not have to sleep alone that night. Tonight is no different. I pair my boots with my sleeping gown and make my way down the hall.

I run my fingers along the cold, perfectly dusted statues of Goddesses that sit on either side of the library's entrance. They are older than the ones that filled the Luz castle. They hold more meaning, too. It's more about the art, the history of it all.

Father's were always meant to send a message that he could *afford* more *have* more than others. I wonder what happened to those statues after the passing of Hansel Luz. *It feels like so long ago.* I shake my head to keep the memory of my Father from coming to the surface.

I move across the large room. The lights are dimmed at night but perfect for reading. I've had Ava explain to me how the school works many times. The magic that flows through Spartus. The same as the castle that she once worked at. Apparently, the whole Kingdom ran on such magic. When there was more to spare, I suppose.

I know I should catch up on reading but sometimes I disregard Sofie's list and choose a book from the same shelf of fiction for myself. Then I find a place to sit, which there is no shortage of. Other times just hearing the echo of my boots against tile, knowing that no one else is near is enough.

I move across the library, doing just that, listening to the sounds of my steps, staring up at its stained-glass windows that line the ceiling. They are not as intriguing in the daytime. Besides, I don't mind listening to Sofie's lectures. She's an infinite library of knowledge all on her own, no books needed. Perhaps that's what her gift is, the eye that occupies the space on the back of her head, knowledge.

My eyes do not peel away from the glass above me as I walk. I don't need to watch where I am going. I've memorized every pedestal that holds a worn book at its center, every marble statue, each priceless piece of silver armor, and every table and chair.

The windows above tell a story, I realized many nights ago. I've never asked of the true story it depicts because whatever it is, it's not as good as the one I've made up in my head. A man on the first frame of glass and a woman on the opposite end.

They look as if they are pushing magic from their palms towards the center. The woman's hair is in locks of fire red. While the man holds a two-pronged pitchfork. His face glowing from the crown that circles his head.

Each step casts a different color onto my face as I decipher the different magic of each piece between the lovers. Dark and light. Life and death.

Blue, then green, yellow- "What are we looking at?" Red. The color that falls over the dark-haired man's features. The Raven. My heart jumps into my throat.

I've been caught. What's worse is that I didn't even notice that he was standing there. He had to have come from behind, through the same doors as I did, but there were no footsteps. Surely, I had not let myself get distracted enough to let him pass by me. I guess I should not pride myself so much on paying attention to details as I once did at House Luz.

His black hair is pushed back neatly. His brows cast a shadow over his cheeks, making his eyes seem to disappear somewhere into two masses of black. He wears what I saw him in the first time, across from me in the carriage, all black and no pins or anything to tell me of who he is. He places his hands behind his back as he stands before me.

All I can do is stare, *think* I tell myself. "I-I could not sleep" I tell him clumsily. I could have lied but I'd promised myself after the jail that I would be better. That I would tell the truth to myself and others. To avoid the mess that comes from lies.

"Agnus could get you a tea for that." He retorts, his voice low.

I hope he cannot hear the hammering of my heart against its cage. "I prefer reading," I say honestly. "To put me to sleep." I can't see his eyes, but I search them still. My head slightly tilted upwards at him, not as far up as I have to move my head to see into Kirian's eyes.

"Your studies cannot be that boring as to put you to sleep." he leans forward slightly, the red light illuminates half of his face. He looks down at the book in my hand, not a part of my studies at all. A smile, or at least what I think is a smile, tugs at the corner of his mouth.

"It's not the books that put me to sleep." I almost take a step away but refrain. This man scares me, but I do not want him to know that. "It's the... emptiness." I decide on the word last minute.

His incredibly dark features, worsened by the red that cascades onto him, brightens when he takes a step forward and into the yellow light that shines down through the glass. The same yellow that is on me. *Too close.* Again, I do not move, do not show my rising fear.

"Are you not afraid?" He tilts his head to one side. I swallow hard. *What is he suggesting?*

Of course, I am afraid. I can't remember a day that I was *not* afraid. Of Father, of Cedric and Medla, of the Shadows. I will not show him how afraid I truly am. I will never show anyone that again, I promise to myself. "Should I be?" I try to say with as much confidence as possible. The lights that were already far off seem to dim further as he watches me.

He snickers under his breath and tilts his head back up to look beyond me, over my head, towards the dormitories. "Let's see. A girl with no power in a school filled with magic users that could..." He pauses for a moment, his mouth twitches upward. The smile doesn't quite fit his features. He crafts his next words carefully, words that are meant to get under my skin, and they do. "Steal the air from your lungs, tear you limb from limb, bury you ten feet under without so much as breaking a sweat." He lists easily. My brows raise, surprised at the unmistakable pleasure he gets from making me squirm. But Madam Christoph has done as much as rip the fear right out of me or at least taught me how to ignore it for a short period of time.

I make sure to even my breathing before I give my answer. "If it is death that I should be afraid of, then no. I am not afraid." His smile drops. He searches my face for a moment too long. "And if this is meant to scare me." I have to stop mid-sentence to swallow again, "If *you* are meant to scare me, then I am not afraid of that either."

He finally takes his eyes off me, and the cloud that had been covering the light of the moon must have moved because the room brightens again. "Stay as long as you want." He barely misses me with his shoulder as he walks past. The herbal smell of lavender overwhelms my senses as it wafts into my face from the quick movement.

I release a much-needed breath. When his footsteps fade from earshot, I am left with the actual feeling of emptiness, the one that I so gladly welcomed before in this library, now felt heavier with his words on my mind. *No power.* Not that having my gift would help. The Shadows were suffocating. They only pulled me along for the ride.

Maybe, here, I could have found their true purpose. I have thought all my life that I did not want them, I tried to hide from them, and I guess they have finally listened. Perhaps I got exactly what I asked for. One of the reasons for coming here, to rid of my gift. This is what I have dreamed of, wished for.

Chapter 18

Ava walks into my room without so much as a knock and sits on the bed beside me. This is not unusual. She spends more time here than in her own room. She lets out a dramatic sigh when she sees the stack of books on my bedside table. It gets higher and higher every day.

My reading is getting faster, but not compared to the others who drop off the books and look longingly at the ones that they haven't gotten to read yet. Ava helps me with the pronunciation and meaning of some words. She doesn't seem to mind, and I have grown used to her presence.

To no surprise there is now a small plant on my bedside table, overgrown and spilling out the sides of its pot. Ava tends to it, holding her hand above it as she shares her magic with the leaves and the dirt. *"Bury, you ten feet under"* he was talking about Ava. I know she would never do such a thing, not to anyone.

"Do you know who runs this place?" I say over my shoulder at Ava nonchalantly. Being careful of the questions I ask in order to stay out of trouble. I've learned my lesson in meddling. On the wrong side of the belt when Cedric caught wind of the questions I was asking the servants.

"Lord Andres." She says with confidence. This does not answer the question that I really have. *Who is the dark-haired man?*

Instead, I ask, "What do they want with magic users?" I decide to keep the secret of my encounter with the man to myself. I'm already a target here. No magic and a gardener as my only friend.

Ava adjusts the pillow on the bed as she thinks. "Gordon once told me that there was a decline in mages after the war." She yawns big before continuing. "King Meron declared those with The Connection an abomination. That's why there were trials. Maybe now that King Aron has ended the punishment, they take us here instead to be used where needed. We are an endangered species." She shrugs her shoulders. "Thanks to his Grandfather." Ava huffs like she thinks it's funny that the now King is paying for his Grandfather's decisions.

"Have you met the King?" I ask Ava.

"Gordon never allowed it. He said that King Aron was known for his reputation around women." She states as if I should know what that means.

I change the subject when I see the sadness that comes with the mentioning of her lover. "After you take The Vow, what job do you think you will be assigned?" I ask Ava. Her eyes close slowly before opening again. We do not often talk of what happens after The Vow. There are so many rumors circulating, especially now that it is only weeks away. That it's painful and intense. That you do not come out of The Vow the same as you went in. Although there is no proof that is the case.

Ava shifts so that the blankets cocoon her. "Hopefully something in a garden" She coos, then smiles. Her eyes close all the way this time.

At this time any other night I would be out the door but tonight I stay. Because our boring conversation was a welcome change of pace. And Ava actually went to sleep with a smile on her face, which I haven't seen her do in a long time. Not to mention I was already caught once this week and have been waiting for punishment ever since.

She usually talks of her brother, holding back tears every time she brings up his name. Her sadness reminds me of her quivering shoulders as we stood before the obstacle course. *"Don't try to fly again little bird"* I'm reminded of those harsh words. She hasn't brought it up and I haven't asked about it.

It's not hard to put the pieces together myself, especially after seeing the state she was in when I first arrived. At the time, I didn't notice her skeletal body from lack of sustenance, her tired eyes, and her quiet demeanor.

I don't know what the days prior to my arrival held for her, but I can imagine that they were filled with grief for her brother. Grief for the loss of her lover, not dead but gone all the same.

I rise from the bed and saunter to the desk to write things down that I do not wish to forget from today's lectures. Avas body sinks into the soft bed as she relaxes completely. She wore herself out today on the course. Every day she proves herself to the others that once did not believe in her, but it drains her. I can see it.

Soon her breathing becomes steady and when I look back, she has pulled the comforter over her face, her head shoved into the pillow. Unconscious.

I turn my attention back to the desk and pick up a book that I promised I would finish by the end of the week. I listen to the shuffling of bodies, the closing of doors of students that have found a bed for the night. The hours slip by, I catch myself bobbing my head as I too almost drift into sleep.

My dreams often bleed into reality, so I almost do not notice as a light comes from beneath the door, its flicker distant but growing. Shaking off my sleep, I make no noise as I walk my way to the door and crack it open enough to see out. Agnus walks down the hall coming towards me, her head down with determination. I slip back into the room, closing the door quietly without letting its hinges click into the frame.

When she passes and her footsteps fade, I open it again glancing back at Ava's sleeping body before deciding to follow Agnus, watching as she takes a turn that leads down the stairs. I make sure my footsteps are near silent as I walk in her direction. Surely her services are not needed at this time of night.

When she stops at a door and looks behind her, I push myself against the wall into the night. For a second, I expect the Shadows to embrace me, hiding me further, they do not. *I'm still not used to their absence.* She shakes her head slightly and continues, unlocking the door then pushing it open before closing it again.

As I pressed my ear against the door, the hushed voices of Agnus and a man float through the air. Their words muffled. I try to decipher their meaning as best as I can. My heart races and unease settles over me.

"I didn't expect you to come." The man murmurs in frustration.

"Like I had a choice" Agnus tells him, her words soft and low. "Look, I have done what you have asked. More than once I might add." She lets out a breath, creating a pause where I can hear my heart pounding. "My debt is paid, I'm no longer a part of this." She tells him but it does not come out as confident as I think she would have liked.

The sound of an object being set on wood, then, "We are *all* a part of this, whether you like it or not." The man's tone is harsh. "Your sacrifices will be well worth it."

"We are running out of time." Another vaguely familiar voice says aloud, a student maybe. This man's voice is lower and younger than the one before. "We have our commands. If what you said is true, then we need to act now."

"Tomorrow." the other man says. "Convince him—" his words are cut off by the sound of a chair sliding across the floor.

This has my feet moving from beneath me before my mind can catch up. I slink into a door frame nearby, hoping that it's dark enough that no one will see me. "I do not wish to know of your plans," Agnus says, clearly excusing herself from the men.

Before she can open the door I move for the exit, hearing the door open and shut from the safety of the hallway. I've nearly memorized her shoes on tile and thankfully I am silently walking much faster than her, even though my legs will me to run as fast as I can. By the time I reach the dormitories and am safe on the other side of my door, Ava sits awake on the bed, waiting for me. I push down the bile that is threatening to spill.

"Gods Katsia. You scared me." she rubs the sleep from her eyes. "Where were you?" she asks.

"I just went for a walk." I lie, then quickly curse myself for breaking the rule I made two and a half months ago. But it's for her own good she can't be wrapped up in this. I head to the bed and pull at the blankets that she disheveled. Busying my hands with the task so that she does not see my face.

She snakes her way out of the covers, stands and places her hands on her hips. I don't dare look up at her. Ava lets out a sigh at my silence. "You shouldn't do that." She scolds. She takes a breath like she wants to say more but I cut her off.

"Listen, if you want to tell on me, just do it." I still look down at my hands, which have run out of things to do.

She takes a tentative step in my direction. I ready myself to feel her put a hand on my shoulder. Ava thinks better of her decision and quickly places her hand back at her side. "Tell on you? Why would I do that?" she asks.

I turn to her, trying to figure out if she is genuine or not.

But I have been on the receiving end of deception one too many times, and it's harder to tell than you think. Adriel's kindness often came at a price. *"You can tell me,"* She would say. Telling her meant telling Cedric and Medla as well. Which came with consequences. I don't say anything. In fact, I push my lips together so that I don't accidentally tell her anything at all. No more lies.

"I'm just telling you to be careful. You're not exactly well-liked." She says, and Gods do I know. I hear the whispers, the taunting from the sidelines of the course. Every now and then, I show up to a destroyed room. Not to mention all the wounds that I have patched alone, no thanks to Cora. She huffs, clearly annoyed at my lack of response. "You *have* to take The Vow with me, Katsia. You- "

"I'm not going to make it to The Vow." I snap at her, throwing my hands up at my sides. Her eyes go wide, and guilt floods me for scaring her, but it's true. I have thought about it plenty of times, just never said it out loud. "I have no magic, Ava." I lower my voice now to near whisper. "I wished it away." I turn away from her once more. She's silent for a while, and I can tell that she is waiting for me to say more. "So, it doesn't matter if I'm out at night or if I have a target on my back. I'm not even sure I am allowed to leave this school alive."

Chapter 19

"No classes today." Agnus stops me at the door. She looks me over and adjusts a loose hair on the top of my head that has fallen out of its braid, scoffing her frustration.

My heart races as I search her eyes for answers. Her presence here the day after I overheard her conversation seems too strange to be a coincidence. She gives nothing away, neither do I.

"Why not?" I question, hoping that my face does not reveal my thoughts. I'm dressed in my uniform and have a book in hand. A book that I now throw onto the bed, knowing that I will not need it. If I had known I was leaving I would not have thrown my hair up so messily or picked up a dirtied skirt from the ground, I would have put on my trousers and sleeved shirt in case I need to run.

She shakes her head but doesn't answer the question, not really, anyway. "Not for you." She says instead. I peer out into the hallway and see the others making their way to breakfast. Ava walks towards us, but I give her a look and tell her not to wait up. Her face contorts with worry. I know what she must think, and I am thinking the same thing. When she hesitates, I can't help but wonder *if this is the last time I will see her.*

If it's not about my magic or lack thereof, then the dark-haired man had to have told Lord Andres I was in the library at night. Or worse, I was seen in the servants' quarters listening to a conversation I had no business hearing. *Either way, I am fucked*. Agnus also gives Ava a sideways glance before pulling me away.

The other servants follow Agnus as we turn the corner. She shakes her head that has them stopping dead in their tracks when we get to a separate wing that I have never been to before. Of course, I tried, but the door was locked.

Agnus moves forward once more, her heels clacking on the pristine tiles. I glance behind me. The group of servants are still in the door frame. They have their mouths pressed up against each other's ears, their hands concealing secrets. *So many secrets, don't believe anyone,* I remind myself as I turn back to stare at the back of Agnus's head.

The servants are the only shadows that seem to have stuck around, always lurking in the corners. They probably know every detail of conversation had in this place. People tend to overlook servants when sharing their secrets. This was true at House Luz as well. Lupita often knew exactly what was going on while I was left in the dark. So, I took to the servants' quarters, my ears open and ready for information. Just as I had done last night.

Distant voices come from behind the two large white doors that are now in front of us. The room I wait in is just a wide hallway with paintings and statues. Much nicer than the ones that fill the hallway of student's doors. Agnus points to a spot on the floor, telling me to stand there and wait. She turns swiftly on her heels and makes her way out. I trail her with my eyes as she goes. Then, they wander to the paintings that line the walls.

Flowers paired with women. Swords with men. The others do not stray from this variation. *Boring*.

Most of the words spoken from beyond the door are muffled like they are talking with their backs turned. Some are clearer as they most likely face the other direction, their words coming towards me.

They exchange harsh words about The Vow. "Would be against our customs!" Someone half-shouts from the other side. The voice sounds familiar, but I cannot place it.

My eavesdropping is almost identical to the kind I did last night. This time I am supposed to be here. They cannot blame me for listening in.

Then, "We shall find out soon enough," Lord Andres's soft, elderly voice. None of the voices beyond this door match the ones from last night, not that I can tell anyway.

Silence falls over the room, making me uneasy. I hook my hands behind my back, swinging back and forth as I wait. My skirt tickles the back of my legs with every move.

Far off, from where Agnus left, the sound of heavy footsteps make their way towards me, I straighten my top and adjust my hair nervously.

The smell of mint hits my nose first, an intoxicating scent that I spent countless nights trying to forget, Kirian. And sure enough, he opens the door on the other side of the hall and enters in one swift step. His nonchalant demeanor changes as he spots me across the room, his face turning from arrogance to worry. He stalks towards me. I can't help it. I take two excited steps in his direction as well. Ignoring Agnus's orders to stay put. "What are you doing here?" I ask, looking up at him as he reaches me. I have forgotten just how tall he is.

I've suddenly forgotten what to do with my hands as well. I settle for balling them into fists at my sides. "I've been called by the court." He says plainly, but his eyes frantically search mine before tracing my body from top to bottom, causing heat to rise to my face. "You look...different, well fed." And there is that smirk, his signature smile paired with playful words. Although I can't say that telling me I have gained weight is quite the compliment that he thinks it is. I look down at myself for a half second, and sure enough, the shirt no longer droops in the shoulders, and the collar seems to fit around my neck. Just as I had noticed Ava's appearance change, I suppose I have as well.

"You look the same." I tell him, and it's true. His uniform is neat and his posture tall and unmoving, like a statue.

He just shakes his head and points to the door before us. "This meeting is about you, you know. I'm here to testify about your gift. A little shy, are we?" He looks to me for answers. You can see the disappointment in his eyes, as if I have let him down in some way.

Which is really a kick in the stomach after the months of torture I've had. I have undoubtedly changed, more than physically. I want to tell him everything. The air around him is much lighter than the air of this old school.

I had thought that I would never see Kirian again, I suppose if my magic did not disappear that would have been true. Maybe I should not put so much thought into our last night together, the kindness that he showed me. My chest is tight with unease as I think of what it meant. The way he looks down at me, with that look that I cannot place. A friend, I realize, just as Ava.

"I-"I begin to say, but then the doors open, and Kirian stands face to face with the raven. The same man who sat across from me upon my delivery and the same man who darkened that library with words of doubt.

The two men who stand before me could not be more different. Kirian is taller, but not by much, and broader in the shoulders from years of hard labor. His light eyes and hair are a stark contrast to the brooding features of the man before him, black hair, brown eyes, and a permanent scowl. The sun and the moon.

I make sure to look down to avoid remembering our encounter in the library. "Hello Augustine." Kirian says as he straightens his spine. *Augustine Nero?* That's the name of the man that Kirian told me about. The man who delivered me is the King's right hand. Why would he be doing something so insignificant?

Suddenly I have so many questions but no time to ask them as Kirian strides past Augustine and into the room. The softness that I saw for just a moment is long gone. I look between the two. Kirian's muscular back as he confidently walks into the room and Augustine's flickering eyes as he looks me over. That same look of disgust as when we first arrived. Augustine gestures for me to enter. I walk too close to him, so close that I can feel heat radiating off of his body.

He closes the door gently behind me. Augustine then takes his place at a long white stone table. Behind the table are large windows overlooking a garden. The head of the table belongs to Lord Andres, whose voice I had recognized earlier and the other one must have belonged to Augustine. There are others lining the wall in observation. Sofie is not here. It's her time to be in the library with everyone else. The others I do not recognize, aside from Madam Christoph. I cringe at the sight of her, evil woman, but she pays no mind to me at all. Kirian has already taken an empty seat and leans back in it nonchalantly, as if he has done this a million times, I expect nothing less from him.

Augustine is next, he pulls out a chair closest to Lord Andres, eyeing Kirian the whole time before he takes his seat. And finally, it's my turn to choose a spot to sit. Surprisingly, I do not hesitate long. The chair next to Kirian squeals as its legs drag on the floor. I think I hear Kirian let out a breath of air, but I pay no attention as I take my seat. As soon as I do, the room grows unbearably quiet.

Hopefully, the thump of my heart is only in my own ears and not loud enough for Kirian to hear how nervous I am.

Lord Andres finally speaks, and I can't help but to stagger at the break in silence. "Katsia, how are you enjoying your time here?" he asks. *Enjoying* is not the word I would use to describe my last few months here. And I know better than to try and lie to the man before me, it would be no use.

Truth, something I used to avoid. Now I speak it without a second thought. Ava being the only one to listen. She does not ask many questions and I do not offer many explanations. My only lie was one that was trying to protect her. Maybe even from whatever *this* is.

I make sure to look him in the eye, silver and milky, just as they were when they first looked upon me. "It's been rather difficult," I answer clearly and loud enough so that all can hear. Not allowing the fear I feel in my chest to transfer into my words. Kirian's presence aiding in my confidence somehow.

"We do strive for the best." Andres says as he folds his hands on the table before him. His posture relaxed and much unlike the time we were in the carriage he barely even glances in my direction, as if he knows what decision I have made.

"Tell us, where do you think you stand amongst the others?" What strange questions. Questions that are leading to something bigger, I can feel it.

"The bottom, I am afraid," I tell no one in particular. Augustine shifts in his chair and the others nod in agreement. All except for Madam Christoph who now wears a small but visible smile as she scratches her chin. I ignore her and find Kirian's eyes instead.

I tell myself that it's not embarrassing to be failing at something in which I took no interest in the first place.

My cheeks still flush as I try to decipher what he is thinking from his expression. Nothing, he sits motionless, his attention elsewhere, I follow his eyes to see that he is studying Augustine Nero intensely. Augustine himself seems not to notice at all. Except for a small shift of his eyes in our direction, then back to the task at hand.

Lord Andres nods his head slowly. "I see. Do you know why we have all gathered here?" He spreads his hands and gestures to the people seated in the room.

"It is my understanding that there are questions regarding my gift." I guess from the small indication from Kirian's and my conversation outside the doors.

"Kirian, tell us what made you think it was so urgent to get Miss Luz enrolled here." Now it's Kirian's turn to be under judgmental eyes. He is unaffected. I feel a bit defeated, like they moved on from me too quickly.

He no longer has his attention on Augustine and instead addresses the room. "Unfortunately, I was not there when it occurred." He tells them nonchalantly. Augustine suppresses what I think is a laugh.

Kirian pays no attention as he continues. "What I can tell you is that she escaped the western jail in Thorn Row, but not a single man saw her leave, nor was a key missing." He looks at me before continuing.

I nod in approval of what he wants to say next. "Then after the escape, she was stashed in an Inn, close to the wall, when the guards were on a search for her, they found no trace, yet she never left the Inn itself. Tell them what you told me that morning after the search." His confidence never wavers as he turns to me. I try not to think of what else transpired that morning, forcing the image of us entangled together on that mattress to the back of my mind.

"I was there, and not there. Stuck in between." I have no better explanation than that, nor do I try to think about the traumatizing event itself if I can help it. Every face scrunches together in confusion all at once, all but one, Augustine Nero, in fact. *Escaped many prisons, much worse than the one you were in.* Kirian's words from the Inn when he told me of someone who shared my gift.

Everyone's attention falls on me, and their judgment seems to settle into me like a knife, making it hard to breathe. Augustine crosses his arms as if bored by the whole thing. "I was pulled into an abyss of sorts." I try again, looking over to Kirian, who nods his head at me, making my unease settle for only a moment. But the words came out weak and unsure.

"How are we supposed to believe a word she says?" My attention is pulled from Kirian as Augustine's deep voice echoes through the large room.

"Just say what you mean, Augustine." Kirian blusters.

"I mean." Augustine stands quickly and walks over closer to us but still on the opposite side of the table. His features darken even more with the light from the window at his back. He sets his hands on the stone and narrows his eyes at Kirian. "You made a mistake. She has no magic, and you have convinced her that she does to spare her life." The room is so silent that I can hear my own heart beating in its cage. I want to speak, to tell them that I have had the Shadows a long time, since before I knew of Kirian Bears' existence. Before I can speak, Augustine beats me to it. "That *is* within your power, is it not?"

I swallow my near spoken words and look to Kirian for an explanation, but he doesn't offer one. "What is he talking about?" I ask. He doesn't look at me. He doesn't move, it's infuriating. I look about the room. The others whisper amongst themselves, for they do not have the answers either. All but Madam Christoph, who stares out the window past the garden and to the lake that I have come to know well over the last few months, its platform still untouched. For a short moment, I wonder what could possibly be more interesting than what is currently happening in this room.

My thoughts are cut off as the man before me speaks again. "Tell her," Augustine demands. "Or shall I?" This time his words make

Kirian move but only slightly and away from me. Augustine slowly turns his fiery gaze away from Kirian and stares at me for what feels like an eternity, all I can do is wait. There they are again, those red eyes. "Your friend has a knack for getting women... and some men, to do his bidding."

"Do not take out your frustrations with me on her," Kirian says through gritted teeth.

"I can't help but notice the similarities." Augustine sneers. He cocks his head to the side. Kirian's face turns a shade of red, but he does not offer a response.

Again, and for what I'm sure is not the last time, their not-so-subtle accusing faces and words of past events are not something that I can make sense of. Always, these people speak of things that only confuse me further.

"You may choose not to believe me, but I have magic. I may not have always known what it was, and I have never known how to use it, but it was there until I got here anyway." I try to get back to the reason we have gathered and away from the tension that has built between Kirian and Augustine.

"For God's sake," Augustine turns his head to Lord Andres and then back to me. "Well, if you say so." His sarcasm so pointed, no doubt to make me squirm. His eyes catch fire once more, like they did when I first saw him upon his horse. No one seems to notice, but I can't help myself. It's as if the House of Hades lives behind those eyes. I become entranced by this new discovery. He catches my eyes for only a second. His eyebrows pinch together, but only for half a second, long enough for only me to see. Then the flame extinguishes, and he pivots slightly so that I can no longer see his face.

"Let's not get ahead of ourselves." Lord Andres finally speaks up. "Kirian has not led us astray before. He would not send us a girl with no magic. Especially if he wished for her life to remain intact, isn't that right, dear boy?" A chill runs down my spine. There it is. What I already knew. What happens if my gift never returns. *It was always meant to be this way. You were not meant to live a long life. Medla and Cedric's wishes for my death have come to fruition.*

Kirian, who has not shown an emotion in so long that I am beginning to think that he may very well be a statue, doesn't even acknowledge me when I look at him.

Everyone waits for Kirian to speak but he does not, and if I say anything now, they will only think it is Kirian's words flowing from my mouth, as Augustine suggests, so instead I stand. My legs wobble beneath me before I force them to straighten. My chest pounds and the room becomes a blur.

Beyond furious, beyond confused. But one thing is for sure. I have fallen victim to another one of Kirian's tricks. One that he has so obviously perfected if what Augustine says is true.

A distant voice, one that I have heard before, like a dream, threatens to make those around me disappear, make *me* disappear if only it could reach me. The Shadows or my own thoughts, I cannot tell. Fear and anger swirl in my stomach, but I do not, will not, let it take me to that dark place that has me hunched over and expelling my guts like it used to.

No one says a word, or at least their voices do not carry over the ringing in my ears as I slide the chair out from under the table with a screech. Then, I leave without so much as a glance at the faces behind me.

Chapter 20

I stomp through the great hall, its florals long since changed into spring flowers. Not the roses that were here when I arrived.

The magic is still in the air, suffocating me. Soon, I land on the same red brick that I entered this damned place on. If I wasn't so angry, I would have thought out my destination much more thoroughly. As I make my way to the fountain, I look behind me to see Kirian gaining distance. I circle the water that flows from a woman's hands and into a bowl below. My body feels like it's on fire, the anger rising up onto my face, surely making my face a deep shade of red.

Kirian stays opposite of me, the cascading water sometimes blocking out his features as we circle around in a sort of dance. He stops, I stop. "You have to let me explain," he says. Now, he takes a step to the right, I take a step, not letting him get even an inch closer to me.

"It's been explained," I tell him, but that is not true. I was only given a hint of what the truth is. I can't think. My head is spinning as I think of all the things that he said, all the things I felt, none of them were true. My feelings that day in the Inn, my senses so heightened to the physical world around me, I couldn't fight his magic even if I tried. I felt the aura around him many times. Dangerously welcoming. *His bidding* Augustine's words are in my head. Was I subject to that?

"You don't get it." He pleads, and while I was thinking of Augustine's damning words, he has taken a step to the left, his hands up as he tries to convince me to listen to him. I correct myself by taking a step as well. I wish the fountain were bigger. The more distance between us the better. He lets out an annoyed sigh "It's not something I can turn off." He takes his hat off to run his hands through his hair. Much longer strands of blonde fall into his face than the last time that I saw him. Then he places it back on his head in a huff and takes a step to the right in another attempt. I take a step to the right.

"I get it. You were just doing your job." I point towards the many windows, one of which is my own room, although I do not look out of it often. I wonder what we look like from that view, perhaps two children playing tag. "And you did it well, I'm here, aren't I?" I say sarcastically. My throat feels tight, and I can't think. I just keep replaying our time together. From the beginning, when he saw me in Thorn Row, then again at House Luz, the Inn. Which words were laced in silver, and which were not? "All of it?" I ask. He just looks at me. "Was all of it a lie?" I rephrase the question.

"No," he chews on his words. "Not all," he says. Unspoken, but there, *some* of it was a lie. He just doesn't know how much. Or at least he won't tell me.

Fine, I'll give him this one time to explain, just once. "What was he talking about in there?" I ask him, my voice barely carrying over the sound of falling water.

He sets his lips in a flat line. He doesn't want to tell me. I can see the struggle behind his eyes. "I- I was a dumb kid." He stutters, takes a deep breath, and continues. "I had just taken The Vow. Then, joined The Guard. I began to truly understand my gift." Again, his lips press together, and I can see the pain behind his words. *Damn, why do I feel bad for him?* I wait for him to continue and to my surprise he does.

"Once The Spent figured out how easy it was for me to... persuade people." The word *persuade* comes out of his mouth with double meaning, of which I know exactly the kind of *persuading* he means. "They moved me to Thorn Row. Gave me a job." He pauses and takes a deep breath. "To convince others to join."

I feel it in the clenching of my fists, the heat that rises to my cheeks, and the tightening of my throat. It's steady pressure, an unbearable weight on my chest, threatening to suffocate me. It comes to the surface in pure hot anger as I recall our conversation, a*nything to get a taste,* he said to me that day. I now know those words were placed strategically to make me believe that one day, I would be wanted, loved. *As long as I joined The Spent, did as he told me, of course.*

I think of that morning at The Charlie after I climbed my way out of the abyss. When this world hurt to exist in, but it hurt in all the best ways when my body was against his. When the world seemed black and white, drained of all its color. He was the only bit of color I saw. His *gift* was the only color I saw. Not him, I realize.

Although my anger is directed at Kirian at this moment, I know that I have felt it many times before that. With Cedric and Medla and even Adriel's fake niceness to make herself feel better. All of it.

Just as I crack the floodgates, ready to let the rage fall out of its perfectly crafted dam within my mind, Kirian looks at me. His head cocks to the side like I am a curiosity that he is making sense of. Then a flicker of something else before he lights up with a half grin that has the gates closing back up slightly. Does he get off on seeing me this way? Angry and confused and on the verge of breakdown? The same breaking of me that he did in Thorn Row at the jail.

Kirian keeps that same grin that forces a dimple to his cheek as he speaks. "Yes, they didn't choose me purely for my good looks" *He's cracking jokes? Now?* For a split second, I think that the Shadows shift, that they have finally returned to keep their promise of making my foes disappear, but when I look past Kirian, in the shade of a well-manicured sarro tree, I see nothing. *I don't even know why I bother looking for them anymore.*

Hot liquid drips past my knuckles, blood, from my nails digging into the flesh of my palms, but I don't care. I could do much worse. "You are joking right now?" I shout. My shins hit the stone edge of the fountain, more blood spills. It's no matter. "I'm soon to be dead. Did you not hear Lord Andres?" I throw my bloodied hands into the air. Kirian doesn't even look me in the eye. He seems to be looking all around but never directly at me.

Satisfaction takes over his features. He wants me mad. He is encouraging it. This time I am the one moving a step closer to him, he makes sure to take a step as well, away from me, and that infuriates me further.

Before I can take another step, I catch sight of myself in the reflection of the water. When I see who looks back at me, it's not the same girl who looked back at me from this very fountain when I first got here. Her cheeks have filled, and the hollows beneath her eyes have gone. She looks not like her Mother or like a scared child but like... me.

The sight of her has me dropping my anger like hot coal. It is replaced with something that I can't place my finger on. My head is too filled with cluttered thoughts of my impending doom. *Dead, dead, dead. Just the way it was supposed to be.* I remind myself.

What may have been my magic, the Shadows, the voice that called so distantly, is now gone along with the rage that threatened to release itself upon Kirian. There are no words or shifting of the darkness. They truly have left, and for the first time, I call out to them. *Come back to me.* I say to that voice in my head. Just like I shouted to Kirian when I was trapped in the abyss. Nothing, nothing at all. I close my eyes. *Please.* I'm unsure if I say it out loud. Doesn't matter. There is no answer.

I reach my hand gently into the water and do not realize that I have sat down upon the fountain's ledge until a hand reaches in with mine and a curious boy with blonde hair stands next to the woman with black eyes that seem to bore holes into me. A tear escapes and makes its way down my face, swallowed by the moving water. "I'm dead, Kirian," I say so quietly that I am unsure that he has heard me.

For a moment, we say nothing at all. As I sit wrapped in Kirian's arms, I decide that I do not care if it is a trick of the mind, the same trick that Madam Christoph plays in such a cruel manner. I do not care because if I am soon to be dead and the only comfort I receive before my end is the kind that I feel right now, real or not, that it is better than nothing at all.

Kirian walks me back to my room in silence. There are no other students around because it is half past noon, they are sure to be at training. He peeks his head inside the almost empty room but does not enter. The gentlemanly thing to do, I suppose. *Women... and some men to do his bidding.* I can't seem to get the words out of my head.

I push them out of my mind for now and look about the room myself. Kirian's Jacket lays over the mirror. Ava's plant on the table. The schools' books stacked high. Truly, nothing of my own. I suppose it doesn't matter now. You cannot take them with you when you die.

Before, I can think of all the things that I did not get to do, the things I did not get to experience, the life that I did not get to live, thanks to Hansel Luz. Before I can let the anger take me away again, I take a step into the room, rambling on about something that Sofie had told us earlier this week. Distracting myself from my own thoughts, thoughts of goodbye. It's a short list. Ava and- When I turn to face

Kirian a look of worry takes up his features as if he knows all too well the kind of goodbye that we are about to make as well.

"Katsia" Kirian's voice is hushed as he scans behind him for any listening ears. "My men will be here for several days. We are staying in the south tower." He says as he takes another nervous glance down the long hallway.

I take his arm and pull him in, taking one more look around and finding no one in sight. *You take more risks when you are about to die.*

I only think of the consequences for Kirian *after* I close the door. Softly, the way I always do. When I turn back, I find myself much closer to Kirian than I intended. I take a step backward, only for the knob to hit my backside. *So much for being quiet.* My embarrassment apparent when my cheeks flush and my shoulders straighten uncomfortably. He takes a large step back and runs his hand through his hair as he often does at times like this.

"Did you have something to say?" I ask him in a half-whisper.

He is having one of those internal debates, the kind that makes his eyebrows scrunch together and his mouth set in a line. "You will not die here, Katsia." He tells me assuredly.

I shake my head at him. "What do you mean?"

"I mean if you do not make it to The Vow if your magic has not yet returned… you must find me."

"Forgive me if your words are less than convincing, Kirian," I tell him almost with a laugh. Mostly because I cannot understand why he would help me, why he would risk his career for someone he barely knows.

He takes away the distance that he had created only moments ago and grabs my hand, pulling it up to his chest as if I could feel a lie in counted heartbeats. "This is no magic, no trick, only if you want, I will take you away from here."

I can only stare at my hand, held beneath his. "It wasn't just for my job that I watched you. With my bow and Arram's dagger, I saw you, Katsia, always. That day in Thorn Row, I couldn't believe my eyes when I saw a girl with long black hair and determination on her face walk through the gates. I tried to stay away, let you keep the secret that you and I both know. That you possessed something bigger than your Father, and your sisters, and your fucking brother."

When he releases my hand, I try not to notice the twinge of sadness caused by the absence of his touch. He reaches down to his boot. The sweet mint scent hits my senses as his forehead nearly touches my chin on his descent.

When he straightens with a flash of silver in his hand. I flinch. Until he flips it with ease so that the blade is pinched between his fingers. Then he places the handle in my palm. *A.E.*, the initials engraved on its side. I had not known the name of its original owner until now. "I wish you had stayed away." I admit as I welcome the familiar feeling of the metal that I hold.

"Me too," he says, but I do not believe him. Especially when he runs a finger down the side of my face. *I do not believe him because I promised myself that I would never again. I do not believe him because-*

Kirian leans down and places a kiss on my cheek, just as he had done at The Charlie. I can't remember what I was thinking or doing before this moment. "Goodnight, Katsia." He side steps and walks out the door before I can even turn around.

Chapter 21

"Let's make a deal." Madam Christoph eyes me warily as she ascends her throne, upon which she sits as we entertain her. This is new. I thought there were no deals with this woman. Others have pleaded with her before for an end to the madness. Soon, she leans back, crosses her legs, and lets that wicked smile devour her face.

I find myself staring back at Spartus, back at my prison, bored. Just as I was during Sophie's lecture, just as I was when Ava and I spared just before we got to the course. If I am not going to be around much longer, it's no use to be anything but.

I can't go with Kirian, I thought about it all last night, I didn't get a wink of sleep. If I go with him, it's only going to postpone my fate and put his career or maybe even life in danger. *There is no escape.* These words are on repeat in my head, along with yesterday's events. The meeting, Augustine's words, Kirian's promise.

"Not that it would have made a lick of difference, but yesterday Katsia was not able to participate in our little game." Madam Christoph coos. Her little jab knocks the thoughts from my head. Everyone's heads turn to me. I fidget nervously under their gaze. "If Katsia can make it to the platform alone, you all get the time between now and The Vow to train amongst yourselves." She looks to the lake, and I am the only one left looking at her as everyone else awaits my answer.

She nods her head in the direction of the lake, her silent gesture for me to take a look for myself. I turn my head. I can still feel her burning a hole into the side of my face with her stare. The platform has moved, it's almost on the other side, doubling the distance that I will have to swim. No one says a word, they do not need to.

Another punishment. Oh well, no need to argue or plead. Instead, I walk away from the group and to the start. Cora whispers something to her friend, who in turn laughs at my misfortune as she watches me stretch out my arms in preparation. Ava stands behind me. "I can take care of the vines." She tries, but I have a feeling if I do not do it alone, only me and no one's gifts to help me, there will be consequences. Ones that do not matter to a girl near her death, but Ava is so close to the end.

She will take The Vow, then she will live her life in the gardens of the King's palace, just as she wants. Or at least this is what I tell myself will happen after my death.

I turn my attention back to the task at hand. I will try, and I will fail. It will be embarrassing, and then, if this doesn't kill me, someone else will. So, it does not matter.

"Don't" is all I say to her, then watch as she takes a step back, letting me know that she understands. Her hands shake and her almost too large eyes well up with tears. Sweet Ava.

Everyone else keeps their distance but stands along the sides of the course to watch me. All the nerves that I thought would take up the space in my chest are nonexistent.

Suddenly, I have a chance to prove myself, not only to the people who watch me now but to myself. I am not useless just because my magic has decided to disappear.

This will *not* spare my life. I know that. But at least I will die knowing that I did this one thing. So, as I stand here, awaiting the fear that is soon to be in my head, I feel nothing but complete calm.

Madam Christoph gives the signal, the high-pitched whistle that's now burned into my memory. Before my mind catches up to my body, I'm being hurled towards the nearest object. Just like before, every height is thousands of meters higher and every jump is to my death, yet I still make them, knowing that I will meet the ground below even if my mind thinks that I will not.

When the vines turn into snakes that wrap themselves around my legs and arms, I pull them along with me as I am used to the creatures that I know are not real. Soon, the snakes become hands. Which is not unusual, with the exception of one with an eye upon its wrist. I blink slowly, hoping that it will disappear. Strange. It's never been this way before. Only fears that most would have, not something so unique to me. I do not dare a peek at my tormentor.

Madam Christoph is diving deeper into my mind. I try to concentrate on my next move. Try to keep the things that scare me most deep inside. The hands cross in front of my face, making it impossible to see anything but that damn tattoo. It is no longer just a tattoo on the arm of an old man because it blinks twice, as if it's alive, mimicking me, watching me. I can't look away. Instinctively, I raise my hand to push it away from my face. My forearm hits something *solid*. Not my imagination at all.

Before I can even try to understand it, a warm sensation starts above my knee and drips down my leg, jolting me back into reality. The shock of the pain is followed by a surge of adrenaline. My attention falls to my thigh, where crimson blood falls down the length of a silver dagger. The hands disappear, returning to vines. I blink away the black that surrounds my vision as though I might faint. When I can see again, I look down again and begin to panic as *my* dagger sticks out of flesh. It's like nothing I have ever felt before.

I don't remember sliding the dagger in my boot this morning. For fear of bleeding out, I know I can't remove it. I leave it as I head for the wall.

So close, just past the wall is the lake and I know it's a far swim, but I have made further ones. *Not any with a weapon in my thigh.* Ignoring the pain that comes with every step I speed up to a jog so that I can clear the wall.

Before I can reach it, Stone spins beneath me. I throw my hands out to balance myself. This time, when reality shifts, there is no wall. Instead, I find myself in an empty field. The one outside of House Luz, the one that I slept in to be far from Father and Kirian. There is no course, no shouts from behind me, no lake.

Wildflowers sprout up from the ground, I can only watch as their whole life cycle plays out before me. From seed to bud to flower. I stare up at the setting sun and smile, I *smile*, genuinely, for the first time in a long time. My face falls as I wonder if that too is a fear of mine, an image that Madam Christoph so cleverly places inside my thoughts, happiness, something that I will never attain.

The wind picks up, sending my hair flying in all directions, releasing it from the pins around my head. It becomes so violent and loud that I can't hear myself think, it takes the wildflowers, ripping them from the ground by their roots and flinging them through the air, destroying the once beautiful field. The colors that surrounded me moments ago are now dull. Brown grass and dead trees, gray clouded skies that are on the brink of downpour. *Move.*

A boot that I have felt many times before strikes me between the shoulder blades, sending me plummeting to the ground face-first. An attack I would have normally dodged if I had heard his heavy steps behind me. Cedric. *Move.*

Tousled brown hair and breath of booze. My punishment for releasing the animals that he had caught with snares.

But I am no longer willing to take his abuse for the sake of keeping peace. This is *not* House Luz.

I know his weak points. Madam Christoph's voice is in my head. The same one she would use to dull out commands during training. *If they can't see, they can't attack. Go for the eyes first.* I know where to hit to make it hurt, and I so badly want to hurt him, the way that he hurt me. I turn to him, prepared to make my attack. Finally, he will get a taste of his own medicine.

My leg does not move. I try again, pinned, I look down to see a snare of his design. He laughs at my mistake, his face turns sinister as he walks away, leaving me, just as he did the fox, the doe, the bear, every animal that had the displeasure of ending up in the hands of Cedric Luz. Now, *I* am the wounded animal, but who will save me?

I try again, pulling at the snare around my leg. The ground meets me with a hard *thump.* When I place my hands down to lift myself back up, it is no longer made of dirt. The ballroom. Intricate designs that Father made sure were one of a kind.

My leg is still trapped as men and women dance around me. An upbeat jig plays in the background. The dancers line up. Men to my right and women to my left. The women hold flowers, the men swords. They collide at the center, where I lay helpless. My leg is still pinned between two pieces of wood. I do not bother to ask for help. These people have no eyes, just more skin where their eyes *should* be. If they did, they would notice the blood, my blood upon their skirts as they drag its deep red across the ground, like a brush on canvas.

The men turn to bucks with long pointed antlers, the women to does with white tails that bounce with each movement. Their hooves click on the stained floor as they continue with their choreography.

Suddenly, I remember the painful screams of those scared animals. Perhaps the same sound that should be coming from me. They were set to die in one of these contraptions. Their last breaths used to call desperately for help. But I will not die here. Nor do I have any pain. In fact, I feel nothing. Not even from where the dagger was lodged into my leg just moments ago.

This is not Cedric's doing, but Madam Christophs. She is farther in my head than I realized she was capable of going. *I am no animal*, I remind myself. I know how to release the snare. I know how to mend my own wound.

Before my hands can reach the trap, the revelation sends the image of the dancing herd skittering out of sight. Reality comes crashing back. I see that I am still in the same spot, my hand clutching my leg, but when I look down now, there is no more dagger.

A trick from the very beginning.

When I look up, there is the wall, just where I left it. Ava screams at me from the sidelines to move. Her voice is hoarse as if she has been yelling for hours.

I shake away the dizziness of having another person in my subconscious. Then I pull myself up and over the wall, landing on the other side without injury. I sprint to the lake, and as I wade through the cattail and the weeds, I start to wonder when the next trick will be.

It does not come. I swim for what feels like a long time. So long that I start to think that maybe there are no more tricks at all. *I made it.* All I have to do is keep moving.

I look down and see something long and scaly swimming beneath me. *There are fish in this lake.* It flips its body so that its white belly faces me, keeping my pace as I go. I have never seen a fish like this one, but we are a long way from Thorn Row.

It comes up to me again, curiosity getting the best of it. Soon, every time I put my head in the water, it's there. This is not one of Christoph's cruel tricks. It can't be. There is nothing fear invoking about it.

I keep moving, swinging my arms and kicking my feet faster now, pushing past my limits and ignoring my tired muscles.

My heart jumps to my throat as the fish comes near me again, closer than before. There is something strange about its scales. They shimmer a different color now. Its face morphs into Adriel's. Blue eyes, perfect skin, button nose. I do not stop. Will not. I guess I was wrong, this must be another trick.

My head goes under again for a few strokes. Water seeps into my lungs, causing me to choke when I see Madam Christoph's evil grin take up its features before she changes into a wealthy woman with red hair.

It changes again and again, into a million faces, some I recognize and some I do not. This is not a fear of mine, how could it be, I have never seen a creature such as this one, or even read of it. *Can you be afraid of something that you never knew existed?*

It reaches up to me with a fin that transforms into a human arm as it nears me. I want to take it, the offer now coming from the face of Kirian. *His* hand, the one outstretched, *his* face looking up at me. Kirian's strands of blonde cascade down his face flowing with the water as he moves through it with ease. His hand is so close to mine that I only have to let my own sink a little further.

I will take you away from here. Our conversations play in my head. I come to a halt, my arms and legs unmoving. Kirian laces his fingers in mine. *No magic, no trick.* He promised me. I let myself sink, taking in a breath of humid air before my head goes under. I feel the opposite of fear as the creature with Kirian's face now circles my body, disappearing from my view for a few seconds before emerging in front of me again. Kirian wraps a gentle arm around my waist, pulling me into him. It feels familiar, good.

My eyes close for a moment as I let myself slip into the moment. *Danger, Katsia.* I tell myself. But my body does not listen. The current catches my body in a lulling back and forth. *Open your eyes.* A small voice. The quietest my head has ever been, actually. *Open them.* When I do, all I am left with is the cold water that surrounds me and darkness.

The creature still has Kirian's eyes, pools of green that blend in with the surrounding water but the rest of his features are disturbingly...off. His nose is too long, his chin elongated. As if he has caught on to my discomfort it morphs again. Into multiple faces as if it's trying to choose the right one to show me. I scan its scales reflecting less light as we sink further revealing its ugly nature.

When I look back at the face it has carefully chosen, Kirian's eyes are no longer the ones that look back at me. Augustine's sullen features take in mine. His eyes, not of fire, but completely hollow masses of black, like the abyss that trapped me.

I begin to squirm, a burning sensation starts in my chest before radiating to my back, my throat. It takes me a second to realize that it's the absence of air that pains me so. The distance that we have traveled from the surface is getting further and further, I'm not sure how long I have been below water. Augustine continues to sink down along with me, a nasty lopsided grin on his face. The same hot hatred spilling off his body.

I push my hands through the water once more, propelling myself upwards. Leaving whoever's face, the creature steals next as I make my way back to the top, my lungs nearly exploding as I take in the air once more. All the strength in my muscles is gone, yet I still push forward.

The muddy water drips down my throat and I have to concentrate on not expelling my guts from the taste. The swim becomes a slow crawl, my arms and legs begging for rest. With every swing of my arm, I look beneath the surface paranoid of another run in with the creature that lulled me into the deep. The platform in front of me seems so close and so far at the same time. *I'm going to make it. I have to make it.*

I throw myself into the next few strokes, hoping that it will be enough, that my muscles can take only a few more minutes of abuse.

My hand hits something hard, shooting a pain into my shoulder. I pull myself on the wood and turn onto my back, lying flat as I take in as much air as my lungs will hold and cough out the water that threatened to drown me.

Pain, my whole body is on fire. Just like when I emerged from the abyss, the world hurts, from the tips of my fingers down to my toes. I stand slowly, each movement sending jolts of fire down my back and legs. I squint towards the shore, but I can't distinguish between the figures that stand amongst each other. Some wave their hands excitedly. Others pace back and forth as if something is on their mind.

Suddenly, the world seems to go dark as a layer of smoke surrounds me, making it hard to see. "No please" I half whisper "I made it, please." Why is Madam Christoph still punishing me? Feeding me fear with her mind.

Just as I feel the familiar, relentless, pulling and prodding, whispers come from all around. I spin my head trying to find where the voices come from, but all I see is black. They are so close, too close, the voices I hear are not around me, they are in my own head. They share with me their worries. They plead with me to stay.

Yes, I tell them within the confines of my own mind. All at once, a familiar warmth seeps into my skin, into my bones. I feel... powerful.

A soft, gentle voice comforts me. *"You're back."* She says. *"Finally."*

There, what has been missing for so long.

Magic.

I thought of my plan as I swam back, my gift ripped from my body once more as I dove into the water. It hurt just as much, more, now that I know what it felt like to have it for just a moment. To have it and not be afraid of it. *Is that what it's like if I embrace it?*

My heart ached as though I had lost something, and I had, I was grieving my magic. I didn't realize how incomplete I felt until those few minutes that I spent on that platform when it had filled the hole that was unknowingly, painfully, gaping open.

A feeling that I previously thought I was numb to, and perhaps whoever took it knew that, knew that I would not notice or care. Just as I had not cared if my life were to end. The only thing keeping me attached to Stone at the time of my arrival was the remnants of Kirian's gift, his convincing words, willing me to continue.

That night I knew what I had to do, I was sure there was a perimeter, which meant that all I had to do was leave it, find the distance that I have to travel to gain my magic back again. Then, after that it's easy, the woman, the one inside my head has warned me of this place, the dangers of staying. My death. I know where I have to go.

I did not say a word to anyone, not even Ava, as I pried open the window and descended the jagged Stone with ease. Thanks to Madam Christoph, I was unafraid of the height. Her nod of understanding when I made it back to shore was enough to convince me that what she had done for me today was no accident. Not at all.

Chapter 22

"Don't tell me how you got here." Kirian whispers, a growing smile on his face. "I won't like the answer." He quickly pulls me into the room by my hand. These rooms are not as nice as the ones in the dormitories. They are void of color and definitely not meant for long stays. There are no windows, and the rooms and hallways all look the same amount of plain. I only knew Kirian's room, thanks to his brief description, in case I needed to find him.

He eyes the bag at my side, his face changing from playful to serious in a matter of seconds. It's Kirian's bag that he got from the markets, stuffed with his jacket and a change of clothes that belong to Spartus. It's all I have. "You said you would take me." I remind him of his promise.

"Of course." He runs his hands through his wet hair and buttons his shirt fully. He smells clean, like fresh linen. He must have just come from the bathhouse. "And I meant it."

"You will take me *anywhere* I want to go?" I lift my chin and straighten my shoulders to mask my unease.

He shakes his head slightly and scrunches his brows together as he looks between my eyes. Just when I think he is going to ask me *where* his face becomes neutral again. "Anywhere." He confirms with a nod.

I don't give myself time to dissect the look that crosses his face next. "Good. We need to leave tonight."

The next few hours are spent trudging through mud and marsh, parts of it I thought looked familiar from my journey here, but I soon came to find out that the terrain is all the same. Large leafy plants, sarro trees with their spindly branches that make it impossible to see further than a few feet ahead. When they are not manicured as they are at Spartus, their roots grow together. Exposed and mossed over, making them blend in with the ground. It would be easy to get lost without a guide.

Kirian took back roads to lead us north and side streets when we would come across a town as not to be seen by many. He knows he is to take me to Thorn Row. That's it. There, I will leave through the only gate that grants you access to the mountains. To Shadow Gate.

My legs are sore, and the pack at my side lays heavily on my hip, hitting the bone with every long stride. I would not be surprised to see a bruise there under my trousers. I do not dare tell Kirian of how uncomfortable I am as the sun falls on our second day, and he continues to walk and walk and walk. The man never grows tired. I trail behind him and speak as little as possible for fear that he might be in the midst of deciding I'm not worth the trouble. *Maybe I am not.*

I chug our last bit of water from Kirian's canteen. He grabs it from my hand and gives it a shake, then without a word he continues down a trail that I had not even noticed.

His silence growing more eerie by the second. *What is he thinking?* I fall behind as he walks into a thick part of the trees. My legs feel as if they may give out, but I follow. My mere months of training are not even close to the years Kirian has on me.

When I reach him, I stand at his side, prepared to finally tell him how desperately I need a break. I take a breath to gather my words, but he puts a hand up to stop me. I nearly roll my eyes but keep my words in as he looks at the greenery around us. His head slowly turns as he listens intently to our surroundings. He takes a confident step in the direction of some nearby rocks.

Again, I move and think about begging him for a rest but when I catch him this time he stands in front of a flowing brook, no larger than a foot wide, at which he kneels to fill his canteen. My mouth waters with anticipation, like when you smell a fresh baked pie.

"Drink up," he holds it out to me without taking a drink for himself. When I take it, he begins removing his pack. A bead of sweat drips from his brow, the walk finally showing the toll it took on him as well. I watch him for a few seconds longer. Then I drink the cool water hastily, some of it falling onto my shirt.

"Thank you." I barely get out between swigs.

I fall to my knees. My legs thank me for the rest. I fill Kirian's canteen again before digging my hands into the stream, scooping out some of its cool water to splash on my face. "We will stay here tonight. I'll go gather firewood," Kirian says from behind me. I nod in response as he stands, but do not look at him.

I promptly strip off my dirty training uniform and rinse it in the water then lay it out to dry, grateful for the heat even though the days are getting shorter to signal the changing of the seasons. I wonder if Fauna has changed their summer flowers to winter ones yet. I try not to think of the fact that I will never get to see that happen in person. The paintings of Father's gallery will have to be enough.

Thorn Row most likely has a view of snow-coated mountains by now. I do not miss much about Thorn Row, but that was a sight to behold. And one that is unique to those closest to the mountains.

Lupita once told me that the snow was a side effect of war. That the Gods were angry enough with the king that they made the holy land infertile. That's why it doesn't spread beyond Shadow Gate. The snow will make my journey more difficult.

By the time Kirian comes back I am slipping the long sleeve shirt back over my head. He throws down the pile of wood and sinks to the ground with it. "Rest. I will start the fire." I tell him and to my surprise he listens.

He does exactly as I did a moment ago, taking off his jacket and then his white undershirt before dunking them into the water. I make sure to busy myself, using a greener branch to poke at the flames.

He comes to warm his hands on the fire now that the sun is setting, giving a chill to the air. He sits opposite me, his chest bare and his face scrubbed of debris. Stubble has begun to grow along his jaw that, clenches every now and then like a nervous habit. He places his shirt near the fire for faster drying. I don't stop myself from letting my eyes roam over his twisted torso as he grabs for it. "Where is your tattoo?" the words fall from my mouth without thought. Regret has me chewing on my bottom lip like it will stop me from saying more.

He faces me and holds my eyes. Dancing orange flames reflect back at me, hiding the green beneath. He brushes his hands off on his trousers. Then, he reaches up and pinches his lower lip with his pointer finger and thumb. When he pulls the skin down to his chin it reveals to me an eye. Etched into the skin of his inner lip. I push my hands together nervously when the memory of that lip between my teeth surfaces.

I don't even stop myself when I begin to ramble, anything to keep that particular image from my mind. "Claire is a seer. Hers is upon her forehead. Lord Andres forces the truth from your throat." I think of when the words that I promised to keep in escaped me during that carriage ride to Fauna. Without realizing it, my hand now lay across my collarbones where Lord Andres' eyes concentrated to pull the truth from me.

Kirian trails my fingers with his eyes as they glide over the bone as if he, too, knows what it feels like to be under Lord Andres' glare. "Why is yours *there*?" I finish my thought.

His face flashes red. Even in the growing darkness that surrounds us, I can see it. He is either upset that I asked such a question or the answer is not something he wishes to speak of. I pretend to be interested in the dirt between my boots, kicking at it to avoid the shift in his demeanor. There is no way to decipher what he is thinking. I never can. *I should not have said anything at all.*

Thankfully, he does not have me on the hook for long as an answer crosses his features. "A woman once said my words sounded like honey." His voice is low, but it's so quiet here, in the middle of nowhere, that he does not need to speak loudly. "Like what I say, no matter what it is, sounds... sweet, tempting." He looks down at his hands for a minute before peering at me through his lashes.

Again I put my foot in my mouth. "Your words were not sweet in the jail. When you made me confess to the others of Father's mistreatment." I tell him. The left corner of his mouth twitches as he tries to hide a growing smile.

"No, I suppose they were not." And then. "Where is your magic, Katsia?" he asks a question for me now, one that catches me off guard.

I clear my throat and quickly look away from him, beyond the light of our fire to the trees that are slowly disappearing into the night sky. What were once small whispers and prying eyes are now full apparitions in the dark. Some of them watch me, speak to me, offer me their advice.

One voice among them tells me of their secrets, a female, one who wishes me to find her heart. She told me of the true nature of The

Spent. I do not share any of this with Kirian, and I never will. The woman speaks to me and only me, her secrets for my ears only.

"It will come when I need it," I assure him, not a complete lie, I really believe that. It's a comfort to know they are there, no longer figments of my imagination. Maybe I was not ready to accept them for what they are. Magic, not insanity.

"I believe you." Kirian rolls out a bed from his pack. Offering me his assurance is enough to make my heart skip a beat. I wish that would stop happening around Kirian Bear. I bet his own heart only drums in steady beats, not wavering for anyone. "You sleep first. I will take watch." He pulls the now dry shirt over his head sloppily and leans up against a tree. I do not object. It would be no use. To my surprise, sleep comes easily. The babbling brook and the crackling fire creates a melodic tune.

The peaceful sound does not last long. My nightmares are much louder than the scene around me.

When I awake the fire is gone, only embers remain. The sound of snoring comes from beside me. Kirian's back against my own pushing me back and forth with each breath. My stomach lets out a heinous growl and I carefully slip from the bedroll and place it over him before setting out in search of something to eat.

This forest is bountiful, much more so than the ones of House Luz near Thorn Row. I find onions in the ground and three eggs in a coffin-birds nest among the trees. Called that because they lay their eggs at the bottom of tree trunks. Mothers bury their eggs in the dirt and debris while they are away. I knew the misshapen clump of dirt from drawings in books from the library at the school.

As I walk back, I think of Ava. She won't know what has happened to me. I must have scared her with talk of death, but maybe it would be better if she thought me dead. Besides, I don't think that I will be returning from my journey. Not if what the woman whose voice is in my head says is true.

The Spent is searching for a weapon, one that will destroy Stone. Their need for magic users, an army. *"An opening of the realms, the same war that was fought and lost long ago."* She told me. Stone and Understone were always meant to be separate. This world was not meant for magic. It's only been used for abuse. She wishes to take away magic from Stone forever. The way it was always meant to be. The way *I* was meant to be. Normal.

When I return, I see Kirian shoving all of his things into his pack once more. He curses loudly as he throws in the last of his things. I hurry towards him. A twig breaks beneath my boot. He turns so fast that it startles me, his face that of a predator.

Suddenly, he is the man who once wiped his blood along my cheek. The man with the same face as the one that I see before me, with a goal to break me. He stomps towards me with that mask that he is far too good at wearing, and I can't help but stumble backward. Turning my face from him in preparation for what comes next. But when he lets the pack fall from his shoulder at my feet, its contents rattling against the hard ground, he lets out a ragged breath of... relief. I am no longer scared.

He pushes my face towards him. "Gods, I thought you left, or-"but he stops when I find myself having nothing else to do besides hold up the eggs to show him where I have been. I look from my fingernails filled with dirt from digging into the ground to his face. His worry turns into a smile that tugs at his mouth forcing a dimple to his cheek. *This is the Kirian I want to keep.*

"I was only searching for these." I tilt my head up at him. He grabs them from my palms. In his hands, the eggs look much smaller. They will not fill a man of his size. I should have searched for more. When I reach into my pocket to grab the onions his smile turns into laughter, the contagious kind.

I let myself laugh along with him. It's been a long time since that noise has left my chest. Kirian starts the fire again, and we sit on the damp ground while we wait for our meal. Kirian feigns satisfaction as he scoops up an egg and downs it in one gulp, leaving the others for me.

"You're full of surprises, Katsia."

The next days are the same, we walk until our legs can no longer move and then we rest as we wait for the day. When night comes, Kirian always takes watch, with promises of waking me to take a turn, but he never does. My nightmares never cease causing me to wake throughout the night, finding Kirian at my back for warmth. Mine or his, I don't know.

One morning, as I often do, I woke before sunrise to see the glow of light from somewhere far off. Letting me know we are finally close to a city, maybe even Thorn Row, but we will not make it there today, even if we keep walking into the night. I don't say anything as Kirian trudges forward with what looks like no plans to stop. We walk for a few hours before I feel a drop of water from the sky, then another, and soon it soaks the jacket that Kirian gifted me all those months ago, and I begin to shiver from the cold.

Kirian slows but does not stop. "It's only a little rain. Let's keep going." He says over his shoulder. I nod my head in a response that he does not see and take one more step with my head down to keep my face dry. As if Zeus himself heard Kirian's words, thunder roars in the sky and the wind swirls around us.

The rain begins to pour down so fiercely that we have no choice but to find shelter. Kirian heads for two large rocks that lean against each other nearby. He tries and fails to keep a fire lit beneath them. The bedroll is already damp from the hike up the hill to get here, and the temperature is dropping quickly.

We lay back-to-back, and soon I am curled into a ball to keep in the warmth, but it's no use, my teeth chatter and my ears sting against the wind. Kirian's breathing is uneven, and his legs shake from the bitter cold. He rolls onto his back, clearly uncomfortable. I turn to face him using his body to block some of the wind.

He has let me use his jacket to lie on, but I do not need to be comfortable as much as I need to be warm. So, I take the jacket and pull it over the both of us, using his shoulder as a pillow. With my ear pressed against his chest, I can hear the hammering of his heart, a steady but fast beat. I nuzzle into the crook of his arm, feeling the heat from his core. His heartbeat grows faster, harder.

His annoyance at my actions is apparent when he swiftly spins me back around and onto my side once more, he lets out an exasperated sigh. My cheeks warm with embarrassment. I'm glad that he cannot see my face. I meant nothing by it, simply to stay warm. "I didn't-"I begin but I am cut off when he wraps his heavy arm around my waist and pulls me firmly into him, his chest against my back.

"You will be warmer this way." he breathes into my ear. The rain does not cease, but the wind slows. And he is right. I am much warmer this way.

I'm surrounded by the scent of mint, the sound of Kirian's breathing, and the rise and fall of his chest. Soon, I am drifting into sleep.

Chapter 23

When I awake, his arm still grips my body, but I face towards him now and not away. His face is mere inches from mine. I carefully push his disheveled hair from his face to study him. All I would have to do is let my face fall forward, and I could kiss the freckles that line his nose. *He doesn't want me*, I remind myself. He made it clear at The Charlie, and last night, he could hardly stand me so close to him, and he won't like it now. So, I turn on my back as the sun rises. Its heat seeps into my body. I stay as still as possible so as not to wake Kirian.

We do not speak when he finally stirs. He dries his things as best he can, but the rain leaves nothing that we could use to start a fire. Then he packs away his things, and we begin again, just as we do every day.

The terrain becomes familiar, and I know we are approaching Thorn Row, but Kirian doesn't go down the road with a sign pointing to the city. Instead, he heads for a small village. One that I do not recall seeing on any map.

As we enter, I can't help but cough. It's filled with a thick black smoke that comes from its core. Everyone seems completely unbothered by the stench that lays like a thick cloud over the village.

We head for a blacksmith, whose shop is in the center like the whole place revolves around it. And it does. There I find the source of its pollution as black smoke plums from the round building with a hole in the middle.

A man with bulging, veiny arms swings a hammer while a woman collects broken weapons and tools from the crowd that surrounds them. They push at each other, trying to get to the woman first. She shouts something at a man with a hammer. The man just shakes his head at the weapon in her hands, upset by something. We get closer and I hear her say "Sorry, not interested." As she shrugs her shoulders and turns to the next person. The man whose hammer lays in his hands in pieces curses but takes his leave.

The clinking of metal against metal fades as we push past men and women in what can only be described as fighting leathers. Reinforced at the elbows and knees, masks to protect their faces, and chainmail falling down their torsos.

One woman, dressed in the purest black, tight to her figure and a hood that only lets a single braid fall to her face, passes us in silent steps. She looks Kirian up and down. Her piercing blue stare and tan skin make her a unique beauty, one that many men around her seem to notice. All but Kirian, that is, who keeps his focus in front of us, busied by the thoughts inside his head, which seem to plague him. I have made it a game to keep track of his subtle change in disposition depending on the circumstances. Maybe it's the soldier in him, being able to adapt to his surroundings. Hot and cold. Has been from the start.

I bite away the feeling of jealousy that swirls in my chest as she trails us. Then, there they are, just as I felt them seep into my body beyond the walls of Spartus. My Shadows rise to the surface at every not-so-subtle glance in Kirian's direction. Thankfully, no one sees them or hears their promises of carnage. *Some men and women*, Augustine's repulsive voice is in my head. There it is again, the darkening of my vision. This time, it was paired with a crackling of power in my fingertips. Jealousy and rage are all I can see. All I can think about. The Shadows are offering me their services. *To dig their eyes out of their skulls. Then they cannot look.*

The woman's voice, the one that tells me her secrets. *"Not yet."* She tells me in a calm, soft voice, and with that, she has the Shadows settling back into their dark hiding places. I try not to think of what might have happened if she did not intervene.

We stop at a peddlers stand. Kirian peers down to inspect the wares. I become confused when I see the merchandise: fine jewelry, amulets and rings that are far too gaudy. With swirling bits of silver that would get caught on whatever you touch. I never much liked jewelry for that reason. In the corner of a glass covered display, I think I see the reflection of a yellow stone embedded into a copper arm band. The same as the one I gave to Lupita.

For some reason, I begin to search for her face amongst the crowd. It's of no use, of course she would not be here. I am pulled from the thought when a short older woman approaches us from behind the counter.

Kirian tosses her a coin, which she inspects thoroughly before sticking it in her shirt. She eyes me from the corner of her wrinkled eyes. "And for the girl?" She crows. Kirian bunches his fist at his side, well out of her sight. Then, he reaches into his pouch once again and tosses another coin at her. "Follow me," she says, satisfied as she turns around without another word.

Kirian gently pushes me in front of him as we follow her to a building nearby. We do not go in through the front door. Instead, she opens the cellar, and down we go, the light of day disappearing as we descend. Thankfully, Kirian stands close. I reach behind me, grabbing the hem of his jacket so as not to lose him as we walk down a dim hallway, torches doing little to illuminate the space.

The elderly woman delivers us to a man who is meticulously running a pencil over paper. His lines precise, his eyes narrowed in complete concentration. He doesn't stop his work as we step further into the room. A mage light hangs over his desk as he works. Illuminating the small space, a door to another larger room is cracked open. Distant sounds of shuffling feet and tinkering noises from beyond.

The man wears a contraption around his head, two thick glass pieces at the front, to help magnify his lines. The older woman stays at our backs, blocking our exit. *Trapped*. The word repeats itself in my head, it's all I can think about. *Trapped, trapped, trapped*. The Shadows slither and shift as if waiting for a command. I try not to watch them in their dance.

We wait for a few minutes before Kirian clears his throat. At this, the man looks up at us, his gray eyes three sizes bigger thanks to the contraption. He takes them by the metal that holds them together on the edge and places them on top of his head. He then shifts his attention to the old woman, back to us, then to the woman again. "Papers?" I can't place his accent, not that I have had the chance to talk to many people with any accents at all.

"Mmhm" she hums almost bored sounding, like it happens every day for these two. I do not dare turn my head in her direction. The door shrieks as she opens it, then it shuts, and her footsteps fade down the long hallway once more. Leaving us here. *Trapped, trapped, trapped*.

The man is silent for a moment. He studies me for far too long as if he recognizes me. Which is impossible because, of course, no one knows *me*. He tilts his head to the side. Kirian shifts uncomfortably behind me. When the man stands, he is much larger than I originally thought as he emerges from behind the worktable. He takes the few steps it takes to get close to us, his head still cocked to the side. I make sure to look straight ahead. He all but pretends Kirian is nonexistent as he looks me over. "A pretty penny in the east for a lass with hair as black as yours." His accent is harsh on the r's with a seductive flow to it. He towers over me now as he pinches a stray strand of my hair between his lead-stained fingers for inspection.

After his hand moves from my hair to my chin my breathing becomes shallow. My heart races wildly as he lets out a low growl. Fear...and something else takes up the space in my chest. He pushes my face up so I can no longer avoid his gaze. The man has a chiseled jaw, much like the statues in House Luz, the ones of warriors. His almost silver eyes seem to see right through me.

He looks at me expectantly, like he is waiting for something. He is clearly after a certain type of response, one that I am sure women offer to him without a second thought. Afterall, it's what all men want. To feel powerful.

"That's why we are here." I bat my lashes, offering him what he is so desperately after. Men rarely want anything else but to know that women would fall at their feet if they asked. *Disgusting.* I continue my act. Hoping that Kirian catches on to my ploy. "My friend here told me you were the best in Stone." Even I am surprised at myself as I let my head lay into his palm slightly, as he still holds me in place.

Satisfaction is written on the lines between his brows. *It worked.* I praise myself silently. But he still looks between my eyes, searching, still rubs his thumb across my chin in a gentle stroking motion.

Then a thought must cross his mind because where I saw satisfaction just moments ago is now a knowing, lopsided smile.

Then, he lets out a laugh that echoes through the small room. The back room grows quiet, shuffling and tinkering, stopping for a minute as if whoever is beyond that door knows that sound all too well, or perhaps not at all. The confident mask I wore seconds ago cracks, but I will not let my fear to the surface. Not even the Shadows let it be known that I am afraid as they keep to their corner, watching.

He takes a step back, releasing my face but making sure that our eyes never part. "You will do just fine." Again, his gaze falls down to my toes and back, accessing me. *What does that mean? Do just fine at what?*

Kirian takes a safe step forward. "We don't want any trouble," he tells him. The man ignores him, circles back to the table, and places the glasses back on top of his head. He takes a seat and nods slowly before turning in his chair to grab something.

"Don't worry." He says as he holds out folded papers. This time, he addresses only Kirian. "I need not to draw attention to myself. Not yet." He holds his knowing grin, one half of his smile higher than the other. Kirian practically snatches the papers from the man's hands. Silver eyes snake their way across Kirian's features before landing back on me. "Let me know when you grow tired of this one, Love." He says through a huff of laughter. "Just call for Damien. I promise my name will sound good when coming from your lips." He gives Kirian a wink, then looks down at his drawing again.

I can't help but to take a peek for myself. I now understand the nature of his work—an instrument firing metal from an elongated brass tube. Next to him, papers I have seen many times before. Export and import documents containing trade routes and pick up times. This man is dangerous. Just like Father.

Kirian turns swiftly for the door, grabbing my arm tightly and dragging me along. It might be stupid, but I am already doing so many stupid things so I don't stop myself from looking over my shoulder at Damien. There are those silver-gray eyes. *Straight through me.* A devilish grin stretches his face, disappearing as we make our way up the stairs.

My eyes slowly adjust to the light and when they do I catch sight of Kirian, his face that of a scared boy, he takes in a large breath of air, and I realize that he had been holding his breath the entire way up the stairs. "What's wrong?" I ask him but he just glances behind him at the cellar door and pulls me away from the building.

He doesn't stop, his much longer strides have me jogging to keep up, and I can't get out of the white knuckled grip he keeps around my wrist. Not until we come to a sign on the outskirts of the village, that says we're headed towards Thorn Row, does he stop and turn to me.

He grabs my chin between his thumb and index finger. The fast movement causes me to flinch slightly. His hold is less gentle than Damien's. His calluses scrape at my skin as he twists my head to the left, then the right. He looks down at my feet and up to my hair, assessing every inch. "Kirian." I try to break him from whatever has him in such a state. "Who was that?" I try again. This time, he blinks hard and straightens his posture. He releases my face, his arm now swinging loosely at his side.

"Ever heard of the boogie man?"

I can hardly stop myself from laughing, but this is no laughing matter. Not when I see Kirian's fear. "Like the story meant to scare children?" I ask confused when I realize there was no hint of jest to his question.

"Well, that was him." He grabs my arm, and we begin our walk again. I do not say anything more. "And you will never utter his name, Katsia. Not even once." He doesn't look over at me when he speaks.

We just keep walking, like we always do. I think of the boogie man, the tale, the one that I read many times over. *Say his name, and he shall come.* But it's not real.

Chapter 24

Kirian has assured me that with the papers in hand, it will be easy to get through Thorn Row. Still, I can't stop thinking of all the things that could go wrong. I'm obviously wanted by The Spent if what Damien said is true. Not to mention whoever wants a chunk of change lining their pockets for turning me in.

The gates open, and a woman in a tan Guard uniform walks towards us. Kirian has long since changed his clothes into citizen attire, which he bought from a traveler that we passed. He was also headed into Thorn Row to sell his merchandise. While I have wrapped my hair in religious garb to conceal some of my features. It's white silken fabric long enough to hide my hair. The dress made from the same fabric is plain, mostly comfortable, as comfortable as a dress can be anyway. Kirian snickered as I picked it out but did not protest. It was the loosest fitting garment I could find, no corset, no lace or frills.

The woman takes our papers. Then, looks between the two of us. She eyes me wearily for what feels like an eternity, sending paranoid spikes of anxiety down my spine. She holds it up to the sun for further inspection. Then, takes one last look at the papers to read the name, *my* name, or at least the one Damien put on paper for us. "Mrs. Thurrow." She says with a nod of approval. "Mr. Thurrow," she then says to Kirian, who stands beside me, her tone softening. She gives him the same once-over as all the rest of the women who look in Kirian's direction. I ignore it. "Safe travels." She resumes her post, awaiting the next who enters. I note that this is the second time I am known as Kirian's false wife.

I am thankful for the bustling streets. The more people there are, the harder it will be to spot two individuals on the run. Although it makes concealing our identities easier, hiding my gift here has not been so easy. Their apparitions were easy to spot on our journey when it was just the two of us. Now I am finding it hard to decipher between the movements I see in my peripheral. Are they human or Shadow? We are almost done gathering things for our journey through the mountains, and I have managed not to raise suspicions, neither Kirian's nor the people around us.

Before I can move out of the way, a flood of people surround us, or maybe we walked right into them. All I know is that they are too close, all of them. They suffocate me. They talk amongst each other in a language that I do not understand. They brush past me as if I do not exist. The women are dressed in robes of many colors, the men in black or white. Their group carries the thick smell of a strong floral perfume, a nice scent when it's not all around you.

The Shadows whisper to me, *a warning,* for what I do not know.

The traveler's step between me and Kirian, separating us from one another. My breath becomes short and quick, and an ache starts in my chest. I push out the fear, the same as I did when Christoph was inside my head. I try to step between two men, but they block the path that would lead me to Kirian, whose head is turned as he walks away, freeing himself from the crowd of people.

When I finally get past the blur of colors, I've now lost sight of Kirian completely. I search each face frantically, but none of them are him, and some are faceless altogether. The panic that has been building within me comes to the surface when I realize that I am alone.

The Shadows groan in what I think is discomfort, the same that I feel. They promise to take me away if I wish. "No" I say quietly to them. I receive a strange look from the woman nearby.

The heat from the day amplifies every bit of panic that I feel. My stomach stirs. I try to collect myself in the shade of a vendor, a man who sells fruit. He watches me as I brace myself against the wooden edge of his cart. "How can I help you miss?" he asks.

I try for a smile. It's difficult to keep it plastered to my face as I reply. "Just looking," I say through struggling breaths and gritted teeth. *Fuck.*

"Go North." The woman's voice has the thunder in my chest dissipating. My thoughts slowly become clear once more. *Go North,* I tell myself. If Kirian is to find me again, it will be there. And if he does not find me, I will go alone. I know my role in this life, with Kirian or not.

I begin to move, but as I turn from the now annoyed vendor and towards the crowds of people once more, a man catches my attention, stumbling out from behind a building. His steps are uneven, drunk. Cedric. A man follows behind him, shouting with a shake of his fist. Something about payment.

Cedric doesn't hear him, or at least he doesn't turn around. For a split second, I am afraid. Then I take a better look at the pathetic man before me. Hardly able to stand or speak. Hardly a man at all.

I continue my steps, keeping distance between us until Cedric becomes a blur, then, nothing at all.

That is until another familiar face crosses my path. Her brown curled hair frames her face. Her piercing eyes and catlike smile growing as she looks at me. She grabs a red apple from a nearby crate and holds it out to me. Claire.

A pretty penny in the east for a lass with hair as black as yours. The Boogie Man's words pop into my head. Claire has had to have heard of it. She most likely knows everything if she is part of The Spent. Not to mention the whole seeing the future part. For all I know, her appearance here at the markets is no coincidence.

Claire moves in such a swiftness that it almost seems as if she is floating closer to me over the short distance between us. Her milky complexion and red lips that I know entice men to use her services. "Found what you were looking for yet?" she purrs. I do not answer. I shoot her an estranged look before stepping past her, and she does not stop me. Unfortunately, the white fabric that covers my hair does nothing to deter her. She knows exactly who I am. "Your yellow-haired beauty has evaded you." She says as she turns, taking a step with me.

She follows as I pretend to be interested in the next vendor's furs. She does not leave my side, as if we are two friends perusing what Thorn Row has to offer, even as we begin walking in the middle of the busy street. I am unsure of what direction. I have no room to think. Between all the noise and the panic that lay just beneath the surface. *I need to get out of here.*

Men ogle her as we pass, turning their heads slightly so that their wives do not notice. *Pigs.* I am careful to keep my hands at my sides, concealing my palms, although I have a feeling that she does not need to see them as she did before to know my future. "I wonder who he seeks?" she says into my right ear. "What do you think he speaks of that you are not allowed to hear?" Her whisper tickles my left now. Is she suggesting that Kirian separated us on purpose? And how did she move so quickly?

There is no use in ignoring her, and she hasn't drawn any attention from the guard that stands on the corner. She would have turned me in by now, right? My decision to face her was quick and ill thought out. Especially when I see her lips curl in satisfaction as I fall right into her trap. "Tell me what you know." I demand.

"Everything." She almost hums, pointing a slim finger at the eye that takes up the space on her forehead. *What an annoying answer.* "But if it's about the boy, I do not need magic to tell you how he feels." Her words linger for only a moment, a tinge of satisfaction in my chest. I push that feeling away.

It does not matter, not right now, when everything is confusing, and I am on my way to end a century-old war.

"What of me? You saw it once before, my fate. What does it hold?" She fiddles with a golden locket before taking another step. I follow *her* this time.

"What I see, they see." She turns to me. Stopping us in the middle of a busy cross-section where you can smell meat curing from one side and the floral-scented candles on the other.

I know what she means when the eye seems to stare right back at me. "And it wouldn't be much fun that way, would it?" she adds. I am unsure if this is a courtesy or not. Two sides to the same coin. To use her magic would be to give me away. Yet, if I was told of my future, who knows what I could do with the information.

So, I will take her bait and ask her what she so desperately wants me to. I cross my arms and widen my stance. "Where is Kirian?" I ask, annoyed. She smiles, but not at me. She looks past me. Someone shoves me from behind, I turn to scowl at the face that has almost knocked me over, but they have already moved along.

"We need to leave." Kirian comes from seemingly nowhere and pushes me out of the markets, North, towards the gate that leads to the mountain. I search for Claire amongst the quickly disappearing people, but she is gone. Like she was never there. My question will have to be answered by someone else.

"Where were you?" I demand once we are on a side street nearing the outskirts of the city.

"I had to take care of something," he says. His head is on a swivel, and he keeps glancing behind us. Is someone after him? A bead of sweat slides down his temple.

"You could have told me. You left me," I half shout, to which Kirian sighs but does not acknowledge me. He keeps his stride. I wish I could scream, but there are still many houses around and probably guards this close to the wall. "*Who* did you see?" I ask, Claire's words dance around my head. *Is this what she wanted?* Still, I cannot help it. I need to know.

Kirian stops, holding out his arm to stop me as well. I barely avoid running into him. Then he turns to me, accusation in his words, "What did she tell you?" He holds me in place, his hands so large that they cover my shoulders entirely. I have no time to answer before he continues. "You can't believe a word out of her mouth, Katsia." He shakes me slightly with each word.

"Oh really? *I* should not believe *her?*" The words are coming out of my mouth faster than I can think. They sting, even to me.

His lips curl into disdain. He removes his hands from my shoulders, then takes a step away from me and walks on without another word. He doesn't look behind him to see if I am following him. I am.

We leave the gates the same as we came. A guard takes our papers with a warning not to travel outside of the villages of the North. We pretend to listen, to take heed. Then we walk right out and begin down the road in uncomfortable silence.

Night falls, and Kirian silently hands me a bedroll. Then, he pulls out another one for himself. I notice a few extra things he now carries that must have been picked up from the market in Thorn Row.

He climbs into his, which is noticeably further from me than he has slept since we began in Fauna.

My legs thank me when I climb into the leather, giving them a much-needed rest. There is no talk of who will keep watch. The only noise coming from the grass as it blows under a slight breeze and the uneven breathing of an obviously still conscious Kirian. It's getting much colder the further we travel, evident by the clouds that escape me as I breathe.

Some time passes, I can't help but shift uncomfortably as I try to will myself to sleep. I lay one way and then the other, a rock lodged at my side. I let out an exasperated sigh and shift again. Quickly realizing that I will not be getting any rest tonight. Hopefully, Kirian is already asleep or has the decency to pretend he is.

But when I sit up and look over at him, he is already watching me, his head propped up on a fist.

His stare has me frozen. "Are you sure you want to do this?" he says so seriously, his sharp jaw set in place. The bone protruding further with his knuckles pressed into his cheek.

"Yes." is all I say before rolling over onto my side in a huff and pulling the leather back over my head, regretting my earlier decision. I am still angry at him. He still has not answered my question. I have answered all his questions, including ones that I did not want to answer, if his memory serves from our time spent at the jail.

Suddenly I start to panic, "Do *you*?" I ask as I jolt up from the ground again. He is still on his side, watching as if he knew that I was not done. "I can do it on my own. I only asked you to take me to Thorn Row. I told you-"a knot forms where words are supposed to come out. "I told you I would go North *alone*."

"I told *you* I would take you away from there. Although I'm not sure what you could possibly find in The North." His eyes narrow in accusation. "We could go *anywhere*." He breathes. It sounds more like a plea than a statement.

Suddenly, I want to tell him everything. I want him to know about the woman, what I can do, and how I can help end the abuse of magic in Stone. I want to tell him how glad I am that he is here because I have always done everything alone, and I finally do not mind the company. But instead, "Have you been?" I ask him, making sure to look beyond him to avoid his gaze, hoping that he doesn't notice that I have dodged that conversation. *Serves him right for all the times I have desperately wanted to know all the truths that he keeps inside but he refuses to say aloud.* I stare into the oncoming dark, where a silhouette sways back and forth, its body made of Shadow.

"No" then after a second. "I have seen those who have." He falls over onto his back and crosses his arms in front of him as he looks up at the clouded sky, making it impossibly darker as night draws on. "They never come back right." He admits. "They come back foggy, disoriented."

"What do they go North *for*?" I take advantage of his openness. A stark contrast to the way he has been on this journey. Which has been mostly closed off, secretive even.

"Not sure. After I joined and completed my training with The Spent, I was assigned to a village just outside the wall, that's as far North as I got." Then he pushes his lips together before continuing. "I saw my friends go in with Augustine and come out... like that." he says with a faraway look on his face, as if he is remembering those times.

I remember the burning stare of Augustine. The tension between the two at the school. "What's with you and Augustine anyways?" I have to stop myself from clasping a hand over my mouth at the stupid question.

His chest rises and falls in a sort of laugh. "I got into some trouble. That's when I was placed in Thorn Row, where my gift could be used more... efficiently." He says to the night air. A twinge of pain rests just below my heart at the thought of what could have gotten him in trouble, *who*. I rest my head on my forearms as I sit bundled into a ball to keep the cool of the night at bay. And to shield some of my face from Kirian so that he does not catch on to my poorly hidden jealousy. "I didn't like what he was doing in the North, whatever *it* was. And he didn't like, well, me." A smile tugs at the corner of his lips for some reason, and I cannot imagine for the life of me why he would be smiling at that. Having Augustine Nero dislike you would be terrifying. His handsome face does little to distract from the evil that lies behind his eyes.

"Ah, so your gift doesn't work on Augustine Nero, Light Taker," I say jokingly. Using the same words that he once used to describe the man to me.

"I guess not." He turns his head slightly, peering at me in a sidelong glance. His green eyes look gray under the light of the moon. "I kind of liked it. Not being liked, I mean."

I nod in understanding. Knowing that his gift must make it difficult to know when someone genuinely wants to be around you or if they are only drawn by the magic that surrounds you. I suppose you don't have to make any guesses when someone openly hates you.

It must have hurt his feelings when I hinted that he might not be trustworthy. In my head, he isn't. No one is. Not until they prove that they are. Kirian will have my trust when he delivers me to Shadow Gate. Still, I didn't need to use sharp words like that to get under his skin.

We stay like that for a while, comfortable in the silence that we created. Kirian must have been tired because his eyelids flitter before he relaxes into a peaceful slumber. "Goodnight, Kirian," I say, even though he most likely does not hear me.

The next few days are all the same, we walk, we camp. I've become bored of staring at the back of Kirian's head. His bow strapped to his back, red fabric dangles from the grip. The silences are not daunting or uncomfortable. While we walk, I keep my head up and my ears open. Ignoring the bite in my knees, the pinch at my side as I struggle up the mountain, and the headache that reappears during our short breaks.

The Shadows are mostly silent, minding their own business, only stopping to stare when I get close enough. They steer clear of Kirian, retreating when he nears them and pulling me away with them. I am unsure of what this means.

Kirian assures me that the burning sensation on the back of my head, the kind you get when someone is staring at you, is nothing. But when he thinks I'm not looking, I see his head on a swivel. Maybe he feels it, too. He purposely distracts me. I know it. He makes jokes, assuring me that it is much too cold for snakes and spiders when he sees me carefully stepping over a fallen tree or passing through brush.

We take short breaks, but I can tell that Kirian is faking his tiredness and is only stopping to give me a rest. Which I gladly take.

The air turns frigid as we approach a pass, two large pillars that were once attached at the top providing the perfect entrance past the dense forest that we just came from. Every now and then we would see a patch of cobblestone from an old road, that's what we followed to get here.

As we reach the pillars and Stone flattens, I see that they most likely belonged to the entrance of a city. There are scattered rusted metal bars that likely acted as a gate littering the ground.

The forest covers the old buildings well, making it blend into the mountainside. But if you look close enough you can see the old windows and doors in the darker spaces of the ridges and the streets in the valleys.

Below our feet the dying moss uncovers what used to be brick. We follow it, and see a sign at its corner. It's weathered by time and I can't make out the words on its face. This street must have housed dozens of families or businesses.

Suddenly, the Shadows split into two, with some pulling me towards the city and some away. It certainly has an air to it, one that is not the same as when we first entered the forest. It's more...sinister than that.

"It's too open. We should find a place to set up camp." Kirian says as he looks around, taking in the same scene as I do. He steps through the old entrance and into the city. Then picks a direction and begins to walk again.

I could stop right now, curl into a ball on the damp forest floor, and close my eyes. I am somewhere between exhaustion and death. But I keep the warm fire that Kirian is sure to start in mind as I take another shaky step in his direction.

As I step through the old entrance, using one of its pillars to balance myself, the hairs on my neck stand up. Something shifts in the mountains. I stop to see if Kirian notices as well, if he does, he doesn't show it. That scent, the same as it was in Spartus, when I first entered, copper, blood, magic.

Things begin to transform around me. Evergreens that were once bleak and uninteresting are now vibrant as their branches float up and down softly in the light breeze. Flashes of gold flakes circle in the air like mosquitos over water. *Maybe I am more tired than I thought.* I take another step.

My Shadows rejoice, *home* they say. I take in a large breath of the new air and suddenly I feel rejuvenated, like I haven't walked all the miles it took to get here, like I haven't hiked the mountain side on weary legs and blistered feet.

With my eyes closed and my arms spread out, I let it lay over me like a soft blanket, warm, welcoming, like I belong. I hardly notice as Kirian approaches me from the side. He gives me a strange, confused look.

My features mirror his, I am also confused. How could he not notice? "Break is over, let's keep moving princess." He smiles, proud of himself for the jest as he walks in front of me, offering a hand to step over the rocks at my feet.

Does he not sense it? Does he not feel the water rushing the same as blood through veins, hear the mountain's heart, wild and unending? Its hairs standing on end as we walk across its jagged spine? See its breath in the white fog that cascades down its sides? For a moment, I can only stare at him, search his face for an answer but he clearly feels nothing, *sees* nothing.

He has changed as well. Magic. Kirian's magic. His aura that I sometimes felt but could never see. I could reach out and touch it if I wanted to. It sticks to him, a yellowish light that emanates from his hands, his head, his mouth. It's beautiful.

I reach my arm through the yellow and take his outstretched hand. His magic sends a shock that travels up my arm, almost like it seeps into my skin through our palms that touch. This has me immediately retreating. His face scrunches with concern when I nearly snatch my hand away from him. "Let's go, yeah?" I half-whisper, turning away from him and pretending to need my free hand to hold my bag.

For a moment as I trail behind Kirian, I swear more eyes are on us, more than there usually are. Coming from the crumpling windows and doors. From the dark spaces that my Shadows are surely occupying.

There was a war here, that much I know. Many lives were lost right where we stand. Maybe that is what I feel in the air.

My second wind is gone, replaced with paranoia. A bead of sweat tickles my back, sending me into a frenzy that turns my stomach in on itself.

I haven't heard the woman's voice in a long time, which makes me spiral into thoughts of what if: What if I am in the wrong place? What if I am in over my head? What if my coming here was a terrible mistake? What if I am not what she claims I am?

Chapter 25

Night changes Stone once more. It brings peace to the land that I have never felt before. All the nights that I would sleep in the field near House Luz, the one that I spent evenings in, watching as the sun fell over the west side of this very mountain, was nothing compared to this. As we lie down for a rest, I feel Stone go into what I can only describe as hibernation, as if it too is replenishing its strength.

I am nearly asleep when a piercing cry rings through the cold air. I sit up fast, searching, ignoring the excruciating drumming behind my eyes. The fire is on its last legs, making the ring of light around us dull and hard to see in. Sweat drenches my hand when I reach up to soothe my headache. *I should be cold.* My jacket lays next to my bedroll, and my socks are absently left over the dying fire to dry.

So hot. I rip the blanket off, freeing my body. There it is again, the cry of a woman in the distance. Kirian is sound asleep, his back turned towards me. I shake him violently to wake him. Unsure of how I got over to him so fast. The Shadows attempt to peel me away from him as he stirs awake. I ignore them.

"What, what is it?" he asks frantically when he sees the terror on my face. His own chest beating from the abrupt awakening. He takes me by the shoulders as I find the words.

Stone spins beneath me as I find my words, and I have to concentrate on not falling over. "There is someone in the woods," I tell him breathlessly. As if whatever is out there heard me, a horn blows, low and... triumphant. His head snaps to the noise behind him, then he looks back at me calmly, too calmly.

"There are said to be settlers in these mountains. Those who did not leave after the war." This does nothing to slow the panic that is running rampant through me as I think back to all the times I thought there were eyes on us as we walked. If there are settlers here, there really could have been someone trailing us. It isn't the strange energy of this mountain or my imagination.

Kirian sees the thoughts as they pass behind my eyes, sees the terror that I now feel. "It's okay, *you're okay*," He tells me in a soothing voice. The glow of his aura brightens. An opaque light that drifts from his mouth. Using his gift to convince me of what is most definitely not true.

I am *not* okay in many more ways than one.

Right now, in this place, where I need to *feel* every emotion to survive, to keep track of my surroundings, to let the bile rise to my throat at the threat of danger. To retreat from it if need be. I shake my head violently. *Get away from me.* That is all I can think. *Get away from her.* The Shadows join in. They lay their slender fingers over his wrists. As if restraining him.

I fall backward in a rush to get outside of the reach of his power. My backside hits the ground in a painful thud. A rock catches my trousers and tears at my skin. I continue my retreat. *I don't want him to use his gift on me. I don't want to be manipulated by him or anyone ever again.* His face turns from worry to realization to anger. Then his large shoulders rise and fall in a heavy sigh before he turns his back to me again. "Get some sleep, Katsia. We have a long day ahead of us." He says to the night.

"Kirian, I-"I try, but it's no use. What could I even say?

All the heat falls from my body, my teeth chatter and my bedroll no longer holds heat. I flinch at every noise throughout the night. Soon, I start to think that I was wrong about Stone going into hibernation, no it's much worse than that. Kirian once told me of *creatures that steal babies and beasts that eat livestock.*

The mountain has gone quiet for no other reason than to hide from whatever it is that lurks in these woods. We are well past the villages that live beyond the wall. We are in The Uncharted Territories. Where maps mean nothing. Where no one knows who or what lives beyond. Not even those who live past the walls of Thorn Row travel this far north.

Except Augustine. Who supposedly takes soldiers to The North and brings them back in a daze, which sends me further into the part of my mind that thinks of what could happen to *me* if I stay in these mountains for too long. I can't help but grip my dagger until the sun rises.

My suspicions of possible madness taking hold of me are proven correct. The gray surrounding us slowly bleeds into color. A sight that only I see as I flip over to Kirian who still sleeps in his bedroll, his large body sunken into the ground.

Twigs snap under light feet behind me. The kind that you would hear under a fawn's footing. *Where a child is, a mother is sure not to be far.* I think to myself. All my years of hunting for myself have told me that.

When I turn my head slowly to the noise, far in the distance beyond trunks of trees that grow in rows, a woman stands. A white veil over her face, concealing her features. It falls over her breasts, landing just below the curve of her womanhood. Her skin porcelain with the help of chalk or paint, the color runs all the way down to her toes. Not a fawn at all and yet her steps are just as such, as if she has walked upon the pine needles and creeping vegetation many times before.

This time, I do not wake Kirian. I only watch as the woman raises her arms with the sun. Her movements like liquid as she takes methodical steps in an almost dance. She is not alone. Others join her from somewhere, only blurs of perfect white figures in my periphery. They step with her, all moving in a circle before dispersing in different directions, the same as a star in the sky, its points shining all around it, filling the black. The woman who I saw first starts towards me. The southern point of the star. *It's not real,* I tell myself. *Something is wrong. With me.*

A heavy weight falls over me, like the air has condensed. I do not take my eyes off the woman, and if I am not mistaken, she sees me as well. Her arms come around, her hands cupped and outstretched in front of her.

In her palms she holds light, white and steady. Not like the flickering light of a candle. More like the light I saw around Kirian, but much brighter, consistent.

She keeps a steady pace, closer and closer. *"Take it"* the Shadows demand, their sudden presence startles me, my whole body jolting before settling again. *"Take it, all of it, it's yours."* But I am unsure of *what* exactly it is that I will be taking.

I want to. I almost can't help it, as if it really does belong to me. *If I wield it in my hand, will it look like that? Pure and white? Like the angel and her sisters?* I wonder. *Or will it be black like the Shadows?*

Kirian stirs behind me, breaking my concentration for half a second but I won't look away, I can't. I lift my hand and begin to point, in hopes that he will follow my finger to what I see before me. *Will he see her?* "What are you looking at?" He answers the question without me having to ask it out loud.

When I do not reply he moves beside me. My finger is now up and shaking slightly in front of us. The woman who bears a gift to me gets closer and closer, completing the southern point of the star. "What?" he says confused as he scans the forest before us. This time I do not move away from him as he nears me, the pull to the woman much stronger than the one that pulls me to him. His magic is...weaker.

"Katsia" he says my name as a hoarse whisper. Then "Katsia" louder.

The woman walks nearer until she is right next to us. I open my mouth to speak, but no words come out. She kneels in front of me. Kirian's eyes are only on me. He does not see the woman. He even reaches a hand up to my forehead between the two of us.

She holds out her hand filled with light.

Then, it's just her. Kirian is no longer beside me, and her sisters have disappeared. On my next breath, I feel the weight of the airlift.

I blink, I hadn't realized that my eyes were stinging, dry. That I have not closed them in a long time for fear that I would lose her, and I did. She is no longer there, she has taken the light with her.

I turn my head to Kirian, whose face is that of a scared child, the same look that took him over outside of the village, after our encounter with Damien. *I wonder what color surrounds the boogie man.*

A tear that I had not felt falls from my cheek lands onto the fabric of my shirt. I meet Kirian's concern, looking back and forth between the green pools, my reflection looking back at me. I take in as much air as my lungs can hold, this breath different from the last. This one is ragged and painful.

I haven't gotten any sleep. My mind could be playing cruel tricks on me. Or worse, the forest is playing its tricks, maybe the same ones that affected the soldiers that were once sent here with Augustine. Kirian takes a tentative seat onto my bedroll of which I am only half in. Even in the cold of the morning I still feel as though my body is on fire, one that I cannot get rid of.

I can't imagine what I look like right now to Kirian. I, myself, feel like I'm falling apart. Like every emotion I have ever felt, is all present at the forefront of my mind all at the same time.

We stay almost bundled together in silence like that for what feels like a long time, until my eyes become heavy. I think Kirian says something as I drift into sleep, but I can't make it out, no light emanates from his words this time. I only feel his calloused finger as he tucks my hair behind my ear and places the leather-lined cover over my shoulders. *Too warm* I think to myself but I'm too tired to remove it.

Chapter 26

When I wake, the fire is roaring nearby. Stone has grown colder as clouds lay low in the sky, casting a white haze over the top of us. Some of the mountain's peaks in the distance have caps of white atop them. Making for a beautiful landscape if it were not so deadly. I have slowed us down enough already. We need to get going if we are going to make it before the snow falls.

A savory scent fills my lungs. When I turn to the fire, I see a rabbit on a spit. Kirian's bow and arrows resting against a stump nearby. Kirian sits with his arms hung over his knees, one hand rotating the rabbit and the other held up to capture some of the fire's warmth.

He takes a quick second glance at me when he notices that I am awake. My throat feels dry, and my head pounds when I try to sit up, so I stay put. I hear the crumbling of pine needles as Kirian shifts.

He clears his throat before he speaks. "Hungry?" he asks. Yes, I can't remember the last time that I had something of sustenance in my stomach. Looking at the position of the sun, I was only asleep for a few hours, but my stomach growls like I haven't eaten in days. I nod my head in response, followed by a small "Yes." My mouth is so dry.

"I'm sorry." I tell Kirian as I wipe the sleep from my eyes. "about last night-"Kirian lets out a sigh and shakes his head, but I continue, "I shouldn't have reacted like that towards you... I'm just afraid-"but

I stop when I notice he is no longer paying attention. He walks over to me and places his hand on my forehead before taking a damp cloth and laying it over my forehead. "What are you doing?" I ask, my brows scrunch together in confusion.

He doesn't answer right away, and I start to wonder how upset I have truly made him. Then, "How are you feeling?" he asks as I take the cloth from my head and discard it nearby.

"I- I'm fine," I reply. He's acting so strange. Something must have happened while I was asleep. I just needed a few hours. I wasn't feeling myself. "Why? What is going on?"

"You've been asleep for two days." He rings the cloth out on the ground. "A fever." He says plainly. "In and out for the last few hours." There's that soldier voice again. Only using phrases that get the correct information out as quickly as possible.

A fever, that explains the mirage of the woman. Not to mention the dreams that filled my sleep. Some were nightmarish, Augustine's hands through my hair, a pinched look of concern on his face. Which seems impossible considering he would never be worried about *me*. After all, he was set on having me killed.

Another image of Cora hovering above me, her hands outstretched, healer's hands. Blue light spilling from the tips of her fingers. *All in my head, of course.* Again, easily identified as a nightmare due to her hatred for me. She would *never* heal my wounds.

Others were not as terrifying. My cheeks warm at the thought as the dream comes back to me in images. A hard body pressed against my own, his chest steady with ins and outs. I didn't see a face, but it was Kirian, I know it. That dream felt all too real because it had happened once before at the Inn when his hands were gripping my back, pulling me into him. I shake my head, trying to get rid of the image. When that doesn't work, I sit up, which only makes things worse because now our faces are close together, so close that I can smell him, mint, and musk.

Thankfully my head hurts so bad that I have to rest it on the inside of my palm, diverting my attention away from Kirian. From the corner of my eye, I see his hand reach up to comfort me. It hovers there for a moment. The Shadows rush forward slightly as if the touch is a threat. He thinks better of his decision, setting his hand back down at his side.

"Come on, let's get you something to eat" he says and heads for the fire again, he peels the leg from the rabbit and hands it to me. When I eye the leg with apprehension, Kirian pushes it towards me further. "Just try." With one bite, I know he is right. I needed something to eat. He sinks back down near me, further than he was just a moment ago, I note.

My stomach is now full, and my head has stopped its incessant pounding. "You tagged a rabbit." I tease. "With your shooting skills?" I ask sarcastically while taking another bite so as not to waste it. An image of Kirian's arrow just above mine on the target comes to mind.

"I am no Katsia Luz, but I got the job done." He smiles through the left side of his mouth. I ignore the skipped heartbeat that smile causes.

One second it's all smiles and jokes and the next his face falls. "Your Shadows don't like me." he turns so that he can see what I'm sure is pure shock on my face. I almost choke on what's left of the rabbit in my mouth. He leans back on his arm and lets the realization settle over me.

He clears his throat in the way he does when he's uncomfortable. Kirian lifts his arm, rolls his sleeve at the cuff and shows me a hand shaped bruise. The purple, blue, and yellow in contrast to his light skin. *I did that? Or rather someone did it for me.* My eyes widen and guilt pulls at my chest. I run a finger over the discolored flesh.

Shit. This is bad, so bad. "How long have you known?" I ask, ashamed.

"I felt...something... before, in the jail, just a fleck of your magic, then it was gone." The memory floods my thoughts taking me back to the moment when my vision blurred, and I could have sworn they were ready to tear, Kirian, to shreds. "Once I knew what it felt like, it was easy to spot. Outside the school." He almost laughs. "You didn't even notice." I think back, and he is right. I thought I saw them move, even thought I heard them after Lord Andres informed me of my nearing death, and the truth about Kirian's sweet words were finally revealed to me. "Not again until we got here. When you-" He inspects the bruise once more, and his words trail off.

"I didn't think that they could do that." I try to layer my emotions so that the correct one is at the forefront. Although I am amazed at my gift, the one that had hardly helped me before, left me to be beaten, forgotten by my family, the one that took me to Hansel Luz to die, held me captive in its unending embrace. *That* gift had protected my unconscious body.

But I should feel guilty, after all, I harmed Kirian with that same gift. "I'm sorry, truly," I tell him, and I am, I didn't ask them to do that. I've never asked them for anything.

"I don't blame them." He shrugs. His jaw clenches once, twice.

"What is it?" I ask as he rubs his hand over his chin.

"Listen, I have to tell you something. You need to remain calm, you-." But I am no longer listening.

Three cups are lined up on a rock near the fire. *Three.* There are only two of us, and one of us has been unconscious, so whose is that?

Kirian's bow, it's also different. I've stared at his back for days and days with that very bow strapped behind him. I've memorized the red fabric that circles its shaft as a cushion for his large hand. There is no fabric. *Maybe it fell off*. I try to convince myself.

The Shadows snake out of their hiding spots just as curious as I am. "Kirian." It comes out faint, strained, not quite a question. My eyes are now locked onto those cups, what they symbolize. *Betrayal*. One of the Shadows drags its fingers across the rims of silver. "Kirian," I say louder now, ignoring the bile that threatens to expel from my stomach. He follows my gaze. He sees what I see. He knows. The pieces come together so fucking easily. "What have you done?"

He stands, placing his hand in front of him as he begins to explain.. "You were so sick." He tries. "You wouldn't be here if I didn't." his words ring true. There is no light that falls from his mouth. He is not trying to convince me. He really did think I was on the brink of death. Still, someone must have known we were here, and who would have told them if not Kirian.

"How?" I ask. *Say it was Claire. Say it was anyone but you.* But Kirian just shakes his head. "How. Did. They. Know. We. Were. here?" I try again with a much firmer voice. Again, he says nothing. He knows that whatever words he says next will be nothing but lies. Lies that I can see, and I think he knows that as well.

I reach for my nearby boots and struggle to get them on my feet. I'm so tired, so weak, damn these laces. Then I reach for my jacket, throwing it over my body as I stand. My head spins, my legs threaten to come out from under me. Kirian mumbles something under his breath, but I pay no attention. I need to get out of here. I have to. With or without Kirian.

The bow, the Shadows point.

I lunge forward but I have been incapacitated for two days so my legs are not at full strength. *So slow*, I curse at myself. Kirian reaches for it as well and just as his hand grazes the weapon as it lays over the rock. "No." I say to him, as the words leave my mouth, his body flies backward, and his arms and legs flail as he tries to find his balance. The air leaves his body as he hits the trunk of a tree, hard. He holds the back of his head with one hand and props himself up with the other. When his hand comes away, it shines bright red.

This time, unlike during my interrogation, the Shadows do not skitter, dissipate. Because I do not feel bad. Never will I again, this is who Kirian is. Finally, the real Kirian, no masks. A trickster, a cheat. Darkness surrounds me, they stand at my sides, waiting for me to move so that they may follow. He knows all too well that I have put all the pieces together. There is no mistaking the anger behind his eyes.

"How much of it was true?" I shout at him. He has barely had time to recover from the way the Shadows threw him. He wipes the blood from his hand onto his trousers. His eyes scan the trees before landing on me. Behind him, beside him, the apparitions wait for his answer just as I do.

"I. knew. it." he says instead, the words come between heavy breaths. *Wrong answer.* Kirian looks around at those who surround him, my Shadows, my companions, my gift.

He can see all of them because I have finally let them be shown. Even to me, the once blurred figures are now full beings with arms and legs, each unique in their stances, some with more masculine builds and others with long flowing hair and wide hips. They peek out from behind the trees, surrounding him as well as me.

As if he senses their unease, their readiness, willingness, "It was the only way." He tells us in a hurried excuse. Damn, already on the brink of begging for his life. *As he should.*

"Only way for what?" my voice doesn't sound like it belongs to me. It sounds louder, stronger.

He opens his arms and gestures for me to take a look around. "You led us to Shadow Gate. It had to be your own choice." He admits. "Gods, it was so easy." He almost laughs. "They were so ready to believe that you had no power, but I saw it." He pauses and sucks in a breath as he adjusts his posture. "We have been looking for you. You have no idea how long we have waited."

We? As in Kirian and The Spent?

I am here. And this is what *I* wanted. What *she* wanted.

"*You have done well, Katsia.*" The woman's soft voice whispers to me. But I am confused because I have not done well at all. I have failed.

"I know what you are after." I tell Kirian in a last ditch effort. "The weapon. I know it exists." My words started strong, confident. But it ended soft and unconvincing.

Kirian laughs. Fucking laughs.

"Oh, it exists alright." He tells me, his eyes rolling back into his head. He has lost a lot of blood, but I have no time to worry about his life. After all, he has never cared about mine. "She will use it to open the gates to Understone." He lets out a ragged breath. "Finally."

She. Tricked, jailed, kidnapped, trained. All for me to be here, right now, right where they want me. The Shadows all move at once, towards me, comforting me as I nearly collapse.

Kirian looks at me as if he actually feels bad. As if he *cares*, and that absolutely pisses me off. His head lulls backwards, creating a wet smack on the trunk of the tree.

"You thought you could take it away from us just like that." *It,* as in magic. "You thought you were the chosen one." He is barely conscious at this point, but he just keeps going. "She doesn't want you to close the gate between Stone and Understone." He laughs at my stupidity.

"She wants me to open it." I complete his thought.

There it is again, that burning sensation in the back of my head, the one that lets me know I am not alone.

The dreams that plagued my fevered mind. Not dreams at all. I whip my head around furiously, momentarily taking my attention away from injured Kirian. Whoever he is working with must be nearby. *Run.* I scan the trees beyond the broken city, it's my best bet.

My Shadows move as I do. I am so slow. My body is still recovering from illness.

They pull me in the direction of the old city, away from Kirian. I follow them, or at least I try. More and more of them come from the trees, from beneath me, from my own darkness that I cast on the ground.

The trees shake, and the crumbling bits of brick fall from old buildings. The darkness swirls around me in a relentless storm, blocking out my vision. I can no longer see an escape or Kirian.

It only takes me a second to realize that these Shadows do not belong to me.

In fact I am useless against whatever surrounds me now. My apparitions pull at me, begging me to run, some are swept away in the smoky wind. *Take me away.* I beg of them. I will not be afraid this time, "Take me away," I say aloud.

Nothing happens. I try to use my remaining strength to get away. I take a step forward, my hair spills over the side of my face with the wind, its long strands wrap around my neck and torso. My feet threaten to come out from under me as I continue. I do not stop. Instead, walk into the storm further, into the wall of black. Soon, the air is pulled from my lungs, and I can't seem to breathe it back in. Still, I move forward.

Just another step, then run, I tell myself, forcing my other foot forward, then reaching an arm out to pierce the black. For a moment, I think that I see the swirling black cloud's part for me.

Crack. The chilling sound of snapping bone, followed by intense pain. My arm is slammed down to my side. Something digs into my wrist, sending a spike up to my shoulder. My left hand is broken and bound. I wince with every gust of wind against exposed bone.

Just. One. Step. But I can't, my feet are bound as well. Vines grow all around me, up my thighs and around my arms. They slither up to my face, around my neck, crackles of light dance around my vision before I start to fade. *This is the end.* I tell myself.

Darker, darker. It feels like I'm falling. This is what death feels like. With my eyes closed, I see my pathetic life flash before me. I did nothing. I was nothing, insignificant.

The walls fall, the wind stops howling. The vines release their pressure slightly. I blink heavily, and my sight begins to return. I gasp for air, but my lungs fill with fire. Or what feels like it.

The first person I see is Ava, her small body firm in her stance. Her arms outstretched, her palms facing me as she holds the vines across my body, releasing the tension on my neck slowly but it does nothing to ease the pain.

An eye, not her own, stares back at me. Ava has taken The Vow. There, on the palm of her hand, is the mark that separates her and everyone else who has taken it from the rest of the world.

My heart breaks when I see what she has become. Her once gentle gift is being used to drain the life from me. Just the way The Spent intended for her to be. My body falls at the realization. The vines that were holding me upright are now around my ankles, I don't try to catch my fall. Not caring about the sharp burning sensation as I slam to the ground. Thorns embed into the thin flesh of my knees.

Beyond Ava is Cora. She kneels before Kirian, her hands outstretched over his body, healing him. Kirian lays limply against the tree. *What have I done?*

My attention snaps to the other Shadow wielder, his eyes alight as they were when I first saw him outside of Thorn Row. Augustine. His body becomes a blur, and then my vision clears. He steps closer. A blur. Clear.

He has been taking people to The North. *He* has been trying to find the weapon and open the gates. They can't. I won't let them. Magic is evil. It was not meant to be on Stone.

Understone, a place that was once thought to not even exist. But I knew, the woman told me, and I've all but confirmed it for them by coming here.

Return the weapon to Understone. The war. The one fought all that time ago. When the realms were split. She wants me to- she said I can rid of magic on Stone forever. They are not meant to have it- wield it to be used in armies and given to servants to benefit royals. Jailed, taken, trained. It's not meant to be that way.

"The weapon shall be used to open the gates." She confirms Kirian's earlier words. Stone spins beneath me.

"No- you promised." I can't tell if I say the words aloud or not.

"Then you will close them." A long pause. *"After I take back what is mine. Stone will not have my magic any longer. In fact, it will have nothing when I am done with it."* Gravity threatens to have its way with me.

"You lied," I tell her.

"Not a lie. The weapon will be returned to Understone, after I am done with it."

My world collapses. I thought I had finally found a way to be useful. To be worth something. All I had to do was this one thing.

My Shadows, my loyal companions, surround me in a protective circle. Their voices, soft and apologetic, fill my ears as they express their regret for their weakness. But they are not weak. No, it's me who is weak.

I burn with anger. At myself. At Stone. At those who have wronged me.

"You will get your revenge, child." She sings. The ground rushes towards me, and I can hardly keep my eyes from rolling into the back of my head. Her presence is stronger than ever.

Before I hit the forest floor, with its hidden cobblestone streets, warm arms wrap around my torso, keeping me upright.

Scarred pink X's litter the tan skin. My chin hits my chest. All I can do is stare and stare at those X's holding me up until my eyelids become so heavy that I can't stop them from falling. *"You will do this one thing for me, child. We will both get what we want in the end."*

Then the world goes black.

Chapter 27
Augustine

A fucking parasite. That's what she is. Just when you think you've rid yourself of *her*, she shows up in a less suspecting place. I should have killed her when I had the chance. When she showed up at my doorstep a broken woman with a knack for destruction. It was fun at first, I will admit. Until I realized she would not only destroy one realm but two.

When Kirian confirmed with our contact in Thorn Row that Kirian was to bring the girl to Shadow Gate, all hell broke loose. *Should have killed him, too.* King Aron sent for his commander-in-chief, who decided to send half his fucking numbers north. *Just what she wants, idiots.*

And here I am, with a direct order to take two newbies fresh from taking The Vow while they gather their useless army. They can hardly wipe their own asses, let alone wield their gifts. I had taken many North in my time with The Spent. All came down with the same madness. The kind that mortal men are subject to when they enter the city. It doesn't take long for them to succumb to it.

King Aron the 1st had once captured me and placed me within the city himself. He did it to all of us just to see who would break and who would not. When I was the remaining survivor, he let *her* get into his head with promises of a new world. The one that his Grandfather let slip through his fingers, supposedly. Of course, I was still navigating the mortal realm with half my powers, but by the time I regained my strength, it was too late. She had worked out a deal with the King, and I had already made a deal myself. One for freedom. Or what I thought was freedom. All I got was a mark upon my wrist, granting her a peek into the mortal realm.

When we arrived, the girl was near death. Shades floating around her with their mindless chatter. They bowed to me as they should. *They bow to her as well, but she does not see.*

Kirian stood his ground for all of five seconds after they flung him from her sleeping body. Stepping aside to let the girl that Lord Andres forced along with me, Cora, to mend her.

But it wasn't enough. She was sick with a whole other kind of illness. What the Shades were calling moonstruck. Her powers have manifested and she has done absolutely nothing with them. Forcing her into a catatonic state. A bunch of busy bodies the Shades are, but they usually know best.

Chills took over her whole body. Sweat dripped into her hair. Words fell from her mouth without her even realizing what she was saying. Something about Kirian, then about *her,* was in her head, no doubt. She lay wrapped in my arms as I slowly talked her through using a small bit of her magic until she was coherent enough to use it herself. Even still, it was weak, minuscule compared to what she could and would do.

I had already contemplated her death. It's not like I hadn't tried before. Her Father's beast was too injured to do the job. And keeping her trapped in purgatory was never going to do me any good, not if *she* has any idea how to use the in-between. I highly doubt it, but I wasn't taking any chances.

I intended to kill her again in the library. Not the cleanest kill, I will admit, but I would have gotten the job done. It had gone too far. Keeping her magic from her was only a temporary solution. Lord Andres might have saved her that time, actually. Calling that meeting to discuss her magic or lack thereof because of me. By the time we were in the library, I had known what her fate was, death, by the hands of The Spent.

I knew that her death would only send the half that rightfully belonged to me skittering around Stone until it met its next body to inhabit. How *she* did it I have no idea. Neither do I know how Katsia, the human girl, was able to wield it without it killing her. So when Kirian took her from Fauna to Shadow Gate I did not care. Petty mortal things that I should not have to concern myself with. What they do and why, I will never understand.

Besides, I have spent far too much time here.

It was time to go home. Time to face the music, as they say. Time to take back what was rightfully mine, and if the girl was the answer, so be it.

When I caught the girl in my arms, when her head lulled, and I could feel her soul reach out to me in death. I was struck with a vision. Given so kindly to me by *her*. The night that we had both been drunk on God's wine so that she would be none the wiser as I left. Trapping her there. Where she could no longer destroy. "She will be the life and death of you." She had told me as she placed her hands haphazardly on the sides of my head. Nothing gentle about it in her drunken stupor.

Black hair. The same tall, steady figure. In the vision, she had picked up a flower in the mortal realm, tears streaming down her face.

And when she peered up at me from death... I saw fire behind her eyes.

Chapter 28
Augustine

Everything happens all at once.

Stone cracks and crumbles, a thin hairline fracture marring the ground, extending from beneath our feet and snaking its way outward. It's as if the very ground recognizes her as the key. All while I am still trying to get those damned words out of my head.

Katsia stands and runs her eyes over me as I remain on my knees before her. A look of satisfaction on her face. One that makes me believe it is not just the human girl that occupies the space behind those black eyes.

She leaves me, floating over to Cora, ignoring Kirian's dead body at her feet. "Heal me." Her voice is too soft to be anything but maniacal. Cora shakes her head. Katsia holds out her twisted, broken hand. "Heal. Me." She demands of the girl.

Cora does no such thing. And what happens next has even me sucking in a breath, and I have tortured souls. She grabs Cora by her braid pulling her inches from her own face. Then, places a gentle hand around her wrist and moves Cora's hand to her own mangled, broken one.

When nothing happens, Katsia smiles. *Beautiful*. Then, Cora's body hits the ground in a lifeless splatter.

Katsia looks down at her arm watching as her fingers snap back into place. Not flinching an inch as she steps over what are now two bodies beneath her.

She is about to put on a show, and who am I to stop her. After all, it is a sight to behold.

Stone gives way entirely, a large gaping chasm from beneath her. I have front row seats as I watch beasts with flaming hair and hoofed feet crawl out. Passed only by men with wings as black as night and women with bloodied white feathers and a nasty look of revenge on their faces.

Katsia looks to the distance, where they seem to be accumulating. I couldn't think of why until I see the speckles on the hillside. Beyond the crumbling city. The army. King Aron, presumably at the front.

It will be quick work, my undead army has never been beaten. It has been over a century since they last got to satiate their blood lust. Bodies fly in all directions when they make their way to the men on horses with their measly swords and wooden bows.

Katsia heads straight for the battle, presumably to join in on their destruction. The shades circle around her with excited energy, a reflection of her own emotions.

Ava, who I had not even realized was still near, takes a step in her direction as well. Her blond hair stuck to the sides of her face from sweat, her arms trembling. Stone's magic is so weak, so insignificant, I can't wait to see how the human girl with immortal powers is to deal with this... pest.

When Ava reaches out towards Katsia, the ground obeys. Twisted tree roots that were once hidden in the dirt make their way to her ankles. Stopping Katsia in her tracks. Katsia lets out a laugh, low and terrifying, even to me. I can't stop a smile from sneaking onto my face at the sound. Katsia cocks her head at the girl, her black hair cascading down half her face like a waterfall. The shades do their job of disintegrating the splintering roots at her feet before she takes her time closing the distance between the two.

If I'd blinked, I would have missed it. There was already a half-decaying crumpled girl on the ground before Katsia. Her magic is now in her veins. The ground shifts and sways and I know it is her connection to Stone with Avas' gift.

It looks much more handsome on Katsia than it ever had been on anyone with the gift. And I had seen many in my miserable human lifetime. The trees want to be near her, the grass tries to crawl up her legs. She could literally move mountains if she so chose.

All of it is so... splendidly entertaining. Until a tear falls down her cheek, and my stomach lurches. Katsia is not in control. I know that much. But she is there. She has nothing but mortality, and a mere human death to me is heartbreak to her.

I had been so caught up in the show that I had not realized how much damage it was doing to the girl. I take a step forward, and for a second, I think I see her eyes shift to mine. Fire, but sadness, and guilt.

I'm not sure what I intend to do, and it does not matter, because before I can reach her, black engulfs her body, a cloud of dark sand. Then she is gone. Appearing again before the mortals fighting a losing battle.

I follow her, conjuring the same Shadow and using it to gain distance on her. Light Taker, they called me on Stone. Now I knew why as I saw all the light from around the girl disappear.

She moves methodically, like a dance. When an arrow hits her shoulder, she pulls it from the flesh and heals the wound in seconds. Nothing can stop her, and I can't stop myself from observing her from the Shadows, well out of her sight. Well out of her way.

She lets out a cry of fury and pain but presses on, the darkness around her growing when needed and dissipating when she wants to be seen again. I watch as she drains the life from body after body.

That same cloud of black hangs low above our heads. The one she used to move in without being seen, is now used to suffocate men. Another cry erupts from Katsia's body. Another. And another. As weapons clatter to the ground, creating a symphony of metal on metal, only the remnants of beasts fighting far off remain, their screeches loud and triumphant as they end the lives of the remaining soldiers. Some fly further down the mountain, sure to have orders from *her* to destroy as much of the mortal realm as possible.

More and more death. I could feel it, more souls snaking their way into the chasm that she had created only moments ago.

Her cries turn into sobs. The black disappears as quickly as it had appeared. The ground is nearly stained red beneath us. Katsia falls to her knees, continuing her crying until she has no more left to give. She looks up at the sky with what looks like one final howl, but nothing comes out. White flakes fall from the sky. At first a flurry and then a downpour. Covering the destruction that she has created.

Only she and I remain alive.

I get closer and closer, watching her as she closes her eyes and takes in a breath, the shades wiping her tears as they surround her in a cocoon of black. I am merely feet away from her as she hangs her head, staring straight but not latching onto anything. Her hand shoots out abruptly, I nearly jump at the movement.

Then she bends over and picks up a flower that had somehow not gotten destroyed in the battle. It is yellow and curved. She holds it up to inspect it. Then, crushes it in her fist.

When her tear-filled eyes meet mine, something unnatural but magnetic has me scooping her up into my arms. She does not deny me. In fact, she lies her head against my chest. We walk away from the carnage and towards the city once more.

The gates to Understone are now open, and we are free to go home.

Chapter 29

Screams of men and women and beasts. Silence.

Ava's face as life drains from her body. Silence.

My own screams as I tried to free myself from the body that was moving all on its own. Silence.

I wanted this, or at least I thought I did. The woman told me I would get what I wanted, and I wanted revenge. It was all I could think about.

Those who hurt me. Betrayed me. Starting with Father and ending with all humans, all men. All those who looked at me and saw nothing but someone to take from, to use.

I am not a killer, but when I saw Cora fall to the ground. When I felt her gift seep into my veins, it felt all too good. I was a willing subject. The woman knew that, knew that this day of destruction would come, that I had it in me all along. I had given her permission to take my body and turn it into a weapon. The one that she had promised me when she first spoke my name.

It was too late. No matter how much I protested, no matter how hard I fought. When Ava appeared before me in my distorted view of the world from the back of my own mind. I had not wanted her to die. *Too late.*

I closed my eyes, but I could still feel it, her magic, as it became my own. Something beautiful that she had shown me many times was now mine. By the time I opened my eyes again, there she was, lifeless and unmoving. I hardly had time to process her death, I wanted to cry, to scream, but nothing came out.

The rest was fueled by my rage for my only friend and the revenge that burned in my heart. It was not only mine. I know that now because I am alone. There is no longer someone occupying the same space as my subconscious. The revenge I felt on the field was ten times that of my own because it did not belong to just me.

Metal crashing on metal. Silence.

Men's last breaths as they coughed up blood. Silence.

The scarred arms of an angel carrying me away. Silence.

White curtains, and a white room. Even the door is painted over. I sit up in a panic before pain rings through my head. This has me falling back down on white sheets. It smells of spring, and when I look over. White flowers.

My chest hurts in more ways than one. The flowers are a reminder of death. The other reason is that I feel as if I have been run over. My body is sore in ways that I never thought possible. I sit there staring at the ceiling, unable to think of anything other than death. My own, for starters. I am obviously somewhere past Stone. Maybe all the lives I took are also here somewhere.

I close my eyes, accepting of the fact that I am no longer living. I wait and wait until I hear voices in the distance. They are full of anger. I can't make out what they are saying, so I carefully peel the blanket from my body and step onto white tile. Ignoring the pain in my arms and the dried blood that runs through the ends of my hair, I make my way slowly to the door and press my ear against it.

"It was easy." A familiar woman's voice says on the other side. "After all, her Mother asked the seers the same question as I." she pauses for a moment, and I hear the other person sigh. "You thought you could just lock me up here? After what we built together?" The words make no sense to me.

"What *I* built, Hecate. Alone. Me." His voice is deep and unforgiving. "If you think I'll let you keep this up, you're wrong."

"Whatever, dear, we will work out the details later." I can almost hear the smile she is sure to be wearing. "For now, we have bigger problems. Problems that *you* created this time; might I add." She takes a breath. They are closer to the door now. All I would have to do is open it to reveal them. "She was weak. I made her strong. And she's going to need it. You're welcome." She sings. They are sure to be speaking of me. I do not feel strong. I do not feel anything but guilt.

"I will return her. Is that what you want to hear?" he tells her. Return me? No, no, I can't go back. Where would I go? They would lock me up. After what I've done, they will- then the door opens, and a woman stands before me. She looks at me up and down. Hecate, he had called her. Slender with wide eyes that narrow at their ends. Her hair is up, aside from two strands that fall on the sides of her perfectly high cheekbones. Her dress is blue like the sky, tied around her body of silk skin.

Behind her stands the angel with raven's wings. Augustine.

"Persephone."

Epilogue

"With fair judgment, she'll rule the land,
    Balancing the scales with a steady hand.
Life and death, forever entwined,
Persephone's reign, an eternal bind.
But remember, mortal and divine,
The Underworld's fate shall align.
For should Persephone falter or waver,
The realms shall shudder, and all shall quaver."

Acknowledgments

A special thank you to my husband. When I second, third, and fourth-guessed myself, you were there, reassuring me at every turn. Late-night conversations with good and bad ideas got me through. I wouldn't have been able to do it without you, my love.

To Cat, my best friend, and Linda, my sister. I'm so glad you got to see it go from the first draft to this! I can't thank you enough for just being there. You both have a special place in my heart and in this book.

Cole, thanks for being the comedic relief. When I get into my head you always pull me out. Thank you.

Hi mom, we did it! You have helped in every way possible, and that means more to me than you ever know. Thank you, a million times, not only in this project but in life. There is nothing I will ever be able to do to repay you for all the shit you've had to put up with. I love you.

No, I didn't forget you. Dad, I know it's not your kind of book. It has no cowboys or inspirational quotes that we help you transform your life or business, and certainly no craps strategies. It does have something that you do like, proof. Proof that you instilled a great work ethic into me. Proof that your words stuck. "Don't start something unless you can finish it."

Hire a developmental editor! Julie Cameron at Landon Literary/Gemini Writers Studio. Thank you for all your hard work and kind words.

C.K Hart is an exciting up-and-coming author. She writes fantasy and thriller books in her spare time. She lives in a beautiful mountain town in Wyoming, where she and her husband own a thriving and busy Barbershop.

Most of her summers are spent hiking, fishing, and camping in the mountains. In the winters (which are long in Wyoming) she stays curled up with a book, often with a cat or two on her lap.

You can find videos of her and her two cats (Darth Vader and Havoc Rifle) on TikTok @author_c.k._hart

If you like this book and are looking forward to the release of the next book in the series or any of the other books she is working on you can follow her on Instagram @author_c.k_hart

Found in Flames- Teaser

Angelic, and that is what I thought him to be. When he picked me up from the ground and brought me here. That day on Stone when the ground split and I could hear both my thoughts and hers. Intertwined so perfectly that it was as if we were one person.

My dreams are mostly nightmares, but when I dream of him, I feel calm. He is there, in my mind's eye, always with those Xs down his arms—the same ones that I see now with his sleeves rolled to his elbows. Angelic is exactly the correct word because behind him lay wings, obsidian in color and beautiful.

Made in the USA
Monee, IL
06 May 2024

d90a1f11-0a4e-4bd3-9aa4-1b1a191f57e8R01